ACORN

OTHER BOOKS IN THE WHITE OAK TRILOGY

Sapling   *out now*

White Oak   *anticipated September 2023*

ACORN

The White Oak Trilogy, Book 1

KELSEY PARPART

For Jim, still a better love story than Twilight

CHAPTER 1

The trees grew so close to the narrow two-lane road that Erica wondered how they didn't hit her mirror as she drove. It was one of those late afternoons in August when she could feel fall setting in and see it in the pale gold sun that spent most of the day low on the horizon. The evergreens cast long shadows on the road, which was uneven from several seasons without maintenance and was beginning to give way to the roots underneath. As the road took a turn to the east and the Cascade Mountains shot up in front of her, she could just make out the edge of a small town.

The town was Juniper Falls, and Juniper Falls was central to Erica's understanding of herself. This was the town where she was born, where she took her first step, lost her first tooth, and made her first friend. And even though she hadn't lived there for more than ten years, it was still the town of family Christmases and long summer vacations. The name was even stenciled in silver letters across her car: *Juniper Falls Farm & Feed ~ Serving Oregon since 1973.*

Erica wondered, as she did whenever she was headed to Juniper Falls, what it would have been like to finish growing up here instead of Portland and how different she would be if she had continued living in a full house with her parents, grandparents, and uncle. Having left when Erica was eight to open their version of *Farm & Feed* in the big city, it seemed like her parents were always at their store. Her mother in particular was so eager to prove that they hadn't made a mistake, that they were independent and thriving. Erica remembered the tense conversations between her mother and grandmother in the days leading to the move all those years ago, conversations about opportunity versus loyalty. Having to decide between the two, she was choosing loyalty. Loyalty was there to catch you when opportunity pulled the rug out, and right now, she felt more like she was falling than flying.

She reached Main Street and passed the municipal buildings, the tiny grocery store, the furniture store, the gas station with original pumps, and the *Farm & Feed* barn, set back from the street, painted midnight blue with silver lettering. In the middle of the previous century, when there was talk of releasing some of the forest to logging companies, young men—and in some cases, young families—had flocked to the area and almost overnight constructed a series of sturdy, modest buildings. Chatter about easy money coming any day from the timber industry had never died down among the residents of Juniper Falls. People were held there by the ghost of a promise of steady jobs and good wages, and in the meantime, they, her grandparents among them, became amateur tradesmen or shop owners.

Erica headed further down Main Street before taking a right onto a narrow residential street. In front of a plain, yellow, two-story house, her grandmother sat in the driveway pruning the withered heads off her dahlias. Two trucks, the same shade of deep blue as her car, sat under a sagging carport.

Granny rose to meet Erica. While she hesitated slightly when it was time to straighten her knees, she was as graceful as ever. Tulip, the old red and white corgi dog laying on the porch, was not so limber, and merely lifted her head. Erica put the car in park and threw the door open.

"Granny! How are you?"

"Better now that you're here." Granny grabbed Erica's elbows and pulled her into a close hug. Granny always smelled faintly like the store, like fertilizer and sawdust, with an undertone of coconut.

"Have you heard anything about Uncle Keith?"

"What, in the last two days? No. I've decided to pretend until I hear otherwise that he ran off with some girl. A nymph or a prostitute, maybe. It's strange not having him around. I have to be responsible for things again. I didn't realize how spoiled I've become."

The couple of months since Keith disappeared had been hard on all of them, but on Granny most of all. Keith was an experienced hiker. Friendly with the local rangers, he had access to all the Forest Service roads around Juniper Falls. It wasn't unusual for him to grab a backpack and head out overnight. What was unusual was him not showing up the next day to open the store. Granny had called Erica's mother that Monday in June, less than two weeks after they had all been together in Portland to watch her graduate from high school, and told her Keith was missing. Erica listened in as her mother suggested that he might be lost and that they should notify the rangers and the police. A few nights later she heard her parents whispering to each other that Keith may have just decided to leave. He was forty and single and may have finally gotten fed up with small town life and filial responsibilities. Erica didn't believe this for a minute. The Keith she knew was content with his simple life in a simple place in a way that contrasted starkly against her mother's constant push for more.

For the next three weeks, Granny called every day but had little to report. She couldn't tell the search and rescue team which direction Keith went in or what clothes he was wearing. They had limited resources to search the forest. Granny sent photos of the flyers that were posted all over town. Then his truck was found fifteen miles from the nearest public area by a summer intern doing wildlife surveys. Erica's mother rushed to Juniper Falls.

Days passed and Keith kept not coming home. Erica worked at her parents' branch of *Farm & Feed* with her father nearly every day, but it quickly became clear that her mother couldn't stay in Juniper Falls forever. The Portland store was her mother's baby, and it didn't work without her. As she listened to her parents lament her mother's absence on nightly phone calls, a small, selfish thought began forming in Erica's mind. Her last year of high school had felt like a nine-month marathon and Keith's disappearance cast an unshakable pall over the future. Facing down college and having to start over at a new school in a new town, to choose the direction of the rest of her life, was something she did not have the energy for. Living with Granny and helping her run a business that did a quarter of the volume of her parents' store was the port in the storm Erica needed to sort out what she wanted out of her next step.

As the hopeful search for her uncle turned into a series of unanswerable questions, Erica called the school she was supposed to show up at in mere weeks to tell them that she would have to postpone. She tried to explain the situation, but was met with no barriers, just an apathetic understanding. She might as well have called to say she stubbed her toe and wouldn't make it in until January.

Erica's next step was to call her grandmother. If she couldn't get Granny on board, there was no way she was going to sell her parents. "Granny, I'd like to come down for the summer. Maybe until Christmas or, you know, whenever he—."

"Really, love? You don't have to do that for me." Erica could hear the hope in her voice.

"Really really. I want to come. I think I need to come."

"Then you're absolutely welcome."

"Can you talk to Mom?"

"Of course."

Her mother drove straight back to Portland that night. There was a lot of yelling on her mother's part and a lot of crying and trying to explain on Erica's. *Didn't she know how lucky she was to have the opportunity to go to college? To be the first in the family to graduate?* The accusation lingered in Erica's ears. Erica pleaded that she wasn't ready, that her grandmother needed her, that a lot of people took time off before going to college. Finally, she was forced to play the only card she had: the call had already been made and College of the Cascades wasn't expecting her until winter quarter. She was technically an adult, and Granny had said she could stay.

Their conversation the next morning felt like it happened on either side of a wall of ice.

"I'm going back for a few more weeks to automate some of the ordering and bring some of the systems up to date. You can head down there toward the end of August."

"Thank you," Erica said.

"Don't thank me. This wasn't my decision," her mother said and left the room.

They'd talked since then but had only seen each other once, right before Erica left. Conversations with her mother were short and tense and mostly about the store or any progress they'd made in tracking down Keith, which was not much. Having worked in the Portland store long before it was legal, Erica could do basic operations in her sleep, but the vendors were different in Juniper Falls and she needed to familiarize herself with their inventory. Her father couldn't work in Portland alone, even with support from their part-timers, so she worked during the day and spent her nights studying the emails her mother sent.

Erica felt a pang of guilt for exploiting Keith's absence in this way. They had never been particularly close, but she loved him the way she loved all things associated with Juniper Falls. Keith's unexplained disappearance aside, it was the place where she felt safe, comfortable, and the most herself.

And now she was here, helping her grandmother carry her sparse belongings into the house she knew so well. As far back as she could remember, not so much as a single trinket had moved in the living room. Furnished like a hunting cabin, there was a low sofa made of unfinished pine and plaid wool cushions. A pair of overstuffed recliners, in his and hers red and blue, faced each other on either side of a fireplace that took up almost the whole wall opposite the door. The fireplace wasn't quite large enough to stand in, but Erica remembered it being one of her favorite hide-and-go-seek spots as a child, tucked behind the fire screen, knees against brick.

Granny dropped the duffle bags she had been carrying at the foot of the stairs and offered to make them dinner. Erica eagerly accepted. But first she hauled her possessions to the second floor and pushed open the door to the bedroom she had slept in for the first eight years of her life. The room had once been so familiar to her, belonged to her, but any vestiges of her childhood had been replaced by sensible guest room furnishings. An amateur oil painting of the view of the mountains coming into town hung next to the door. Juniper Falls looked smaller and newer in the painting than even her earliest memories.

She tossed most of the contents of the duffels in the dresser and anything that needed to be hung up she shoved in the closet for now. After placing her toiletries in the bathroom, she made her way downstairs, sliding her hand across the wall before turning into the dining room with its worn oak table, then through to the kitchen. She leaned over the stove next to Granny to check the progress of the grilled cheese, a masterpiece composed of homemade wheat bread, gruyere, and sharp cheddar. Standing close together, the resemblance between them was obvious. They were about the same height, which was a little on the tall side, their eyes fading from brown at the pupils to pale blue, their complexions fair without freckles. Granny's hair had been so blonde that when it went white, almost no one noticed. Erica's shade was somewhere between ash blonde and mouse brown, which was why she usually dyed it. It was currently cut to her chin and shone crimson like pomegranate seeds.

Erica grabbed plates from the cupboard, chipped stoneware that Granny had hand painted as a wedding present to Grampy. The acrylic flowers had almost vanished from wear. The two women—for despite what her mother thought, Erica was a woman now—were quiet as they ate. Tulip had disappeared, likely to her bed by the fireplace.

"Do we need to go to the store tomorrow?" Erica asked as she picked up the last of the crumbs with her fingers.

"It's Sunday."

"I know, but I thought I'd take a look around. Remind myself where everything is. Someone is going to come in and ask for slug repellent and I'm going to have to give them a blank stare."

"There will be plenty of time to get acquainted. You should explore the town. It's been a while since you've been down for more than a weekend. I don't know what people your age do here, but you should find out or it will be a long five months."

Erica nodded, though she was looking forward to spending time alone. There was so much to think about, so many decisions to make. But for tonight, all that could wait. She was home.

CHAPTER 2

Before she could go anywhere, Erica needed gas. Because her family ran a local business, she had to fill up at Gas Guzzler—which was owned by the Hendricks, another long-standing Juniper Falls family—and not the newer, cheaper gas station just off the highway. It took her a whole two and a half minutes from the time she turned on the car to pull up to one of the four antique red and white aluminum gas pumps. Not wanting to draw business away from the grocery store across the street, the Hendricks chose to operate a liquor store instead of the traditional minimart in the building next to the gas station.

It was already ten o'clock by the time Erica had woken up; now it was noon and near ninety degrees. Erica grabbed her wallet out of her purse and headed into the dull brown building to prepay. She wasn't all the way in the door before she heard her name.

"Erica!" a familiar voice shouted. Behind the counter stood a petite girl with a thick brown ponytail and bright, hazel eyes. Though naturally dark-skinned, she was the unmistakable burnt sienna of someone with a monthly pass to a tanning salon. The sight of Erica had her hopping up and down. "What are you doing here? Your mom didn't say you were coming."

"Was my mom stopping by often to sample the merchandise?" Erica snorted, gesturing to the shelves full of alcohol.

Cora laughed. "Well, you guys are just right there." She pointed in the direction of the blue barn next door. "Any news about your uncle?"

Cora asked the question in the same tone one would use to ask about the weather. Cora always went through the motions of being polite but had a hard time disguising her apathy when things weren't directly relevant to her. Some people, like Erica's mother, found this distasteful and abrasive, but Erica found it refreshing. She liked knowing exactly where she stood with people, especially when they liked her. It helped that Erica had known Cora for longer than her memory went back.

Erica shook her head. "No. Granny is trying to stay optimistic. My mom too, but mostly because she can't figure out what to do about Granny and the store."

Cora nodded and the girls were quiet for a moment, letting the topic pass.

"So," Erica said, taking out her debit card. "Can I get thirty on three?"

Cora ran the card through the register. "How long are you here? Just down for the weekend?"

"I'm going to be here until Christmas. You know, until we know what's going on."

"What? That's awesome!" Cora said before catching herself. "I mean—."

"No. It is pretty great. I'll be at the store most days, but we should hang out and catch up."

"Totally. Are you still with that one guy? The one you told me about over spring break. Jason?"

Erica grimaced. Josh had been so boring it wasn't even worth correcting Cora on his name. "No. We didn't make it much past prom. You?"

"Not a lot of variety in Juniper Falls."

"And you've already sampled most of them."

"Right?" Cora laughed. "It's going to be fun having you here. There's a bonfire on Thursday out at my cousin's place in the woods. I'll text you the info if you want to come."

"I'll think about it. I'm not sure what this week is going to be like. I might want to be asleep by seven every night."

"I can think of someone who would be happy if you came. He'll probably ask you tomorrow."

"Who?"

"Seriously, Erica? Think about it."

Erica did think about it. She couldn't come up with any-one besides Cora that she still talked to in Juniper Falls. She had gone to school there through second grade, but who had the same friends from elementary school? None of her friends in Portland were the same ones she met when she originally moved.

"I'm sure you'll figure it out. I'll text you just in case, though," Cora said, handing Erica her receipt. "What are you up to today?"

"I'm going to head to the falls and read for a while. It's too hot to sit around the house and Granny is getting on me about figuring out what young people do here," said Erica, putting air quotes around *young people*.

"Let me know when you figure it out. I'm dying of bore-dom. I should have tried harder to get into college. Remember all those schools I applied to in California? I didn't get accepted into any of them."

"Oof," Erica said, feigning sympathy while feeling supe-rior for the briefest moment before remembering that she too was playing hooky from her education. "I'm supposed to be at Cascades in a month, but I deferred until January."

"It's a good thing our families can keep us employed, then," Cora said.

The door made a sharp *ping* as it opened and a short, bald-ing man wearing a stained muscle shirt came through. Cora and Erica waved goodbye, and Erica went back out into the heat to fill the tank of her car. Unlike the more populated parts of Oregon, Juniper Falls was rural enough that she had to pump her own gas. The metal of the pump burned her hand as she waited for it to click off. She sweat uncomfortably in the swim-suit she wore under a purple sundress. Hanging up the nozzle and jumping in the car, she was hoping that the air condition-ing hadn't completely dissipated while she was inside. She was disappointed. She turned the air up as high as it would go and snaked back through the neighborhood toward the falls.

Erica wondered who—or more specifically, what boy—would care if she was here. She thought back to before her sophomore year when she had spent all summer in Juniper Falls after a big fight with her mother. They had fought about school, hours at the store, whether she could have a boyfriend, whether she could have a car. This was what all her friends fought about with their parents, but for Erica every fight was bigger, the consequences more severe. It took almost nothing to flip her mother's switch. Once the yelling started, Erica felt like she was losing unless she kept up her end of the clamor.

Feeling like a stranger in a familiar land, Erica had been abnormally flirtatious that summer. There were a couple of house parties, a few kisses, and more than that when the kisses were good. In Portland, all the girls were prettier, more confident versions of Erica. Like her, they unironically read Victorian classics, wore just a little, tastefully applied makeup, and preferred high-waisted pants to miniskirts. But in Juniper Falls, which seemed to think the outside world looked much like it was portrayed through television sitcoms and pop songs, she came off as cultured and unique. It was easier to be herself when she wasn't feeling like she was ripping off someone else. None of the hookups from that summer had lasted, but Erica assumed she must have made an impression on one of them.

Not that it mattered. She had three goals for the fall: work hard, help her grandmother, and figure out what she was going to do with her life. None of those had anything to do with kissing country boys. This trip to the cluster of waterfalls at the edge of town was meant to clear her head. Something about the sound of the water, the deep green of the plants around it, the smoothness of rocks eroded over centuries of steady pressure soothed Erica and stilled her usually racing mind. It reminded her how insignificant the decisions she made were to the rest of the world, though that didn't always stop her from remembering how important they were to her.

The drive out of town was much the same as the drive in, a narrow road winding through a dense forest. She knew she was close when the trees opened enough to see the Juniper Falls

Cemetery, which sat on a hill overlooking her destination. When the town was first founded, there was hope that industry would boom. That boom was going to require land, so the cemetery was built as close as possible to the state forest that encompassed the waterfalls and thousands of acres beyond them. It was a romantic idea, creating somewhere beautiful for the dead. The entire hill was cleared, and a winding path built up to its peak. The result was a sunny oasis in the middle of all the hemlocks and firs. A holy-looking light shone on the graves and the two oaks that overlooked them.

Another quarter of a mile and Erica pulled into a gravel lot empty of other cars. She parked and grabbed a waterproof bag out of the backseat of her car. It contained a copy of *Great Expectations*, which Erica was reading for the second time, a bottle of water, a turkey sandwich that Granny made her that morning, and a towel. She swung it over her shoulder and walked down the dirt and gravel path to Peace Falls. Though not the largest waterfall in the area, Peace Falls, named in honor of its view of the cemetery, was Erica's favorite. About forty feet tall, the water came down in a wide sheet rather than the small trickle or chaotic rush of the other falls. The cliff surrounding it, slate gray mixed with ruddy brown, was almost a perfect half-circle, the land seeming to want to curl around and protect something so beautiful. Bright green foliage grew around the top of the cliff, and small shrubs clung to the edges all the way down.

As Erica approached, she took off her cheap flip-flops and navigated the slippery boulders down to the water. At the edge, she slipped off her dress and put it in the bag. She approached the water, walking in until it came up to her hips. The stark difference in temperature between the chilly mountain water and the stagnant air almost made her decide against getting in. But she had to choose, so she opened her arms and took one large stroke into the middle of the pool. The water was lower than she remembered from previous summers but deep enough that she couldn't reach the bottom and keep her head above the surface.

Erica tread water for a few minutes until the nylon straps of the dry bag irritated her skin. She swam to her favorite feature of Peace Falls, a small cave behind the sheet of water that poured over the cliff. The summer had yielded little rain, so the cave was mostly dry, though a fine mist hung in the air. Erica threw the bag in and lifted herself into the cave, which was just large enough for two people to sit. One of Cora's brothers had shown it to them during that long summer three years ago. Cora had been interested for about fifteen minutes, but Erica was drawn to the space. It felt otherworldly, a hideaway, a secret place rarely touched by other people.

Pulling out the towel, she dried her hands and arms so that she could take out her book. She promised herself a reprieve from her life, a moment not to think about Keith or her mother or whether she was making a huge mistake skipping her first quarter of college. She was going to let the rush of the water drown out her thoughts and read Dickens.

The steady sound of water hitting water drowned out most other noises, so Erica was surprised to look up from her book and see a man standing at the edge of the pool. He was tall with dark, close-cropped hair, wearing plain blue swim trunks and a white t-shirt. He used his height to his advantage, scanning the area, lingering perhaps longer in the direction of the cemetery than anywhere else. When he was satisfied that he was alone, he took his shirt off. Erica noticed that his stomach curved slightly, and she could easily make out his collarbones. The tall boys she knew were always slouching, wanting to be on the same level as everyone else. This boy—Erica thought he was about her age—carried himself much differently, with a certain dignity and gracefulness that she didn't associate with her peers. Not wanting to scare him off, Erica tucked herself up against the back wall of the cave and watched.

She could barely make him out as he waded into the pool and swam underneath the sheet of water. He was close now, eight or ten feet away, but his features were obscured by the rush of water. He put most of his body under the fall, letting it pound down around his shoulders. Erica knew it took a lot of strength to hold yourself above the surface, but he was hardly moving. She studied his tanned, muscular back, watched his shoulder blades almost touch as his long arms worked to keep him up. Then he relaxed completely and went under. Erica drew in her breath and held it as she waited for him to come up, but he stayed down longer than she could go without oxygen.

Seconds later, though it felt like minutes to Erica, he popped up just outside of the fall. He was laughing, looking like he was enjoying himself for the first time since she saw him. Erica couldn't help it—his laugh was infectious, deeper than she would have thought—she laughed too.

His face closed immediately as he looked her way, and she could finally make out his features. Bottomless brown eyes, skin that was rough and deeply tanned from time spent outdoors, a small mouth, and a straight, long nose. His eyebrows were thick and brown. Judging by the stubble already forming on his face, he had been acquainted with a razor since early puberty. He looked somewhat familiar, but she couldn't put his face in context.

"Hi," Erica said, moving closer to the mouth of the cave.

He studied her for a beat. She realized how she must look—hair a mess, holding a damp book, intentionally hiding from him on top of slippery rocks and some dead foliage. The situation, or maybe just him, made her feel self-conscious.

"Hey," he said. The laugh didn't return to his lips. He took his eyes off her and headed back to the far edge of the pool. He threw his shirt on—he had no shoes or towel—and walked back up the trail as quickly as he'd come.

Erica sat there, barely making out the sound of his vehicle starting—a truck, this was Juniper Falls after all—and kicking up gravel as it left the parking area. His demeanor had been so calm, but his reaction was so strange, like startling a deer in the woods. There was something tense about him. He was intriguing. And distracting. After a few minutes, Erica threw *Great Expectations* back in the dry bag and swam over to the edge of the pond. Today wasn't going to be the day she forgot all her problems. Today was going to be the day she daydreamed about a mysterious boy.

CHAPTER 3

Though she was no stranger to working hard, often, and early, Erica's job at her parent's store never required her to do the receiving. In her role as Keith's temporary replacement, she had to learn all facets of the store's operations. This included waking up before dawn on a Monday morning to greet the supply truck.

Last night, after she came home from the falls, Erica asked Granny if she was planning to join her in the morning. Granny had smiled pleasantly and said, *"If that was the case, why would I have wanted you down here so badly?"* Even so, Granny rarely slept these days, and black coffee and eggs were on the table before Erica made it down the stairs. Erica was already wearing her uniform—khaki Bermuda shorts and a blue embroidered polo shirt. The front of her A-line bob was pulled back in a clip to keep it out of her eyes.

"Thanks for breakfast, Granny."

Granny waved her cup of coffee in greeting and gave Erica a warm smile. Her hair sat over her shoulders in two long braids like a young girl's. "Are you ready for today? I'm sure Joe will be able to show you everything you need to know. Everything your mother hasn't already told you."

"I'm sure it'll be okay. Kind of worried about all that lifting in the storeroom, though."

"Oh, there are plenty of strong, young backs to help you out," Granny said with a mischievous uplift of her eyebrows.

Erica walked to work that morning, as she would most

days, even when it rained. Juniper Falls was almost silent this early in the morning. There were no streetlights, but the porch lights of friendly neighbors, most of whom she knew, lit her way. She was excited to be heading to the store as the sole representative of the family; it gave her a sense of ownership and responsibility for something larger than herself.

Juniper Falls Farm & Feed was a large building, built by hand by her grandfather and a few other Juniper Falls pioneers in the early 1970s. Every five years it was refreshed with another coat of paint—midnight blue with pale gray trim (*silver*, Granny always insisted, though Keith never let her shell out the money for metallic paint). From the front, it looked like a long, two-story barn, but was L-shaped, with the bottom of the L serving as a loading dock and storeroom. As Erica rounded the corner, she saw there was already one car in the parking lot and a light was on in the office. She grabbed her keys out of her pocket, but when she turned the handle, the office door was unlocked. Erica walked into the small, wood-paneled room, which was crowded with a desktop computer, a printer, several bookshelves of hard copy records, and two large men looking at a clipboard.

The minute Kyle Zukowski's eyes met hers, Erica knew who Cora and Granny had been hinting about. Kyle was a couple of years older than her, the son of *Farm & Feed*'s longest-lasting employee, Joe. Joe began working for Grampy in high school in the late 1980s and never left. Grampy, and then Keith, were the kind of men who believed in the value of hard work and were more than happy to pay Joe a wage that kept a roof over his family's head and put food on the table. Joe was a kind and loyal employee and eager to please. Kyle was cut from the same cloth and had already been working at the store since his junior year of high school.

Erica and Kyle's lives had always overlapped in small ways. As children, they were friendly during the store's anniversary picnics and the barbeques their families hosted. Erica was too reserved to make much of a splash then, but shyness somehow turned into mysteriousness that summer she spent in Juniper Falls three years ago. Kyle, then entering his senior year, was no valedictorian, but he was one of the few decent athletes the town had ever produced. He was built like a concrete pillar and his features were oddly, almost imperceptibly smushed, but his reputation guaranteed him a girlfriend when he wanted one.

"Hi," Erica said.

A huge smile overtook Kyle's face, radiating up to his eyes. "Erica!"

"You're both here early."

"We've got a lot to take in today," Joe said. "We'll be glad to have the extra hands." Erica had been worried she might be stepping on Joe's toes coming here after he had spent more than thirty years earning the kind of role she was just given. As if he could read her mind, Joe pulled her into a rough but genuine one-shouldered hug.

Outside, the piercing sound of a tractor-trailer's backup beeper meant that it was time to get to work. The three of them walked through an interior door into the open storage area. Rectangular spaces were mapped out with duct tape, and the names of their intended contents were spray painted onto the cement—grains, tack, garden, etc. Noisy fluorescent light fixtures hung twenty feet above their heads from bare wooden rafters.

"When did you get here?" Kyle asked though she knew that her mother had told them she was coming.

"Saturday night."

"Cora said she ran into you yesterday. Are you going to make it to the party on Thursday?"

"Is this secretly a homecoming party for me or something? You guys are relentless."

Kyle laughed. "No, more of an end-of-summer thing. One of Cora's cousins, I think he graduated a couple of years before me, has a place way out and likes to have everyone out before it gets cold."

"Everyone?" This was sounding less and less like somewhere Erica wanted to be.

"The under twenty-five crowd."

"I guess that's what passes for old in Juniper Falls. If you're still here at twenty-five, you're probably married with three kids, right?"

"Ouch. That's pretty bitter for someone who is *throwing her life away*." Kyle's voice went up at the end in imitation of her mother. Even though he was joking, Erica felt the shock of the words hit her stomach and send embarrassed blood to her cheeks. Kyle didn't notice. "Super weird about your uncle. You okay?"

"Yeah, I guess so." Erica attempted to use a casually dismissive tone that told him the conversation was over. Being hit so bluntly with the one-two punch of her current life problems was more than she could take before sunrise. Luckily, they caught up with Joe who pushed the big red button that brought up the roller gate. The tractor-trailer moved expertly into position, and the driver came out of the cab to help them open the door and situate the ramp.

"Is this all for us?" Joe asked.

"Just the front half," said the driver. He hopped back down on the gravel and walked to the front of the truck to have a cigarette.

Registering the look of surprise on Erica's face, Joe said, "He'll stay right there until we get unloaded. Keith used to be able to guilt him into helping sometimes, but he doesn't even hear me."

"Fun," Erica dead panned.

Joe deftly removed the merchandise from the truck with a pallet jack and left it in a big pile in the back of the storeroom. It was clear about half an hour in that if Erica tried to match Joe and Kyle pound for pound that she was unlikely to be able to move the next morning. Joe said nothing as her pace slackened, and she began grabbing only one giant bag of dog food at a time or taking charge of the inventory clipboard for a solid ten minutes to catch her breath. Kyle, however, was more than happy to point out her shortcomings.

"C'mon, Erica. You'll never put any muscles on those arms if you don't push yourself." He playfully grabbed her non-existent bicep. "We're going to be hauling more stuff than ever now that the Forest Service finally struck an agreement with Kriners Lumber."

"They did?" This was unwelcome news. She thought Juniper Falls' timber dreams had died decades ago.

"Yeah, it's all but wrapped up. Kriners bought the logging rights to ten thousand acres pretty much right up to the border of town," Joe said, gently placing three boxes in the area designated *glass*.

"That sucks," Erica said. "I always thought of this place as kind of—."

"It does not!" Kyle interrupted. "We're all going to be rich. Rich lumberjacks." He brought the spade he was carrying across his body like an ax, almost knocking over a couple of large clay pots decorated in garish broken tiles, crudely shaped into formless mosaics.

"Kyle! Careful!" Joe said.

"Because it would be a shame to break one of those beautiful works of art."

"Let me guess," Erica said. "My mother?"

"Oh, um, yes," Joe said, uncomfortable with saying anything negative about her family.

"Those things are ugly. We haven't sold any, but they keep coming," Kyle said.

"Kyle," Joe warned.

"No, it's fine. They're awful. My mom's friend makes them. They're supposed to look Grecian, I think. I'm sorry. I'll send them back."

"Thank god," Kyle said. Joe gave him a look that said, *Watch it.*

"What else did she order?" Erica asked.

"Let me show you," Kyle said. They left Joe to handle the pallets and walked to the far back of the storehouse where someone had spray-painted her mother's name—Danni, with a tiny heart over the "i"—on the floor with pink paint and outlined the area in pink duct tape.

Stacked higher than Erica was tall were boxes scrawled with familiar names. Erica knew they were full of hand-painted angel ornaments and delicate kittens made of paper mache. Cans of premium three-dollar-a-can cat food came up to her hips.

"Some of this might sell, but I think she's confused about the volume," Kyle said.

"She's not confused, she's cleaning out our storeroom up in Portland."

"Seriously? If you can't move it up there, there's no way we're going to get rid of it down here."

"I think she knows that, but she was probably being given hell by my dad about having it up there." Pointing at the floor she asked, "Did she paint this?"

"No, I did that," Kyle said, the corners of his mouth twitching. "Sorry."

"Stop apologizing about her. I know what she's like. You'd never know from looking at her that her tastes were so——." Erica couldn't find the right word.

"Cute?" Kyle offered.

"Precious."

Kyle laughed and bumped his meaty arm against hers. "I'd much rather have you here."

"Because I'm going to save you from having to peddle letterpress greeting cards?"

Kyle shook his head and smiled.

Erica had not quite forgiven him for throwing her for a loop earlier and she wasn't sure how she felt about the brand of attention he was paying her. She smiled at his boldness, at the simple way that he viewed the world. In Kyle's mind, he was still an almost handsome athlete, a big fish in a small pond, and that was probably how he would always see himself. For her part, all this flirting and physical activity and cleaning up after her mother planted a seed of doubt in her mind. Perhaps she was making a huge mistake choosing this over college.

"Are you guys going to help me finish this?" Joe called from the back of the room.

"Coming," Erica yelled back, thankful that she was saved from having to respond to Kyle who was looking at her as though he had the answer to a riddle on the tip of his tongue.

It took a couple more hours to move everything to its rightful place in the storeroom. Joe and Kyle were going to spend the time until opening using the new stock to fill in what was missing on the sales floor. Erica, sweaty and bone-tired, was headed home for more sleep before coming back in for closing.

"I'll be back at noon," she said on her way out the door.

"Thanks for your help this morning," Joe said.

"I'll work on getting some of that stuff sent back to Portland this afternoon."

"Don't worry about it," Joe said, and Kyle added, "Think about Thursday."

As soon as she had made it out of the office, she texted Cora: *Kyle Zukowski*. Cora texted back: *I knew you'd figure it out.*

When Erica opened her eyes after her nap between shifts, she couldn't shake the image of the boy from the waterfall. The vision of water evaporating into a fine mist around his lithe shoulders was so clear that she wasn't sure if her subconscious was particularly sharp or if her imagination was filling in the details. She wanted so badly to fall back to sleep and study that beautiful face. But the image was slipping away and suddenly she was all too aware that her arms felt so heavy she was surprised they didn't sink through the bed like a couple of anchors. Though she forgot to wind the clock on the nightstand, she knew it was closer to noon than she might like it to be by the intensity of the sunlight spilling from underneath the curtains. With what felt like more effort than should have been necessary, Erica grabbed her cell phone off the nightstand.

"Damn," she muttered. She had to be back at the store in less than an hour.

Pushing herself out of bed, Erica walked to the mirror to assess the damage. She was smart enough to change out of her shorts into a pair of pajama pants when she got home, but she was still wearing a *Farm & Feed* polo. Even though she knew most of the staff, except for a few seasonal part-timers, she didn't think it was a good idea to show up on her first day in a rumpled, sweat-soaked top. Luckily, she owned more work shirts than any other single item of clothing, so she threw on a new one and picked up a brush to fix her hair. Twisting her long bangs up and pinning them back, she deemed that with a quick wash of her face, she could probably make it through the day without too many disapproving looks.

From the top of the stairs, Erica could hear Granny humming a lullaby. She looked over the banister to see her grandmother, in a pink and gray tracksuit, sitting on the floor and absentmindedly scratching a belly-up Tulip—the look on Granny's face one of faraway consternation.

"Were you asleep when I got home this morning?" Erica asked as she descended the stairs.

"No," Granny said, snapping her eyes back into focus and resetting her mouth into a smile. "A few other old ladies and I like to get up with the sun and take a long walk around the town. You'll live forever if you can outrun death."

"I will keep that in mind."

"I made you a sandwich," Granny said, waving toward the kitchen. "I'll get it for you if you help me up."

"It's ok, I can get it."

"Well, I may be here until you get back, then. I don't know how this dog always manages to trick me into getting down here."

Erica laughed. She held out both of her hands to Granny and pulled her to her feet. Tulip gave Erica a disapproving glance and sighed.

"Tulip looks tired. Do you take her on your walks?" Erica asked.

"No. She's been different since Keith's been gone. Before then, you would never have known she was an old dog, but in the last couple of months, she's let all the years catch up to her. I'm trying not to let the same thing happen to me."

"Hence the walking."

"Hence the walking," Granny agreed.

Erica sat down at the dining table while Granny retrieved a tuna salad sandwich and a glass of water from the kitchen.

"Chips?" Granny asked.

"Please. I think I burned a few thousand calories unloading that shipment this morning."

Granny set down the plate and the glass and sat right across from Erica at the big, round table. The history of her family was etched into that table—permanent marker from school projects, paint from homemade holiday decorations, gouges taken out while enthusiastically gesturing with a steak knife.

"Did you know that Keith took Tulip with him the day he went missing?" Granny asked, running her hands over the hardwood, remembering.

"What? No."

"He often took her when he was going on short hikes. Her little legs don't hold up too long, but she loved him and loved being out in the woods."

"But that means—."

"That he wasn't planning to be gone that long? I know. He left Sunday morning but didn't say when he would be back. He was always quiet and private. You learned after more than forty years that he would tell you things when they were actually important. He loaded Tulip and a daypack into the truck and took off. I figured he'd be home before dinner."

Erica had seen Keith do this exact thing a dozen times before. He spent most of his Sundays in the woods. "Nothing seemed weird?"

"Not at the time. He was taking more time off and leaving Joe in charge of the store a couple of months before all this. He went to all those meetings with the hippies who were trying to stop the Forest Service from striking a deal with that timber company. I was happy he was invested in something other than the store."

"Kyle just told me about the logging thing. How long has that been going on?"

Granny splayed her hands out on the table and tapped her fingertips, remembering. "It's always been looming in the collective conscience of the town. But maybe a year in earnest."

Erica wondered how she hadn't heard about it until now before recalling what a whirlwind the last year had been. Usually, she was down in Juniper Falls visiting Granny and Keith every couple of months or so, but her senior year had flown by in a revolving door of classes, dances, and pointless award ceremonies. "Was that what he was doing? Protesting or something?"

"I don't think so. He wouldn't bring Tulip to something like that."

Summoned by her name, Tulip wandered into the kitchen and laid herself at Erica's feet. Erica tore off a piece of her sandwich and fed it to the corgi, scratching the dog's ears while she ate.

Granny watched them, and Erica noticed tears forming in the corner of her eyes. She stopped petting Tulip and reached across the table to put her hand on top of Granny's. "When did you start to think something was wrong?"

Granny shook her head as if it would shake her memories loose. "Well, sometimes he wouldn't come back until after dark. It takes forever for the sun to set in June, so I didn't worry that he wasn't here when I went to bed. I woke up in the morning and didn't register that anything was different. Then I couldn't find Tulip. I walked all around the house calling her. I opened Keith's bedroom in case she was trapped in there, but I expected him to be at the store taking in the shipment, so it wasn't surprising he wasn't there. Finally, I went outside to call her. Keith's truck was gone, which was strange because he usually walks to work, it being so close. I decided to go over to the store, and Joe asked if Keith had sent me over to help with inventory. He laughed when he said it, but it froze my heart. I knew then it wasn't just Tulip who was lost."

"When did Tulip come home?"

"Not for about two weeks. After the police were already involved and your mom was here, I got a call from Sherry who lives right on the edge of the woods. Tulip wormed her way through her cat door in the night and was asleep in her garage. She was dirty and thin and had eaten all the cat food and thrown it back up all over the place. When I went to go get her, she was so scared, and it took about half an hour to soothe her enough to come to me. I've never seen that dog so much as nervous, but she was out of it. It took days for her to calm down."

This was news to Erica. She wondered why her mother hadn't told her any of this during the phone conversations they had during the months she was down here with Granny. Surely, she told her father who also kept her in the dark. Annoyance was rising within Erica, but she didn't want to make the conversation about her. She reached down to pet the dog again. "Poor Tulip."

"I wish I could ask her what she saw. Your mom gave her a bath and swears she saw dried blood. Why would she say something like that?" Erica shrugged, not in the mood to defend her mother. Granny continued, "The walking group ladies keep trying to tell me he's alive. But I don't know, Erica. When I think back on it, he was different before he disappeared. Almost restless. I feel like I'm missing something, but I can't put my finger on what."

Granny grabbed a paper towel from the dispenser on the table and blew her nose. Erica thought about how unpredictable life is. She was so worried about making the right choices that she felt stalled out. Had Keith been living in neutral all those years? And now he was missing, presumed dead, maybe right when he was finding something to live for?

"You being here should be temporary, Erica," Granny said as if she could read her mind. "I think it's time for me to start thinking long-term, and you should too."

Erica left her chair, rounded the table, and wrapped her arms around Granny's slender shoulders.

"We'll find out what happened to him."

"I know. But you're almost late. Better go now."

Erica squeezed Granny one more time before grabbing her purse off the couch. She instinctively checked for her keys, though she knew the door would be unlocked when she got home.

"Are you going to be okay?" she asked.

"Oh yes," Granny said, still dabbing her eyes. "I always manage somehow."

CHAPTER 4

Pulling up the long gravel driveway lined with vehicles, Erica was already regretting giving in to Cora and Kyle about going out. The last four days at the store challenged and exhausted her. She was amazed at how something could be so different and so familiar all at the same time. Keith had custom programmed the computer system, so while it was easy enough to ring up customers, it was near impossible to do anything else. She didn't know what quantities were normal for the floor, so even when she was able to figure out how to flag things for reorder, Joe often had to convince her to wait a few more weeks. Granny occasionally stopped by, but she mostly talked with her friends and long-time customers. It was almost a liability to have her at the cash register. Erica met the other employees, a varied cast of part-time teenagers and bored mothers. She was grateful to have the next day off and resentful of social obligations keeping her from the comfort of the couch and the joys of Dickensian prose.

Erica pulled her sedan between a couple of trucks. Stepping out of the car, she caught the smell of burning wood and could hear the echo of dozens of voices talking over each other. Erica wore a flannel shirt of her father's that she cut the sleeves off of and tied at her hips with a black tank underneath. Her jeans were from an expensive, popular brand, a thrift store find that she was particularly proud of. Her brown leather flip-flops featured a bottle opener in one of the heels, which she had never used and likely wouldn't tonight. She had agreed to be Cora's designated driver since her local friends could not be trusted to stay sober.

"I wonder if he'll be here," Erica said as they made their way toward the plume of smoke.

"Who?" Cora asked, grabbing onto Erica as her ankles, strapped into high rattan-wrapped wedge heels, wobbled on the uneven gravel.

"That guy from the waterfall last weekend."

"I told you. I know every eligible guy in this town under forty and none of them look like someone you of all people would want to sleep with."

"I never said I wanted to sleep with him."

"No one talks about someone that much without wanting to bang them."

The girls walked up the driveway toward the small craftsman house that glowed around the edges from the bonfire on the other side. A workshop, easily twice the size of the house, stood off a short distance, partially obscured by the forest, which threatened to take back the property.

They turned the corner of the house, and the party came into full view. There were more people than Erica had expected, and she was acquainted with about half of them. The fire, taller than anyone there, blazed closer to the house than Erica was entirely comfortable with. A couple of kegs of cheap beer stood next to a card table stacked with red cups that were spilling onto the ground. It didn't look like anyone had thought to bring out a trash can. There was nowhere to sit, but a few trucks had pulled around back and were parked with their tailgates open.

The host, Cora's cousin Jordan, wandered over to them. He too was wearing flannel, but in a way that suggested he was about to go shoot something. Jordan was a true Hendricks, tall and wiry with thick strawberry blonde hair and the freckled skin to match. Cora, petite and tan, leaned much heavier on her Mexican mother's genes and stood out as a rare beauty among the pale residents of rural Oregon. Everywhere Cora went she was admired, and she was doing a bad job of pretending not to notice the stares that were directed their way.

"Beer?" Jordan asked, handing a cup to Cora and then to Erica.

"I'll take that," Cora said. "DD," she added, tilting the cup at Erica.

"Finally found someone new to drive your wasted ass around?" Jordan asked.

"Not new," Cora said, after swallowing a mouthful of tepid beer. "Erica is Keith Schueller's niece."

"No shit. I remember you from way back. Seriously, have a beer." He tried to hand her the cup he'd been drinking from.

"She doesn't need to be roofied by you," said a voice behind Erica. She turned to see Kyle emerging from the line of trucks. Jordan laughed.

"No roofies here, brother," Jordan said, grabbing one of the cups from Cora and handing it to Kyle. Cora huffed but didn't protest.

"I'm already two deep, man, and I'm trying to cut back," Kyle said, though Erica had a feeling it was for her benefit. Kyle did not have a reputation for holding back at parties. "We'll grab you a soda from the garage?"

"That'd be great." Even if Kyle's motivations for staying sober weren't entirely innocuous, Erica welcomed the effort. She let him take her hand and lead her back to the front of the house.

Near the fire, a group of girls in heels to rival Cora's stood passing a joint between them. A few truck cabs were occupied by couples who appeared not to care that the windows were perfectly clear. Erica, whose idea of behaving badly was convincing her friend's brother to let them into a twenty-one-and-over concert and ordering a bourbon that she was too grossed out by to finish, felt her level of regret rise a few more notches. The Juniper Falls she felt such nostalgia for was full of soft daylight and quiet contentment. She had never quite connected the stories Cora told about her nocturnal activities with the faces she saw around her. When she waved at a few girls she knew from elementary school who acknowledged her with a smile and a nod as she passed. No one acted surprised to see her, which made Erica both happy and a little disappointed.

She and Kyle arrived at the utility door on the side of the garage, and he dropped her hand to open it.

"Locked," he said, but he wasn't deterred. Kyle pushed on the large window to the right, and it opened enough to let his hand through. Erica was confused until she heard the click of the deadbolt, and Kyle opened the door. "He never locks that so he can get in, but I don't think he realizes that it means everyone else can too."

"Doesn't Jordan build houses?"

"Yeah. Hopefully they're more secure than his."

Erica laughed, and they walked into the unlit garage. She hadn't realized how loud it was outside until she was insulated from it. She inhaled deeply and leaned against the bare sheetrock.

"I'm getting the feeling this isn't your scene," Kyle said as he started rooting through the first of a series of banged-up refrigerators.

"It's sensory overload out there." It was much nicer in here away from the music and smoke. And Kyle was being so generous with her.

"Bingo," he said, opening the third fridge. "What do you feel like? Coke, Diet Coke, grape soda, Capri Suns? They still make those?"

"Diet Coke, please."

"Obviously."

"Why obviously?"

"Well, all girls drink diet, right?" He popped the top of the can before handing it to her. Erica took it, trying to decide if it was meant as an observation, a jab, or a joke.

"That comment would annoy me if only it weren't true."

"Sorry," Kyle said, a blush forming on his cheeks. The sincerity in his voice made her laugh again.

"No, you're right. If I've learned one thing from my mother, it's don't drink your calories. That's some kind of female mantra, *don't drink your calories*."

"I've never heard that."

"See? You're proving your hypothesis. All girls do drink diet because girls, unlike boys, are taught to have body issues from their infancy."

"You shouldn't have body issues."

Kyle's tone had softened. Erica knew he was flirting. She was trying to decide if she was going to reciprocate when he took another step toward her and brushed a couple of fingers against her hip. Before she could formulate a response, he did it again and left his hand there, his thick fingers spreading almost to her navel. A small voice in the back of her mind reminded Erica that she wasn't interested in having Kyle Zukowski touch her like that, but her skin yelled at her to let him be. This happened to her sometimes. Her parents were touchy people with each other, but not with her. There were times when she craved an arm around her shoulder, a hug goodbye, and, apparently, a hand on her hip.

Erica had only just begun to lift her head when Cora rushed through the open door.

"Erica! He's—," Cora yelled. Then, "oh," as she looked around and found the pair of them standing much closer than expected.

"Who's what?" Erica asked, narrowing her eyes at Cora in a look that dared her to say something about what was happening. She shook her head minutely as both a warning and an attempt to clear her mind of the giddiness that was taking hold.

"I think I've figured out who your mystery guy is."

"Seriously?" Erica pulled away from Kyle to look out the window, conscious of the way his fingers trailed across her stomach, reluctant to let her go. "Who? Where?"

"Well, I don't want to interrupt," Cora said, backing out of the door.

"No, I'm coming."

Erica followed her, putting one foot outside before grabbing the door frame to stop herself. She looked over her arm at Kyle, who was leaning against one of the refrigerators. The dim light was more forgiving of his flat features, and he looked, she admitted to herself, *good*. His eyebrows were raised, but the corners of his mouth drooped in an expression that mingled confusion with disappointment. She briefly considered how it might be to go back to him, to be held, to let herself be adored. But would that choice look as desirable outside of this garage, in tomorrow's daylight or under the store's fluorescents?

"Sorry," she whispered. She left the door open as she followed Cora.

A breeze had picked up. Autumn was threatening to move in, and the whole party moved closer to the warmth of the bonfire. Cora pulled Erica into the crowd of girls that had previously been smoking and were now grinding against each other in time with the music, all bare legs and push-ups bras. Erica looked past them toward the dark line of trees.

"Where?" she shouted over the music and roar of the fire.

Cora pointed to somewhere in the middle distance. Erica strained her eyes, trying hard to focus past the light into the almost pitch black.

"I can't see him," she yelled.

"There!" Cora twisted Erica a few degrees to the left. Sure enough, she could make out a tall, thin figure lurking a good thirty feet away from the crowd. Though he made no effort to hide, no one else appeared to notice him.

"Who is he?" Erica whispered. She didn't think Cora heard her, but she got her answer anyway.

"Alex Reed."

Alex Reed? Erica combed her brain to remember why she knew that name. Reed. Her mind conjured images of a sky-blue craftsman house. A woman lit a candle on the top of the most beautiful cake Erica had ever seen. Mint green fondant. A birthday party. The form of a boy became clearer, only eight years old but already he could lean his head on his mother's shoulder. But they left Juniper Falls shortly after that party. No, not left, something had happened. An accident. Erica opened her eyes, looking for the dark outline of a ghost.

All she saw was fire.

Alex Reed was supposed to be dead. The February before Erica moved to Portland, Alex and his mother had been asleep when a fire, which started in the oven she forgot to turn off, swept through the house. They died of smoke inhalation before waking up. Erica had heard this story a thousand times. She and her father were both rather forgetful when it came to basic household safety. *One day you're going to burn this house down like Alina Reed!* her mother would yell after they once again left an empty slow cooker plugged into the wall.

Yet Cora said *Alex Reed* like it wasn't completely insane that he would be there.

"What?" Cora yelled over the music and the blaze when Erica grabbed her arm. Cora tried to fight her grip, but Erica kept her fingers firmly planted around Cora's bicep. She pulled her in the direction they had seen Alex until Cora shrugged her off.

"Seriously, what's your deal?"

"I thought Alex Reed died when we were in like second grade." Erica could use a normal voice here. The silence from behind the trees was so complete that it pushed back on the din.

"No, remember? He missed a bunch of school but then he came back to live with his uncle. They tried to put him back in class, but he was so messed up that they pulled him back out again."

"I think I left by then." Erica ran her fingers through her hair. Did he look familiar? Is that why she was so interested in finding out who he was? *Probably not*, she thought. The Alex Reed she knew was blonde, exuberant, and had a pudgy, puppy-fat face. While she could see the resemblance in his height and his eyes, she would never have made the connection between the happy kid she had known and the brooding man at the waterfall without being told.

"Erica," Cora said, sensing her mounting interest. "Leave it alone. You know this town. We all know everything about everyone. But no one knows anything about the Reeds. I want to know why he was creeping out here uninvited."

"I thought everyone under twenty-five was invited."

"I'm serious," Cora said. And from her tone, lacking its usual lyrical sarcasm, Erica knew she was. "I shouldn't have pointed him out to you. No wonder he didn't talk to you at the waterfall. He's probably gone a little feral."

"That seems unfair." Erica couldn't make sense of her need to defend Alex. Sure, he was attractive, but it was more than that. She didn't like Cora's rejection of him just for being an outsider. He had lost his mother at a young age. If he was a little off, surely that explained it.

"Look, there are rumors too. I guess no one's sure where they live, but it's got to be in the middle of nowhere. What are they doing out there and who are they doing it with? Keith isn't the first one to die out in the forest in the last few years."

Erica started at this information. Did Cora really think this guy could be involved in Keith's disappearance? Did other people? "What are you trying to say?"

"I'm not trying to say anything other than that he's weird and you're probably better off staying away from him." Erica thought about pushing Cora for facts or proof or even rumors, but she realized she was being led back toward the party. Cora's mood improved with every wobbly step she made toward the music until it was too loud for Erica to ask more questions.

They both noted the glint in Kyle's eye when he spotted them. Cora smirked. "I saw what was happening with you and Kyle back there. If I hadn't broken it up, who knows."

"It wasn't what it looked like," Erica said, cognizant of using the phrase everyone did when it was exactly what it looked like.

Cora made her way straight for Kyle, but Erica hung back for a moment. Cora didn't notice, and Erica found herself alone for the first time that night. She turned her back to the party and scanned the perimeter of the forest. There was no trace of Alex. She crossed her arms in an attempt to fight off the chill that ran through her, unsure whether it was a result of being too far from the bonfire or processing Alex's sudden resurrection.

Standing there in the dark, she realized how silly she had been to think that coming to Juniper Falls was going to simplify her life. She merely dragged along all her existing problems and added a few more. Keith, Kyle, Alex. Men complicated everything even when they were dead—or weren't, as the case may be. Despite all the people she was supposed to care about, she found herself fighting off a deep-seated sense of loneliness. Alex, beautiful and mysterious he was, was exactly the wrong type of person to fill that void, even if he didn't have anything to do with Keith. Cora and Granny seemed intent on pushing her toward someone else anyway. Maybe she should let them.

Erica found Cora, Kyle, and a guy wearing a faded, holey band shirt and a sparse black beard pumping beers back at the lone table. Kyle's back was to her. She approached without him seeing her and slipped her arm through his, resting her hand on his forearm. He instinctively flexed, but relaxed when he saw her. Looking straight into her eyes, he asked a silent question that she responded to with a close-lipped smile and light squeeze. He flicked his eyebrows at her and then at Cora who shrugged and pulled at the hem of her skirt.

"What did I miss?" Erica asked.

"Cora was just catching us up on your Alex Reed sighting. He's bad news," Kyle said.

"I've been warned. Don't worry, I've sworn off zombies."

"I told you he didn't die," Cora said.

"I know, I know." Erica was ready to put the whole thing behind her. It was a short-lived obsession. Time to move on. She turned to the guy with the beard. "Hi, I'm Erica."

"Derek," he said, throwing his arm around Cora's neck.

Cora rolled her eyes but made no effort to get him off her. "Derek is from Alaska. He starts at Kriners next week."

"Mmm," Erica replied, her lips tightening.

"Erica doesn't believe in logging," Kyle said.

"How liberal of you," Derek said.

"It's more of a *not in my backyard thing*. This place is gorgeous. Why here?"

"Gotta be somewhere."

"Sure, I guess, but I don't have to like it."

Kyle extracted his arm from hers and wrapped it around her waist. Neither of them looked at each other, but she leaned in, liking the way the weight of it sat on her hip. Her arm was left swinging at her side, and she knew the protocol was to loop her thumb in his back pocket or otherwise reciprocate his gesture, but she worried about being too encouraging. Cora pulled down her skirt again and took a sip out of her red cup. She wasn't too far gone, so Erica wasn't worried about what Mr. Hendricks would say if she ran into him later in the week.

The silence lasted just long enough to be awkward before Kyle said, "So, I signed up to start at Kriners next week too."

"Seriously?" Erica said, twisting away from him.

"Yeah, on Monday, after I got off. We sorta talked about it."

"Sorta," Erica spat. She crossed her arms in front of her, daring him to try to pull her back in.

"Are you pissed?"

Erica grew up in Portland, where fast-food restaurants offered trash cans marked *Landfill* and *Recycle*. The City outlawed plastic bags when she was in middle school. Her Environmental Science class toured a building with a garden on the top that filtered rainwater for use in the toilet system. Global warming was a fact, not a theory, and it was exactly this kind of inability to protect assets for future generations that contributed to it. Her mind flew through its litany of reasons why she should be pissed. But, she reminded herself, Kyle was not her boyfriend. She shouldn't be any madder at him than she was at, say, Derek. But she was.

"I guess I can't be upset that you got a better job," she said, willing her displeasure to come out in her tone if it wasn't in her words. "Does your dad know?"

"Yeah. I'll pick up shifts, though. Good thing you're here now to help out."

"Only until December."

"We'll see," Cora interjected. To Derek, she asked, "Want to go closer to the fire?"

"By which she means, do you want to make out?"

"Screw you, Kyle," Cora said, but without betraying any actual annoyance.

"I want to get out of here in about half an hour," Erica called to Cora as she dragged a grinning Derek from the group.

"Plenty of time."

Left alone, Erica tried to stay annoyed with Kyle, but he disarmed her by asking how her last year of high school went and was genuinely engaged in her answers. The way he laughed at her stories, his carefully crafted follow-up questions, how he moved incrementally closer to her as the conversation progressed—it felt like it came straight out of some dating strategy playbook. That didn't mean it wasn't effective. Erica knew she was letting herself get picked up, but she found herself without the tools to fight it.

The party quieted down as they talked. Most people had broken off into small groups, slowly sipping their last drinks before sobering up enough to head home. Only those too inebriated to pay attention to the vibe were still pulsing to the music, which had dropped a few decibels. Their conversation slowed down too.

"I'm sorry," Erica said after they sat quietly for a few moments watching people break off from groups and head toward their cars.

"For what?"

She was annoyed he was going to make her say it. "I don't get to have an opinion about what you choose to do for your job."

"Right."

Six rather inebriated girls crawled into the back of one of the pickup trucks parked on the lawn. Another three guys got into the cab, and the lot of them drove off.

Kyle put his hand on the small of her back. "Do you also want to go find somewhere to sit?"

Erica sighed. She looked at his anticipatory face, trying to conjure up the feeling she had in the garage during the kiss that almost was. Instead, she shook her head.

"Can we take this slow? I find myself a little fragile at the moment."

"Of course."

She noted his very noble attempt to conceal his disappointment.

CHAPTER 5

Erica lay in bed the next morning processing last night's events. She found herself thinking more about the brief glimpse she got of Alex than an entire night spent with Kyle. Why didn't he join the party? Did everyone in Juniper Falls share Cora and Kyle's feelings about him? She caught herself letting the minutes slip by in this way and threw her sheets and comforter off. She had promised her mother she was going to use her time here to figure out her college plans, and this morning was as good a time as any to take stock.

Erica got out of bed and fished a binder full of papers and the College of the Cascades academic handbook from the bottom of one of her boxes. Still in her pajamas, she carried all this and her old laptop downstairs. She found Granny in the blue recliner reading and nursing a cup of coffee.

"Good morning," Erica called as she dropped her stuff on the dining table with a thud and beelined for the kitchen to pour her own cup of dark brew.

"Good morning. You got in late last night. Did you enjoy yourself?" Granny replied, not looking up from her book.

"I did."

"Do you need me to make you anything?"

"No, I'm fine. Just going to look through some college stuff. Don't let me bug you."

"Sure, sure," Granny said, already absorbed again in her book.

Five sticky notes stuck out of the side of the academic handbook, labeled with the associated major they marked. Erica had been through this book countless times and all but memorized the course requirements for each program. This morning she was confident that something new would pop out to her as she walked herself through her carefully whittled down options. If the definition of insanity is doing the same thing over and over and expecting different results, Erica had to accept the fact that she was insane. But she felt like a slightly different person every time she confronted the book. Surely new experiences, new people, new perspectives would influence her and make the choice come clear eventually. She opened her laptop and hit the power button. As it warmed up, she hovered her hand over the sticky notes before opening it to Business Administration.

The upside of choosing the business path was that she could wait to select a specific major—Marketing, Family Business, Supply Chain Management—until her junior year. The basic requirements up until then were generally the same, and she could fill in electives that could be used for any of them. The downside was that she had no idea whether she wanted to pursue business. She had been involved in the store so long that she couldn't tell the difference between interest and expectation. Her mother, and even, if she was honest, her father, couldn't hide the light in their eyes when she mentioned pursuing a business degree. Erica was constantly regaled with the story of her older cousin on her father's side who, pursuing a business bachelor's followed by an MBA, was scooped up by a Fortune 500 company and was running her own division by 30. She's a beast, her dad would say. Erica didn't think she was enough of a beast to make the same kind of impact. She flipped the book to Accounting.

Once, maybe five years ago, Erica had been helping at the Juniper Falls store over Christmas break and happened upon Keith reconciling books after closing. She offered to help, and he handed her a pile of cash receipts to enter into a spreadsheet. It took Keith a long time to come around to computers. He used to do everything by hand, then double-check it against the output from the registers. There were very rarely discrepancies, but he believed in his system and thought it kept him honest.

That night, he and Erica spent half an hour reviewing receipts, the only sounds between them the scratches of Number 2 pencils and the mechanical crunch of an adding machine. When she finished, she silently handed her spreadsheet to Keith. He looked it over, making some ticks in the margins, but not changing any of her work.

"This is perfect. You could be an accountant," he said. "You've got a real eye for numbers."

Erica felt a glow come from inside as he smiled at her, putting her spreadsheet into a pile of his and neatening up the edges. He sent her home to Granny as he finished, but she rode that high for the rest of the break. She wasn't used to being told she was good at things. Her parents expected greatness, so any time she managed it, her accomplishments were met with a shrug that asked why she couldn't perform at that level all the time.

Accounting and Biology were the only two STEM majors that Erica could stomach. The technology and engineering paths, she kept being told, were more lucrative, but any time she read about them her eyes glazed over and she contemplated a nap. Better to play to her strengths, such as they were. She received a four on her Advanced Placement Biology test in May and even found the botany and genetics units fascinating. Unfortunately, if she were to choose Biology, she would have to start right in on classes pertaining to her major. There was no room to second guess herself and graduate on time. Erica thought about the look on her mother's face if she didn't finish in four years and felt a light sweat form on her forehead. Worse, though, would be spending their hard-earned money on a liberal arts degree.

Erica logged in to her computer, opened a browser, and navigated to the Cascades course catalog. She clicked on English and scanned the course titles. Multiple surveys of different periods of British literature, Classical Mythology, The American Novel, Introduction to Literary Criticism and Theory. Four years of reading, of talking about books, of not caring about what she was going to do outside of academia—it sounded like heaven to Erica. She took every English class she could fit into her high school schedule without making her parents suspicious. Books built little worlds that were more romantic and consistent than the one she had to live in. She liked tightly wound plots, hints toward spectacular outcomes, happy and fair endings.

It had been the library at Cascades that ultimately made Erica choose to go there. Her mother had driven her to visit the University of Oregon and Oregon State University last fall. It was made very clear to her that a state school was all her parents could afford, and it was expected that she would go to one of the best. But the huge brick buildings and the number of students milling around everywhere she looked made Erica panic. She already felt invisible in high school; she didn't want the same experience in college. But the smaller state schools were farther away—*not worth the gas money*, Danni had said—and less prestigious, so come November, Erica had only pushed submit on applications to those two colleges.

Then a friend invited her along to visit College of the Cascades, a small, private college nestled among the Ponderosa pines north of Bend. She sat with Heather in the third row of the family SUV as they wound their way through the mountain passes. Just before the forest gave way to the high desert of Central Oregon, they turned onto a campus that looked nothing like what Erica thought a college was supposed to. Large timber-built buildings lined the wide avenue that had more space for bicyclists and walkers than cars. The wood was broken up here and there by stucco buildings painted with bright murals depicting Oregon landmarks—Multnomah Falls, the Painted Hills, Haystack Rock.

Heather was interested in their engineering program, so they soon parted ways and Erica wandered around the compact campus. The buildings were mostly connected by covered walkways, and Erica enjoyed guessing which major was housed there by the posters, plaques, and art that littered the walls. In the middle of the campus, she stepped into a three-story atrium. The distinctive smell of old books hit her immediately and was juxtaposed against the newness of the black metal staircases and railings that wound around the circular space. Though the ceiling was glass and the large room bright, the sunlight fell into the middle of it, shielding its precious contents from damaging ultraviolet rays. While Erica couldn't envision life beyond college, this library was the first place she could see herself spending the next four years.

Erica had decent grades and her parents made little enough money that when acceptance letters rolled in, they were accompanied by financial aid packages that gave Erica the freedom to choose. It had always been her mother's dream to graduate from OSU, and so the battle to go elsewhere was a hard one to win. In the end, her father had to intervene. He backed Erica up based on smaller class sizes, the lack of a party school reputation, and the possibility of larger scholarships once she declared a major.

Shaking her head to clear the memory of yet another fight with her mother, Erica clicked through and read a few upper-level English course descriptions before bringing herself back down to reality. The only way she was ever going to escape indentured servitude to her family's little business empire was to graduate with a degree useful enough to find her employment in the real world. Erica's mother was always telling her that only the independently wealthy and those resolved to poverty had the luxury of going to college for the experience. As Erica was neither of these things, she had to be practical and learn a skill or a trade that translated directly to dollars.

This was where she always got stuck, in the gray area between want and need. She could easily start down the Business Administration path and take a sharp left into English if she magically became a millionaire. And would it be the worst thing in the world if she got a management degree and realized in her thirties that she had been dying all along to pursue a Ph.D. in something not even on her radar like, say, international affairs? Why was it so hard for her to take a step in any direction when hundreds of thousands of her cohort across the country were already settled into their dorm rooms?

Erica stared intently at the handbook, willing herself to

commit to a decision. What, in the end, was so terrifying about being wrong? She was eighteen. It was her prerogative to make bad decisions.

"You look very serious," Granny said. Erica hadn't noticed her coming toward the kitchen to make herself a cup of tea. Granny was a fan of caffeine in many forms.

"Too many variables," Erica grumbled.

Granny lit the gas stove and put the ceramic kettle on top. "Your mother desperately wanted to finish college."

"Oh, I know," Erica said, slumping back into her seat and navigating to her email.

"I think she's mostly just afraid of you making the same mistakes she did."

"I love you, Granny, but I am amazingly tired of hearing that. She met a guy she's still in love with and got pregnant. It's not exactly a cautionary tale."

"No, I suppose not."

"She also manages her own business. Her life isn't ruined."

"Erica," Granny said, sitting down beside her and taking her hand. Granny's skin was thin and warm, and the muscles underneath were strong as they squeezed her fingers. "No one thinks they did well enough for their children. When your mother is critical of you, what she is criticizing is what she perceives as her parenting failures."

"Then she must think she did nothing right. I feel like one big failure."

"You are not, and I promise you she doesn't see you that way. She has always had problems expressing her feelings."

"Not with Dad."

"It's always been different with your father. He understands her in a way no one, not even me, ever has."

Erica wished insights into her mother's complicated psyche made her feel any better. If only someone had sat her down a dozen years ago and tried to make her mother seem like a fully realized person, independent of her influence on Erica's life. The two of them had been keeping a balance sheet on each other for as long as she could remember, as though one day they would be able to prove whose fault it was that they didn't get along.

"What would you pick if you were me?" Erica asked, gesturing at the binder, the book, the computer.

"Love, even if I had any opinions, and I'm not saying that I do, you wouldn't really hear them."

"That's not helpful."

Granny laughed. "No, I suppose it's not, but lessons learned the hard way are usually the ones that stick."

"I might be the exception to that rule."

"You are the exception to many rules, but not that one, I think."

It was Erica's turn to laugh. "Why does everyone think that at this point I am even capable of deciding what I want to do for the rest of my life? Did you know that only half of the people who go to college ever graduate? Those are some depressing odds. Can't we all just get sorted by an aptitude test or something? I'm not above a little 1984."

"A life of unhappiness to save yourself from a single decision doesn't seem like a perfect solution." Granny smiled at her. She got up from the chair as the kettle whistled. "Tea?"

"No, thank you," Erica said, pointing to her coffee mug. She scanned her email and found a notification from the Juniper Falls Library. Just the distraction she needed. "I'm going to go pick up a book."

CHAPTER 6

Freshly showered and dressed, Erica decided to stop by the store before heading to the library. Signage for their big Labor Day sale was supposed to have gone up that morning, which was her excuse for checking in. While it was still warm, the unseasonable heat from earlier in the week had dissipated. Stepping out the front door was like being wrapped in a warm embrace rather than set on fire. Erica had carefully chosen to wear a pumpkin orange romper. This was not her go-to look and clashed loudly with her bright red hair, but she liked the way it drew attention to her long legs and away from her somewhat flat chest.

She walked the short distance to *Juniper Falls Farm & Feed*, threw open the doors, and immediately shot a blazing smile in Kyle's direction. She didn't perceive even the slightest hesitation in him as he set down his scanner and crossed the sales floor to her. Erica flashed her eyes toward Joe, who was manning the registers with a scrawny local kid and stepped just out of Kyle's reach as he approached.

"Hey there," he said, letting his hand fall in the dead space between them.

"Hey." She looked around at the aluminum rows of off-white shelves, fully stocked and bearing the fall-colored sales signage she had designed and printed earlier that week, mostly advertising drastically discounted prices for the assorted flea market finds her mother had brought down with her. A dozen or so customers wove in and out of the aisles. "Not a bad crowd."

"We've been having a good day. Have you?"

Erica nodded. She looked down at her feet, then back at Kyle. "Look, I was thinking that maybe we should go out with Cora and that guy tomorrow night. I think I need a real date. Like bowling."

"Bowling?"

"Bowling. I need some good, clean, old-fashioned fun."

A young woman, probably not that much older than Erica, headed straight toward Kyle with her toddler in tow. She was holding a couple of clearance perennials and her face was full of questions.

"I don't want to get held up here, but say you'll come out with us."

Kyle looked at her, and she noted that he approved of her outfit. She tucked her hair behind one ear and met his gaze.

"Yeah, okay," he finally said.

"Thanks. We'll make plans at work tomorrow?"

"Sure." He turned toward the young woman, and Erica took her opportunity to retreat. As she didn't make it farther than ten feet inside the door, she hoped that her stopping by hadn't come off as too suspicious. The last thing she needed was Joe to tell Granny to tell her mother that she was dating Kyle Zukowski. She could hear the argument now, that this had been her plan all along when she wasn't even sure she was capable of planning that far in advance.

The library was on the other end of downtown from the store—that is, about four blocks away. It had only been a week, but Juniper Falls' residents had already acclimated to having Erica there. They were no longer stopping her in the street asking her probing, personal questions about Keith. They were content to meet her smile and return her nods as she walked from the blue barn past the gas station and a little collection of stores, many with hanging baskets out front whose summer annuals were wilting.

The library was part of a batch of red brick municipal buildings with low, flat roofs and industrial concrete entryways. Erica opened the door, and the blast of the air conditioning made the skin on her arms turn to goose flesh. Though it bore no physical resemblance to the perfection that was the library at Cascades, it did smell the same—a little nutty, a little sour, and unmistakably bookish. Speckled beige linoleum connected to green carpet that was older than Erica. A now-deceased townsperson had hand built the maple bookshelves more than fifty years ago. He was memorialized on a large plaque by the circulation desk, but Erica had looked past it so many times that she no longer registered his name.

Juniper Falls wasn't large enough to merit a well-stocked library, so the librarian, Mrs. Shields, focused mainly on maintaining good reference and children's sections and relied on interlibrary loans to otherwise serve her patrons. In Portland, Erica would sit on the waitlist for bestsellers for months, but Juniper Falls didn't seem to be home to many voracious readers. She had learned during her stay a few summers ago that books came in as quickly as she could read them.

Erica walked over to the holds section, running her fingers across the spines and scanning for her last name. Finding her book, she turned toward the library's single public use computer to request the next title on her reading list. She registered that someone was sitting in the children's section in an overstuffed bean bag chair. Erica smiled to herself, noting that he fit about as well as an elephant would in an armchair. It took her a few beats to realize she had seen that lithe body and those deep-set features before. It was Alex Reed.

Erica jumped, pushing her body up against the holds shelf and out of sight of the boy in the beanbag. She startled Mrs. Shields who looked up from browsing social media on her computer at the circulation desk. Erica tried desperately to make a normal face, one that said there was nothing to see here. Mrs. Shields turned back to her computer. Erica slowly peeled her hand off the side of the bookshelf and looked back at Alex.

Her brain racing with the handful of facts and opinions she had gathered about him in the last week, Erica had a decision to make. This was her opportunity to talk to him, to figure out if Cora's dislike—and her incomprehensible interest—had a basis in reality. What were the chances that he was a serial killer? Slim to none, Erica reasoned. Not to mention, he looked so handsome and otherworldly surrounded by undersized chairs and tables meant for kids. He wore a battered white shirt and cutoff jean shorts. A dollar store flip flop dangled from the big toe of his right foot, which was crossed over his knee. She watched his dark eyes fly back and forth across the pages of a thick John Adams biography. Then, without warning, they lifted to meet hers. There was no choice now. She had to engage.

"Hi again," Erica said, picking up her leaden feet and taking a few steps in his direction. He stared at her, cornered, scrambling to stand, but thwarted by the slippery surface of the beanbag, long limbs akimbo. "We met last weekend at Peace Falls. I was sort of, you know, hanging out, I guess, in the rocks by—," she gestured at nothing. He continued to stare at her, frozen. "Plus, we went to school together a long time ago. I'm Erica Wright."

Alex immediately relaxed. He twisted awkwardly, putting his book on a short table, and pulled himself upright. Erica took a step back. She knew he was tall, but she had a few inches on most women and the top of her head barely skimmed his shoulders.

"Keith's niece," he said, his deep voice sounding like the rumbling whisper of an avalanche.

Erica took half a step back, startled. "You know Keith?"

He nodded. She expected him to do what everyone else had done and tell her how sorry he was that Keith was missing, how he was such a great guy. Especially if he knew something about his disappearance. But Alex stood stone still, waiting for her to speak.

"I saw you at the bonfire last night."

"No," he said, a shadow flickering in his eyes.

"You were definitely there."

Alex shrugged. He grabbed his book off of the table but was reluctant to move past her. She wondered why he would lie about being at the party, and how it hadn't come up with Keith that he knew her supposedly dead classmate. But, if she was the only one who wasn't in the know about his continued existence, maybe it wasn't that weird that Keith had never mentioned it. Questions were bubbling up inside her, but she knew she would never get the answers unless she could sustain some small talk.

"John Adams," she said, pointing to the book in his hands. "Seems dull."

"Great men, great lives."

"I'm more of a fiction girl myself."

"There's nothing to learn from the way people want their stories to play out."

"I disagree. Literature is like any art, a window into the artist's soul."

The side of Alex's wide mouth lifted, though she couldn't tell if it was a smile or a smirk. Either way, it caused her stomach to jump into her chest.

"It was nice to meet you, Erica. Keith talked a lot about you." He closed the gap between them in one long step and extended his hand toward her. This obvious dismissal caught her off guard, but she was able to weakly offer up her hand. He grasped it in a rough, tight handshake and smiled in earnest this time.

"Uh, you too, Alex."

"Xander."

"What?"

"I prefer Xander."

He took his hand from her. She ran the thumb of her left hand down the palm of her right where their skin had just touched.

"See you around," he said, careful to avoid further contact as he navigated past her in the narrow aisle. She caught the scent of wet soil when he passed. As Erica watched him practically sprint through the doors and into the street, she felt none of the fear or aversion she had expected, just confusion and the warm tingle of anticipation.

Erica placed the hold on her next book and checked her current one out from Mrs. Shields. She exited the library into the heat of the day. As she made her way back to Granny's, she wondered if the flowers in the hanging baskets had not only perked up, which could be explained by a healthy dose of water but were somehow bigger and more radiant than they had been just half an hour ago. She couldn't be sure if it was a trick of the light or if being around Xander made the world brighter.

CHAPTER 7

It turned out that wrangling four people with full-time jobs for a double date was harder than Erica anticipated. There were a grand total of six bowling lanes in Juniper Falls, all of them in the new community center on the northside of town. The center was the crowning achievement of Cora's father's time as mayor. At the end of his previous term, rather than put up with another few months of being accosted by Bobby Hendricks and his golf cart everywhere they turned, the locals finally approved the bond.

Erica hadn't seen Kyle since he started at Kriners on Monday. Every day since then she received a text message when he got off saying he was too worn out to be social. This worked in her favor because Erica found there was a lot more to do around the store in his absence. She and Joe were busy clearing out their inventory of kiddie pools and hoses, stocking up instead on rakes and leaf blowers.

On several occasions, Erica had to do a double take to make sure she didn't just see Alex, or rather, Xander, but when she looked up he was never there. She was unable to escape him during her first week in town, but now he was nowhere to be found. Her mind wandered to him when she was at her most busy, in the middle of checking out a long line of lunchtime customers or fixing the seed rack after some kid thought it would be funny to throw all the packets on the floor. She asked Joe about Xander on a whim, but he just shook his head and told her *not to get caught up in all that.*

They finally found time on a Saturday night, and Erica let Kyle pick her up despite Granny's knowing smile and slight razzing. The sixty and up bowling league was having a few weeks off between the summer and fall seasons, and the lanes were available. Erica dressed up in an off-the-shoulder top in a deep, emerald green paired with dark skinny jeans. She always felt too tall to wear heels, plus she couldn't stand the idea of going sockless in bowling shoes, so she settled on a simple pair of flats. The flat iron smoothed out her bob, and she applied a deep red lipstick that she found in the bathroom. It was old enough to have potentially belonged to her mother when she was Erica's age, but with a little water, she was able to soften it. The final effect felt too try-hard to Erica, and she was washing her face when Kyle's lifted old pickup, sporting mud an inch thick and significant rust on the rear wheel wells, pulled into the driveway a full twenty minutes after the agreed-upon seven o'clock.

"Good thing that boy isn't this late to work," Granny called up the stairs. She was watching him out of the front window. "At least he's coming to pick you up at the door."

"And here I was thinking you approved of Kyle," Erica shouted back as she rushed to re-apply mascara with a lighter touch. She grabbed her purse out of her room on her way downstairs and joined Granny at the window.

"Oh I do, love, but still, manners are manners."

"I don't know what time we'll be back tonight. Probably not too late."

Granny pulled herself away from the window, trying not to be too conspicuous as Kyle knocked on the door. Erica made sure to open it slowly, to give Granny time to look natural.

"You look great," he said, taking two steps into the house and immediately pulling Erica into a full-bodied hug. She squeaked, unsure of her position on this method of greeting. He let her go, walked right up to Granny, and hugged her too.

"Hi, Vivian."

Granny, a great fan of all forms of affection, embraced him right back, her thin arms only reaching his shoulder blades.

"No worries about the time tonight. Have fun. Take a coat. It smells like fall tonight."

"Too bad it's still summer during the day. I think I sweat off ten pounds this week hauling around that chainsaw."

"You could use it," Erica said, elbowing him in the stomach.

"Both my pride and my side say *ouch*." Kyle's tone was wounded as they walked outside.

Outside Erica took in the trashy majesty of Kyle's old pickup. The smell of diesel hung in the air, though it had been sitting dormant for at least five minutes. The running board on her side was missing. Though Kyle was waiting to help her up, Erica grabbed the doorframe and jumped back into the seat. This was unsuccessful on the first try.

"You do hate the environment, don't you?" Erica said when she landed back on the ground.

Kyle ignored the comment. "Need some help?"

"I've got this." Erica planted her feet firmly into the gravel, then sprung up with everything she had. She landed deftly in the dirty seat.

"Impressive."

"One of my many talents," she said, pleased with herself. Erica waited for him to get in the truck before asking, "How was your week?"

"Crazy. I wish I'd been able to get this job right out of high school when I was in shape." Kyle threw his arm behind her headrest as he looked behind him to back the truck out of the driveway. "Those first few days before we were even cutting anything, it was exhausting just holding those damn chainsaws long enough to figure out the safety. I don't know how the scrawny dudes like Derek do it. That thing probably outweighs him with a full tank."

"Where did you start clearing?" Erica asked, unable to take the bite out of her voice.

"A few miles outside of town. They're nervous that public opinion is going to turn against them if they start too close to the roads."

"I can't imagine why."

"Let's change the subject, okay? I want things to go awesome on our first real date." Kyle reached across the bench seat and opened his hand as if offering her to take it. He had four broken blisters where his fingers met his palm. Erica kept her hands in her lap.

While Erica was not inclined to hold Kyle's hand, she was impressed that he had chosen to wear a button-up—maroon with dark charcoal stripes. It was unbuttoned at the neck, showing off a fine smattering of chest hair. She felt so young, studying his face, noticing that he must have shaved just before he came as she was used to seeing him with a shadow of facial hair. She realized that all the boys she had ever been out with were just that—boys. But now she was out of high school and there was a new group available to her—men. This revelation was both exciting and terrifying. She tried to imagine what the texture of chest hair might be and couldn't come up with anything other than the thick fur that grew on Tulip's shoulders.

"What are you thinking about?"

"Nothing," she said, perhaps too quickly. Kyle grunted like he knew it was something bad. They had turned off the main road and were driving through a neighborhood of little ranch houses. "Just realizing that I haven't made it through this part of town since I got here. Isn't this where Alina Reed's place was?"

"Yeah, but someone bought the lot and rebuilt it a while back."

Erica felt a wave of disappointment wash over her, though she should have expected that answer. What did she think she was going to do, walk through the rubble like some sort of forensic investigator on a television show? She changed the subject to the rec center. They discussed their mutual love of swimming, how she had competed in a few meets in high school but was always middle of the pack. Then Kyle turned into an expansive, black-topped parking lot. He got out of the truck—the driver's side running board appeared to be intact—and she waited for him to open her door. He held out both of his hands, and she placed hers in them, giving him all her weight as she jumped out.

They received their shoes at a counter just inside the

building. The lanes were downstairs in a windowless basement area that also housed half a dozen arcade games. It looked exactly like a miniature version of every bowling alley Erica had ever been to. The lights were dim, the carpet black with neon outlines of pins and balls. The backsplash at the far end of the lanes depicted bowling pins sitting around a table playing poker. A couple of older men sat at the closest tables, each apparently having paid for his own lane, but for the moment they were disagreeing loudly over something she couldn't make out.

Erica spotted Cora at the far end with Derek. He was wearing the exact outfit she had seen him in more than a week ago, but it was Cora who surprised her. She was sporting an oversized red and black bowling shirt that read *Hendricks Hellraisers* on the back with custom matching bowling shoes. The logo was a huge flaming skull. Erica watched as Cora took a little curtsy before making three carefully calibrated steps toward the lane and letting go of her ball in a perfectly straight arc. It hit the middle pin a little too squarely, leaving her with a split.

"Damn," Cora said.

"So when I called you and you were so excited about going bowling it's because you're secretly a pro?" Erica asked, reaching their lane.

"My dad and grandpa are obsessed. They used to haul me to Roseburg for their league when I was little. We'd go early and they'd teach me. This was my grandpa's," she said, pointing to the embroidery on the pocket that read Ross.

"Now I'm intimidated," Kyle said. He and Derek clapped each other on the back.

"Let me help pick you guys out some balls," Cora said.

"Sexy," Derek replied. Cora rolled her eyes, but Erica could tell she was pleased.

Cora hooked Erica up with a hot pink, ten-pound ball and dropped a blue sixteen pounder into Kyle's arms with a wink. They started their game. Erica was by far the worst bowler in their group, but it didn't matter because she was enjoying herself. Derek and Kyle had at first been apprehensive to get excited about something they clearly considered lame, but by the second game their competitive streak kicked in. They cheered on the girls, booed each other, and tried to determine which superstitious actions led to lucky results. Erica was having such a good time that she almost didn't notice how she and Kyle fell into the same pattern of public displays of affection as Cora and Derek. He wasn't so bold as to kiss her, but he occasionally touched the small of her back while they waited for their turns, and she found herself more than once leaning into his big body.

The group's enthusiasm waned as their wrists wore out. They were finishing their fourth game, and Cora had won all but the third. What Kyle lacked in finesse, he made up in sheer force, shooting his ball down the lane like a discus.

"I'm going to need a cigarette break after this one," Derek observed after Kyle failed to pick up a spare.

Erica rubbed her wrist. "I think I might be getting carpal tunnel."

"You're all just pissed that you're losing to me," Cora replied.

It was Erica's turn, and while Cora had been trying to give her tips, it was pretty clear that bowling wasn't her sport. She broke a hundred in her second game, more the result of luck than skill, and her scores dropped off steadily after that. Erica grabbed her ball, pulled it even with her hip, and practiced her walk and swing. When she let go, the ball dropped limply onto the lane and rolled into the gutter halfway down.

"I think I need some food," she said on her walk of shame back to the ball return.

"It's after nine in Juniper Falls. That means The Diner," Kyle said.

"The trucker diner?"

"Yes, ma'am," Kyle said, registering the dismay in her voice. "You up for it?"

"How bad is it?"

"You'll be fine," Cora said, shaking her head. "It's either that or Momma Hendricks makes us some quesadillas at my house."

"No parents," Derek replied, rolling himself a cigarette while the alley attendant was out of sight.

Erica threw her second ball, knocking down a respectable six pins. She wasn't sure why the idea of the diner was so repulsive to her, but a wave of unease that she usually associated with her mother's disapproval struck Erica in the heart as she took her seat again in the gray plastic swivel chair next to Kyle. Cora got up to take her turn. Derek's fingers flew from the packet of tobacco in his jean pocket to the papers sitting on the table, impressing Erica with their dexterity and economy of motion. It took him no time to put six perfectly rolled cigarettes into a battered aluminum case with another two behind each ear.

Cora finished her frame and came back to the table. Derek handed her one of the cigarettes and got up to retrieve his ball. Cora twiddled the cigarette between her fingers.

"I didn't know you smoked," Erica said, trying hard to keep the disapproval out of her voice.

"I don't. But there's something so European about the idea of it."

"It always blows my mind when anyone of our generation smokes. All our parents hid it, right? And we've been inundated our whole lives with the commercials of old ladies smoking through holes in their necks. Even though I know a bunch of people do it, I can't fight my programming enough to not be grossed out by it."

Cora shook her head and smiled. "Portland wore off on you."

"I guess."

"I'm sure we can beat it out of her," Kyle said. He put his arm around the back of her chair and squeezed her shoulder.

"Well, that was shit," Derek said, pointing to their final scores. Fatigue had set in hard in the second half of the game, and they all made their worst showing of the night. "Are we getting out of here?"

They looked expectantly at Erica, individually judging her willingness to spend a couple of hours in an environment that made her less than comfortable. She mentally smoothed out each line on her forehead that could be read as concern.

"Sure, let's go," she said, pushing her mother's face from her mind.

CHAPTER 8

Erica wasn't sure what she expected from The Diner, but the reality was much more depressing. They took both cars since neither Kyle's truck nor Cora's coupe could comfortably fit four people and their destination was a few miles outside of town.

The Diner itself was a tiny rectangular building dwarfed by canopies sheltering dozens of gas and diesel pumps that were tall and long enough to accommodate tractor-trailers. As far as Erica could tell, the building was painted yellow and the roof was red metal, but years of dirt and exhaust turned the whole structure a gray-brown. Kyle parked the truck in the nearly empty parking lot, and they entered the restaurant portion of the building through a dusty mini mart where a lone woman managed the cash register. She had a perm reminiscent of the eighties with bangs that gave her an extra couple inches of height, probably the same style she sported since high school. She did not look up from her magazine when the doorbell announced their arrival.

Two truckers sat in booths on opposite sides of the restaurant, each wearing faded flannel shirts and eating bowls of tomato soup. The younger of the two, Erica guessed he wasn't much older than Kyle, also had a plate of fries that he dipped into the soup in place of ketchup. At first glance, the furnishings looked like those of your run-of-the-mill diner—red vinyl booths, Formica counters with chrome finishings, a jukebox at the back. But if she looked too closely, she saw that tears in the seats had been sealed with duct tape, stains older than her marred the faux-granite finish, and the chrome was chipping to reveal milky plastic. Only the jukebox looked untouched by wear, possibly because an injection of joy was pointless in such a place.

Judging from Kyle's face, however, he had a different reaction to the space. Despite the *Wait to be Seated* sign, he took Erica's hand and led her to the booth closest to the jukebox, facing the highway.

"What do you feel like?" he asked, taking a few nickels out of his pocket.

"What does it have?"

"Nothing you've ever heard of probably." He cracked a mischievous smile that she couldn't help but return.

"Your favorite, then."

He put a nickel in the jukebox, and it slid down the chute before giving a satisfying clink as it hit the other coins. She wondered if anyone ever emptied the coin tray or if she could pull it out and dig through the layers of nickels, identifying the decade in which they'd been used to purchase a song. Kyle pressed two buttons and joined her back in the booth.

Erica listened to the electrical precision of the jukebox as it put away one record and placed Kyle's selection on the gramophone. It began to play: *Well, when I was a young man never been kissed / I got to thinkin' it over how much I had missed / So I got me a girl and I kissed her and then, and then / Oh, lordy, well I kissed her again.*

"Because she had kisses sweeter than wine," Kyle sing-songed. He leaned in and stole a quick peck from Erica before she had a chance to protest. His lips were thin and dry and left no lingering warmth when they were gone. Erica closed her eyes for a moment and waited to feel something—pleasure, anger, flattery—but failed to identify any emotion that had not been there before the kiss. She opened them to see Kyle studying her face, but before she could feign the proper response, she saw Cora and Derek headed their way. Erica eagerly waved them over.

"This place isn't so bad, is it?" Cora asked, sliding herself into the booth. She and Derek reeked of cigarette smoke and an undercurrent of something skunkier.

"Not so bad," Erica lied.

"I like this," Derek said, bobbing his head to the song that was winding down.

The waitress appeared from the kitchen at the front of the diner for the first time. She could have been, and probably was, the sister of the woman manning the convenience store, but with a decade newer haircut, a voluminous shag. She handed them menus and took their drink orders. Derek ordered a beer, and Erica tried to see his birth date when she carded him. She had him pegged as early twenties, but with his thick beard covering most of his face, he could be thirty for all she knew.

"What made you decide to leave Alaska?" she asked him.

The way Derek's eyes darkened, and his shoulders hunched made her immediately regret asking.

"Needed a change, I guess."

"His dad is an asshole," Cora added.

"I can relate to difficult parents," Erica said.

"No. The kind of asshole that hits his kids and his wife when he drinks," Derek clarified, flicking a strand of hair out of his face.

"Oh," Erica mumbled, "I'm sorry." She felt like an idiot for asking, for driving the conversation in this direction. She looked imploringly at Kyle and Cora to change the subject, but neither of them appeared uncomfortable.

Derek took his cigarette case out of his pocket and tapped it on the table. "No worries. We grew up pretty isolated. Not a lot of money. The usual MO."

"How long have you been in Oregon?"

"Just got here. I took a bunch of jobs on the Kenai. Tried to stay close. The good money is on the Slope, but I just can't stand the cold."

Erica had no idea what Derek was talking about, but she also didn't want him to start drawing a map of Alaska on their flimsy napkins. She opted to smile politely. "I'm sure."

"So, yeah, I'm trying to make enough money to help my little sister go to college. She's only fifteen, but she's crazy smart,

and no one else is going to do anything about it. The rest of us
are just tough and dumb."

"Meanwhile, I didn't even get into college," Cora interrupted. Erica didn't get the sense that she was saving the
conversation from awkwardness, but that she needed the spot-
light to be on herself.

"Sounds like she's lucky to have you," Erica said, giving
Derek a perhaps too bright smile.

"My brothers are just dumb and not even tough," Cora
went on. "Manny doesn't realize there's no money coming to us.
We're not going to be able to slide through like Mom and Dad."

"You come from money?" Derek asked. Kyle raised his
eyebrows.

"Ranching," Cora said, unfazed. "My great grandpa owned
half of northern California. That's how my parents met, working on the ranch. I'm pretty sure someone's written a novel
about it—young, rich white kid falls for the illegal help. The
Napa Valley wine insanity was spreading farther north, though,
so by the time they got married, my grandpa sold all the land at
some huge profit and bought half of Juniper Falls instead."

"Are you guys selling to Kriners?" Kyle asked.

"We can't, apparently," Cora said. "Whatever idiot set up
our trust drew our boundaries within the Town limits, so without a bunch of stupid zoning changes, we can't log. And since
my dad spent all our money on that damn community center—
you're welcome, by the way—it's off to college for me."

"There are other options," Kyle said.

"Are there? Enlighten me."

"Sure. I mean, I've been working in Erica's uncle's store
and now I've got this logging gig."

"You're also twenty, and you live with your dad."

Erica laughed at Cora's jab, glad that they had moved away
from Derek's story with relative ease. Derek didn't seem to
mind. He had poured pepper onto a napkin and was using it like
an Etch A Sketch to draw simple pictures.

Erica never thought of Kyle as that much older than her,
but Cora had a point. If Kyle was going to make a case for

manual labor, it had to be more compelling than moving your bedroom to the basement.

"You never thought about going to college?" Erica asked him.

"No. What's the point? You just go over everything you learned in high school and then pick a major and half the time it's just some kind of bullshit. There is nothing I would want to do for a job that I need to learn about in college."

This logic was eerily close to the same lines Erica had been feeding herself for months, but they sounded inane coming out of someone else's mouth. "Aren't you limiting your options?" she asked, but immediately regretted it. She had no leg to stand on and, worse, she sounded like her mother.

"I'm leaving my options open."

"But what are you going to do?"

"Like as a career? I don't know yet. I have about forty years left to work, though, so I'm sure I'll figure it out eventually."

"That's irresponsible, isn't it? Not having a plan."

"Then why aren't you at Cascades?"

Erica sucked in her breath. She saw Cora draw up her eyebrows and make a sideways grimace at Derek. They both trained their eyes toward the menus. Erica grabbed her menu as well and buried her face in it to hide the surprise and hurt. Kyle tried to get her attention back, but she motioned over to the waitress.

"Y'all ready to order?" the waitress asked. One by one, they told her what they wanted. The waitress responded to the tension at their table by getting away as fast as she could. Erica wished she had lingered.

"Hey, I'm sorry. I know about Keith and all that. I shouldn't have said anything," Kyle said, putting his hand on her arm. She flicked him away.

"It's fine. You're right."

"Erica," Kyle began.

"It's fine. Drop it." To Derek, she said, "Tell me more about Alaska."

The mood picked up again as they moved the conversation back toward uncomplicated topics. The camaraderie the group had developed at the bowling alley came back into play, but Erica kept her hands and everything else to herself for the rest of the meal. It wouldn't have felt so cold had she not been so uncharacteristically relaxed earlier, and if she and Kyle hadn't been sitting across from a couple who saw one another as coat racks for their loose limbs. Cora and Derek were conspiring in low voices as the waitress cleared their plates.

"What's the word?" Kyle asked.

Cora hesitated. "Derek was talking about showing me your job site."

"Oh." Kyle's eyes flicked to Erica who leaned back in her seat. She understood why he wouldn't want to take her, but she was interested in seeing the impacts of this thing she was so philosophically opposed to. Maybe it wasn't that bad. Maybe she could understand better if she had some physical evidence.

"That sounds cool," she said.

"Really?" Kyle said. "I don't think we should go. It's late."

"It's eleven," Cora said.

Kyle frowned. "Let me take you home."

"No, let's go. I want to."

Kyle's shoulders tensed, but he nodded. They paid their bill, Kyle throwing cash down for both of them and not listening to her protests and exited back through the convenience store. The site was about half a mile back toward Juniper Falls and down a dirt road that, Kyle argued, Cora's car wouldn't be able to handle. Cora and Derek climbed into the bed of Kyle's truck, and they took off.

They didn't get on the highway but followed a frontage road before taking an unmarked turn. Kyle slowed down and kept a close eye on the contours of the uneven dirt road, doing his best not to throw his passengers from the truck. His concentration made their silence less awkward. Huge trees, hundreds of years old, grew as close to each other as competition for resources would allow. Erica could almost feel them digging their roots deeper into the ground, searching for groundwater after not seeing rain for months. The windows were open, and she took a deep breath, thinking of how different the air was here than in Portland or even in Juniper Falls, still dusty but organically so.

They made it to a clearing that appeared to be exactly as large as a logging truck needed to turn around. Wide tire prints circled the edges, trampling the underbrush. Kyle parked and went around back to open the tailgate. Erica swung herself down to the ground for the third time that night—she was starting to feel straight-up agile—and saw a single-file dirt path in front of them that wound through the trees.

"Do you have a flashlight?" she heard Cora ask.

"No. I'll leave the headlights on." Kyle walked to the start of the path and held his hand out to Erica. "Coming?"

Erica followed him in but did not take his hand. Cora came up behind her after telling Derek she wasn't going to be the one in the back. They only made it in a few dozen feet before the lights from the truck were useless. Erica grabbed the back of Kyle's shirt, pulling the carefully tucked tail out of his jeans. She ran her other hand across the tree line to make sure she was headed in the right direction. All she could make out when he looked back at her were his white teeth. She wondered if she was being too hard on him, if part of the attraction in the first place wasn't his simplicity, his disinterest in the big things.

And then they ran into nothing.

Erica could smell it almost before she saw it—the sweet tang of sap and fresh wood chips. It was a smell she associated with happy memories of camping trips and family hikes, intensified a hundredfold. The moon was waning, but without branches overhead it was enough to illuminate acres upon acres of shin-high stumps, some of them many feet in diameter. Her heart dropped into her stomach and burned in the acid.

"Jesus," Cora whispered. "I thought you've only been out here a week."

"We have," Derek said.

Erica realized she couldn't hear so much as the hoot of an owl or the flutter of a bat's wings. All this destruction in one week. Her stomach twisted into a knot, and she plunged back through the trees toward the truck.

Kyle dropped Cora and Derek back at The Diner. He tried several times to engage her on their way back to Juniper Falls, but she shut him down. It had been a long evening, and she had too much to think about before she felt like she could reliably explain her feelings to anyone. By the time they turned onto Granny's street, Kyle had realized he wasn't going to get anywhere with her tonight. He pulled up in front of the house and opened his mouth to wish her a good night, but she interrupted.

"That's my mom's car," she said, pointing to another blue sedan, identical to her own, sitting in the driveway.

"Are you sure?"

"Yeah."

Erica's mind raced with reasons why her mother would show up unannounced and what she was going to encounter when she walked in. Maybe she was going to make Erica start college in a week despite their agreement. Didn't she know that her deferment was a done deal? The last thing she needed today was a Danni intervention.

"Should I walk you in?"

"No, I'm fine. Thanks for dinner. And for being such a good sport about bowling. It was nice."

"Really? Because I'm sorry," Kyle started, but she cut him off again.

"I need to go in."

"Ok." Erica was too tense to register the sadness in his voice and the concern on his face. "Good night."

"Night."

She jumped out of the truck. She wished the driveway was longer so that she had more time to compose herself for whatever waited for her on the other side of the door. When she was level with the front window, she could see Granny sitting in a chair stroking her temple while Danni paced back and forth talking on her cell phone. Erica turned the door handle slowly and entered the house. Danni walked up immediately and grabbed her into a tight hug, acrylic nails digging into Erica's back.

"Why haven't you been answering your phone? They found Keith's body," Danni said. Then, holding her at arm's length, "Have you been smoking?"

CHAPTER 9

Keith's body was found by the town's on-call gravedigger and sporadic groundskeeper. Juniper Falls didn't boast a large population, and no one—or at least no one who planned on being buried in the local cemetery—had died since late spring. When the elderly patriarch of an established family passed away in his sleep shortly after Erica came to town, the gravedigger headed into the darkness to prepare the plot for a Sunday funeral. The old man was beloved by his family and so they had procured him a nice spot near the top of the cemetery hill that faced west toward the falls. They wanted him to enjoy the sunshine and a view in the afterlife, never mind the six feet of dirt above his concrete casket.

The gravedigger turned on his halogen floodlights and began digging. The dry summer had hardened the soil, and he needed a break after an hour. Opening a water bottle, he walked a few feet away to lean against one of two white oaks that dwarfed any other foliage in the cemetery. The thick trunks of the trees split into more than a dozen branches just above the gravedigger's head, and the beams coming from his work area filled the gaps between the leaves with a subtle gray light. The result looked something like the black and white photographs that he saw hanging in the town's lone art gallery, photographs that were at once beautiful and vaguely menacing in their emptiness.

Turning his focus to the ground, the gravedigger thought something looked amiss to his trained eye. In between the two trees was a large area of dirt that the contrasting light showed to be darker and more even than its surroundings. The gravedigger returned to his worksite and pointed one of the halogens at the disturbed patch. He grabbed his shovel, which he used to tentatively poke at the soil. After giving slight resistance for the first inch, the dirt gave way easily. The gravedigger couldn't say what compelled him to dig, but he was unprepared for what he would find. It wasn't until the hole was the depth of his shovel that he found a hiking shoe with a foot still in it. He called the police.

Granny, Danni, and Erica heard this account directly from the gravedigger after the police decided there was nothing suspicious about his involvement. They did, however, bring in a homicide specialist. No one dies and buries themselves in a proper grave. As the Schueller women prepared for a funeral, Keith's body went to Medford for forensics processing. Even without following this protocol, he would not have had an open casket. Besides having been dead for almost two months, *he looks like someone ran him through the mill* as Sheriff Denman put it. The stout, sturdy, mustachioed man was Juniper Falls' only policeman. He was in his element ordering around County detectives who had been brought in to make up for his lack of experience with potential murders. While they knew the sheriff meant well, he was responsible for tactlessly bringing Granny to tears more than once.

Sheriff Denman did more than spout unwelcome observations. He and a team of County detectives made a thorough search of the house. They spent most of their time cataloging items in Keith's room. She wasn't sure what they were searching for, but now and then they came out with something in a clear, sealed bag—a spiral notebook, a dirty shirt, some well-worn maps. The police were interested in the possible connection between Keith and the death of a young biologist who had been doing early exploration work for Kriners in the spring. He was tight-lipped on the details but mentioned that his injuries were similar, though the young man's death was chalked up to a work accident.

"They said one of the lumberjacks must have got him, but I've never seen a chainsaw make those kinds of marks," the sheriff said. "Five deep gashes, head to toe. I thought it was an animal attack. But money talks and Big Lumber wanted to hush it up for some reason. Now your Keith turns up after participating in those logging protests and his body was moved."

"Do you have any theories?" Granny asked.

"We always have theories," Sheriff Denman replied. Erica got the impression he was enjoying the mystery a little too much.

Erica had naively thought that finding out once and for all that Keith was dead would bring a sense of closure to her family, but, as Sheriff Denman illustrated, it opened a Pandora's box of new questions and emotions. It became difficult to separate facts given to them by the police from the opinions of the residents of Juniper Falls who were pouring in and out of the house supposedly out of concern for Granny, but also to soothe their thundering sense of morbid curiosity. Erica tried to remember if there really no blood was found at that burial site. Was the official cause of death crush injuries or bleeding out? Were they sure that whoever killed Keith had also been the one to move him to the cemetery?

It was clear from her reactions that while Granny had been able to say aloud that she thought Keith was dead, in her heart he was alive until there was hard evidence to the contrary. Erica watched her closely and could see that the truth came at her in waves. One minute she was able to stand tall, carry on a conversation, and even laugh. But when she was alone, she was prone to burying her face in her hands or leaning against the doorway of the room Keith had occupied since he was an infant. In these moments, Erica would do her best to offer physical comfort, as she couldn't figure out how to ease that kind of pain with words.

Erica's mother, on the other hand, never stopped talking. She must have been grieving the loss of her only sibling, but she maintained momentum by making arrangements for the memorial and, of course, keeping the store running. Danni tried several times to engage with Erica on whether she would continue to be involved with the store but was never satisfied by

Erica's answer that she was committed to staying in Juniper Falls through Christmas. After being asked for the fourth time, Erica snapped, and they ceased talking to each other for an entire afternoon.

She did such a good job of keeping busy that it took Erica a few days before she had time to process what had happened to Keith. After the last sympathizer had left and the parade of food that had been flowing in for days was properly packaged for the freezer, she snuck up to her room and sunk into the floral comforter. Keith, gentle, warm Keith, was dead, and there was a person, perhaps even a person she knew, who was responsible. This was something that happened on late-night TV shows, not to people who lived in small towns in Oregon and paid taxes and had families. Not to people so close to her.

Erica turned on the lamp at her bedside and got up to shut off the overhead. She smoothed out her navy jersey skirt before sitting down on her bed, wondering how many more days she could dig up the dark, conservative outfits required by the occasion. Was the dull ache that resided at the base of her skull what mourning was supposed to feel like? Though the saying went that death was inevitable, Erica realized that until the actual event occurred, life was the expectation. All the people who Erica loved, except for her grandfather who died when she was very young, had been with her, her whole life. Her mother, her father, Granny, Cora, and, up until very recently, Keith, were not always present, but they were constant. What made death so difficult to deal with was the sudden shift, the realization that something that brought you comfort has been torn from you forever.

That fact hit Erica with an unexpected force. She folded her legs up into the bed and held them tight. She wanted to cry but felt more surprise than sadness. How had it taken her so long to understand what it meant to cease being? She had never been the type to be afraid of dying, had never felt an inclination toward religious explanations of the great beyond. Death was a large, gray question mark that even considering Keith's disappearance hadn't come into focus until now.

Looking up from her knees, Erica was surprised to see her mother standing in the doorway. She had her cell phone in her hand, but the screen was black. They looked at each other, Erica noticing for the first time the purple bags forming under her mother's eyes, the deepening of the frown lines around her mouth. She sat up expectantly, waiting for an order—finish cleaning the kitchen, iron Granny's blouse for the funeral, tidy up the living room. Her mother took a tiny step into the room, asking to be invited in. Erica moved her feet to the floor and slid toward the head of the bed. Danni sat down lightly next to her.

"Wow," Danni said.

"Yeah."

If Danni took off the dark eyeliner and lipstick, let her self-tanner fade, and managed a genuine smile, it would have been easy to place her as Erica's mother. Her hair was tastefully dyed in a do-it-yourself ombre that covered her grays, and she carried more weight around her hips and thighs than either Granny or Erica, allowing her to pull off the Schueller family height with a more feminine edge. Still, it wasn't her appearance so much as her demeanor that removed the family resemblance. There was a rigidity about her that the rest of the family lacked. A coolness, which read like superiority and tasted like insecurity, radiated from her clear blue eyes.

With these appraising eyes, Danni glanced around at the chaos in the room, which had been neglected in favor of keeping the downstairs guest-ready over the last few days. Books and clothes were bundled in the closet and strewn across the butterfly chair.

"I'll clean up," Erica said, getting up. Her mother grabbed her wrist.

"It's ok. Do it in the morning."

Erica sat back down. They listened as Granny opened her door at the end of the hall, letting Tulip into the rest of the house. The dog wandered past Erica's door, heading downstairs. The stillness between them made Erica uncomfortable. She had never known her mother to seek comfort in her presence.

"I should let Tulip out."

Danni sighed. "Okay."

Erica got up again and headed for the stairs.

"You've been very helpful this week," Danni said.

Erica stopped, putting her hand on the doorframe. She crossed one foot behind the other ankle, looked at the carpet, and waited. A heart-to-heart was the last thing she wanted. These surficial, innocuous conversations tended to result in tears on one or both of their parts.

"Erica, I know that I didn't want you to come here."

"I know," Erica replied, tensing up for the fight. She kept her eyes trained on the banister.

"No, I mean, I'm glad that you're here. Granny needed you. She needs you now."

"But?"

"No. You made a hard decision. I'm still not sure it was the right decision for you, but you made it and it's helped people."

Erica waited for her to continue, but no reprimand came. "Thanks." It came out like a question.

"You've done a lot of good here. Joe says you've been a big help." Danni paused again and switched which foot she was sitting on. "You know you have to go to school in January, though, right? You know that you can't stay here forever. I'm going to put everything in order." There it was. Erica turned to look at her mother who was scrolling through her phone, likely already making plans.

"What about Granny?"

"Granny is going to be fine once we figure out what happened. We sort of knew it was something like this, right? She's in good shape. She's got lots of friends. She doesn't need a caretaker, Erica. You need an education."

"But we might never know what happened," Erica said, but she knew she sounded desperate, grasping at straws.

"You're right. We might not. But we can't let this hold us back forever."

The next thing she said was meant to start a fight. This is how it always happened between them. Her mother beat her down with an air of rationality until Erica felt trapped and lashed out. "Why? What if I want to stay? What if your life is good enough for me even if it isn't for you?"

"Then you can have it. All of it. Just do college first. All I want you to do is to understand all your options. It's not like I'm asking you to join the Army."

Danni brought her hand up carefully to her hair. She spun loose tendrils around her fingers before placing them delicately back under her bobby pins. Erica had a distinct feeling that her mother felt she had said her piece, but Erica wasn't going to let her go with the upper hand.

"How can you be so blasé about Keith? He could have been murdered," Erica said calmly, doing her best to match her mother's cool.

Danni's eyes widened and met Erica's for the first time. "I am not blasé, Erica. If you can't see that, then you do have a lot of growing up to do."

She got up from the bed and walked straight out the door. Erica had to hop out of the room to let her pass. Danni was occupying the next room over—the room where she had spent almost thirty years of her life as an infant, a girl, a newlywed, and a mother. She closed the door with more force than was necessary. From downstairs, Tulip barked in protest.

CHAPTER 10

Erica woke up the morning after the latest dust-up with her mother realizing that she was in the wrong. She had stayed up for hours after the house was quiet trying to come up with one good reason behind her reluctance to go to college and had once again landed on nothing more solid than a deep-rooted fear of making the wrong choice and ruining the rest of her life. While this was not an insignificant concern, it was presently unfounded—an unfortunate hypothesis that could only be proven by sucking it up and attending Cascades. And as for Keith, hadn't they all been feeling his loss for months? Could she fault her mother for her economy of emotion upon having her suspicions confirmed?

But it was clear at breakfast that all was not forgiven, and Erica was not going to be the first to extend the olive branch. Three generations of women ate pancakes and sweet sausages in silence, each as far away as possible from the others as the round table would allow. Granny was largely lost in her thoughts lately, a state that Erica hoped would improve after the funeral.

The funeral—it was impressive how quickly it had come together. Erica thought that they might wait until the investigation was over, but her mother was determined that they all needed closure as soon as possible. Erica suspected this largely had to do with Danni not wanting to loiter longer than necessary in Juniper Falls. Granny surprised them both by giving in to her daughter's practicality, though at one point she had asked

Erica if she thought a soul could rest without its body in the ground. Erica wasn't sure how to respond, as her family rarely showed any religious or even spiritual inclinations. Granny went so far as to insist the funeral take place at a church. This was more understandable, though, as there was a tiny, white, pastoral-looking chapel on the edge of the river with a rolling green lawn and big wooden doors that they all agreed was exactly the right venue.

It was to this church that Erica drove with her family after their awkward breakfast, all of them dressed in black. Granny had pulled out a little black pillbox hat that contrasted startlingly against her white hair and porcelain skin. Erica wore an empire-waisted cocktail dress that had been purchased several years earlier. The dress was now almost scandalously short and tight across her bosom, but Juniper Falls didn't have a decent clothing store and there hadn't been any time to run into Roseburg. Her father had brought it down with him that morning, having grabbed whatever in her closet was most appropriate.

Erica gasped when her father pulled his car next to a large, black hearse. Granny grabbed her hand in response to Erica's sharp intake of breath. The hearse was empty, but it represented so much that she had not been able to process. Erica turned toward Granny, and she imagined that the older woman's wide-eyed, pursed-lipped expression was mirrored on her face.

"Well, let's go," her mother said. "Erica, you're standing with Granny in the reception line."

"What reception line?"

"We talked about this," Danni sighed. "We have to greet people as they come in."

"Right." Granny squeezed Erica's hand again and gave her a small smile. She squeezed back.

"Let's go, Rich." Her mother opened her car door, and Erica's father stepped out to open hers. Erica adjusted her dress and carefully exited the car.

"You're going to do fine, kiddo," he whispered as he put his arm around her shoulder. "You are a lot farther from death than the rest of us. One foot in the grave over here."

"Not funny," Erica said, but she was betrayed by a snort of laughter that she couldn't contain. This caused her mother to shoot her a sharp look. Erica pretended not to notice, rounded the car, and took her grandmother's arm. "Okay?"

"As okay as I can be," Granny answered.

Erica traversed the lawn arm-in-arm with Granny, trying not to lean on her when her heels sank into the plush grass. They had arrived early, but there were already a few mourners milling around outside the church, unwilling to enter without the family's permission. Danni led them purposefully up the steps and through the heavy doors. Rich, Granny, and Erica lingered in the entrance as Danni strode up the aisle like a determined bride to talk with the withered-looking pastor practicing his lines in one of the front pews.

Erica let her eyes wander around the small church, taking in its white-washed walls, faded burgundy carpet, and rough-hewn, heavily lacquered pews. There was little ornamentation to be found, no stained glass or bleeding crucifix—just an enormous cross in the front of the room stained a deep cherry with a matching simple pulpit. Erica could feel, see, and smell the copious dust particles that twinkled in the narrow streams of light coming through the raised windows.

Danni came back up the aisle and pushed them all into their places. She opened both wooden doors wide, letting in the warm September sunlight.

Greeting casual acquaintances and downright strangers at her uncle's funeral was exactly as awkward as Erica feared it would be. She did her best to mumble the *thank yous* and *yes we're very sads* required to encourage overzealous attendees to move on before they made Granny cry. Cora came with her parents and one of her much older brothers. The little church was near capacity, and Danni was just starting to usher the family to the front when Erica spotted Xander at the edge of the parking lot arguing with a man with shoulder-length yellow-blonde hair falling over his face. The blonde man wrenched his bicep out of Xander's grasp. Xander threw up his hands and stalked toward the church as the other man got into a tan truck.

Erica watched Xander take big, steady strides toward her, but his confidence faltered in the face of her mother who looked witheringly at his plain black t-shirt and khaki work pants. He was significantly underdressed compared to the rest of the mourners, and Erica felt a second-hand embarrassment for him.

"In or out?" Danni barked, giving Xander a head-to-toe appraisal and finding him lacking. "We're about to start."

"In," Xander said, and he took the steps two at a time until he was even with her. "Erica." He nodded in greeting but didn't offer his hand.

"Xander. What are you—?"

"Erica!" Danni called, already halfway down the aisle again with Erica's father in tow.

Erica looked at her mother, then back at Xander who was slouching sheepishly, then to Granny who was squinting toward the parking lot. She heard Granny whisper something but didn't have time to ask what it was before Danni barked her name again. Almost everyone in the congregation was now paying attention to the scene at the door. Erica put her hand on Granny's shoulder, which brought her back to reality.

Erica gave Xander a half-smile and escorted Granny to the front of the church like the father of the bride. Everyone's eyes were on them, and Erica briefly wondered why people chose to put their grief on display like this. As she settled Granny into the pew, Erica could feel the heat of her mother's gaze three people over. Its intensity doubled when Kyle snuck into the spot next to her, putting a possessive hand on the back of her neck. She refused to make eye contact and flashed a glance to where Xander had settled himself in at the back of the room. When Kyle moved his arm down to her waist, she shrugged him off.

"What's wrong?" he whispered into her hair.

Danni made a sound reminiscent of an angry lion and then nodded hard to encourage the pastor to begin. The little man looked terrified, shuffled his papers, and began reading. "We have all come here today to celebrate the life of Keith Schueller, whose dedication to our community will ensure his memory is kept alive for years to come."

Erica wanted nothing more than to listen to Keith's funeral service. She knew she was being disrespectful, that surely there would be some karmic retribution for the way her thoughts kept bouncing between staying clear of Kyle's grasp, reasoning out why Xander was here and who his reluctant friend was, and worrying about facing her mother when it was all over. When she was able to tune in, though, all she heard were generic platitudes that had nothing to do with the person she knew. Sure, the pastor talked about Keith's love of hiking and his dedication to the store. But it was shallow, with no mention of his habit of telling bad jokes in awkward situations, the endless patience he displayed during tedious tasks such as teaching her to play cribbage, and his staunch position that a fire should be blazing in the hearth whenever it was below sixty. She imagined that Keith could forgive her for ignoring a speech that had so little of him in it, especially when his body was lying in a morgue somewhere until the police decided they had learned all they could from it.

The pastor ended with a Bible verse. "For everything there is a season, and a time for every matter under heaven: a time to be born, and a time to die; a time to plant, and a time to pluck up what is planted."

Erica, along with what felt like everyone else in the room, let out a breath she didn't realize she was holding. Mourners started to stir in the pews.

Beside her, Kyle asked, "Can we talk?"

Erica ignored him. Her attention was already at the back of the room. Xander had extracted himself from his pew and was leaning against the back wall of the church. Erica noticed that she wasn't the only one looking at him. A few others, including Cora and her parents, were whispering among each other and casting sidelong glances. People were starting to approach her family to express their condolences once again. Erica had a feeling that Xander would disappear if she didn't act soon.

"Erica, you haven't called me in a week. I just want to talk for a second," Kyle tried again.

"Give me a minute." She pushed past him, avoided seeing

her mother's reaction, and cut around the outside of the pews to where Xander stood.

As she approached, his lips turned up slightly, and he nodded to the door. They had been closed at some point, and Erica was worried about the attention they would draw by opening them again. But she couldn't help following him outside when he opened them a crack and slipped out.

Xander was almost around the side of the building by the time Erica emerged into the sunlight. Her heels sunk into the grass once more. She felt herself falling with nothing around her to catch herself when Xander appeared suddenly to catch her arm. With her opposite hand, she latched onto his forearm, and he pulled her back up to standing.

"Thanks," she mumbled. She was impressed by how ropey and strong the muscles under her hand felt compared to how thin Xander was.

"No problem."

Erica left her hand on his arm in case she fell again as they turned the corner and came face-to-face with the blonde man. His eyes were narrowed in a stern look that made her feel cornered. She squeezed Xander's arm.

"This is my uncle, Alden," he explained.

Erica nodded. An uncle. That made sense. Xander had to have been living with someone since his mother died. But Alden looked too young to have taken custody of a child ten years ago. He also didn't appear to be a very good guardian. He was even more worn and disheveled looking than Xander. There were holes around the cuffs and elbows of his long-sleeve shirt and dirt stains on the knees of his jeans. The only part of his appearance he seemed to care about was his thick, luxurious hair that had been brushed until it was glossy like a show pony's mane.

Erica stepped forward to introduce herself, but Alden wasn't here for small talk. "Have you found Keith's journals?"

Erica's eyebrows shot up. Cora's warnings rang in her ears, and suddenly she hoped someone had seen her leave with Xander. As a precaution, she slipped off her shoes and asked, "What journals?"

Sensing her discomfort, Xander answered quickly, cutting Alden off. "When we would see Keith—Alden knew him too—he would write in these journals. They're important to us. We were hoping you could help us find them."

"I think the police took everything they thought would help."

"Oh, okay," Xander muttered, casting his eyes down.

"No," Alden said. "He would have hidden them where Vivian couldn't find them. They're leather, I think. Kind of a tan cover with ties."

"What's in them?"

Xander looked like he was about to respond, when Alden said, "Horticulture stuff."

Xander closed his mouth, the corners ticking up, and gave a brief nod of agreement.

"I didn't know Keith was into horticulture." She could tell they were lying, but she couldn't figure out why. Did these journals somehow link them to Keith's death? But neither of them had asked her not to open them. She waited for someone to elaborate, but they both just looked at her expectantly.

"I can look, but I don't think I'm going to find anything the police haven't."

"We just," Xander stumbled before trying again. "We think Keith was on to something special, and we want to see how far he got with his—."

"Research," said Alden.

Xander nodded. "Yeah, research."

Erica wished wish there was someone else on her side of this conversation. She felt like she was missing something obvious. She could hear people leaving the church. Part of her wanted to stay here and grill them about their request, but Alden was shifting uneasily as his gaze shifted between her and the direction of the voices.

"I should probably get back to my family," she said at last.

"Erica," Xander said, stepping forward to take her hand that wasn't holding the shoes. "This is important. We hope you can help."

Erica looked into his deep brown eyes and saw her heart-shaped face reflected in them. She could feel the pulse in his palm speed up, which caused her own to beat faster. She nodded.

"And not tell anyone about it? Or about me?" Alden interrupted. Erica dropped Xander's hand.

"What is there to tell about you?" Alden crossed his arms and didn't answer. Erica shook her head. "You're asking me to do a big favor with very little information."

Before anyone could say anything else, they heard Erica's name being called from the front of the church. In the time between when she turned to search for the source of the voice and looked back again, Alden had vanished.

"People shy?"

Xander smiled. "Something like that."

"I'll let you know if I find them. That's the best I can do for now." Xander's lips disappeared into a thin line, but he nodded. Erica waited for him to say something else or to leave as his uncle had, but he was rooted to the spot. She gestured with her shoes in the direction of the voice. "I'm going to go."

Xander kept nodding. Erica took a few steps back, wondering if he was waiting for a more formal goodbye. Finding herself tongue-tied, she turned her back on him and made her way toward the parking lot. The ground felt much firmer under her feet this time as if the grass had knit itself into a thick turf. It took all her strength not to look back to see if he was watching her go.

CHAPTER 11

Her mother's eyes were burning a hole into Erica's forehead as she approached the car in her bare feet. Granny was already in the backseat, ready to be taken back to her home to host her son's wake. Erica could tell her parents were having one of those hushed arguments that centered around how to deal with her. She steeled herself for a confrontation about the strange experience she just had, thinking up biting retorts for questions about Kyle and Xander. But right as it looked like her mother was opening her mouth to begin her tirade, her father saved the day.

"Better get going or folks will arrive before we get there." He opened Erica's door, then swept to the other side of the car to do the same for his wife.

They both obeyed, getting in and waiting patiently for the engine to turn.

"How are you doing, Mom?" Rich asked Granny when he turned his head around to back out of the parking space.

"You would think that the biggest shock of your life would be finding out your son is dead and might have been murdered." Granny was staring out the window and twisting an old handkerchief in her hands. "But then someone comes to his funeral looking the same as when you last saw him almost forty years ago, and you wonder if anything in the world makes sense anymore."

"What are you talking about?" Danni asked, using a softer tone than she had managed to all day.

"I saw a ghost. There is no other explanation."

"Whose ghost?"

"Alden Reed."

Erica's heart leaped into her mouth. "You know Alden?"

Granny turned her eyes from the window and looked at Erica. They were wet and red-ringed. "Do you?"

"I just met him today. I—Xander introduced us."

"Xander?" Danni needled. "Was that the boy you had to run out of the church to meet?"

"It's not like that," Erica sighed. She was about to roll her eyes when she saw the look on Granny's face.

"Xander Reed? Alexander Reed, you mean?" Granny's voice shook.

"Yeah, he said Alden was his uncle. They asked me to help them," Erica trailed off. She needed more information before she could decide whether to reveal what they had asked of her.

"Help them what?" Danni asked. She was reapplying her lipstick in the visor mirror.

"Nothing," Erica said quickly. "How do you know Alden, Granny?"

"Everyone in Juniper Falls knew Alden back in the day. He was an incredible carpenter and woodworker like his father. They built almost everything in this town, including every piece of the church we were just in. Then Alden had a sawmill accident. It took his shoulder almost clean off. The recovery was slow, and no one saw him for a long time. He started coming to town again, but he was emptier somehow." Granny paused for a moment, a far-off look in her eyes. "After that, he bought a piece of land outside of downtown and built a cabin on it. When the cabin was done, he stopped coming. As far as I know, no one has seen him since the eighties. And then he shows up today looking, I swear to you, exactly like he did the last time he came into the store for finishing nails. Young and lean when we should be the same age."

Rich pulled the car into the driveway of Granny's house. He was right, cars were already lining the street, their passengers politely waiting for the family to arrive. They were going to have to wait a little longer as Erica's family digested the story Granny had just told, each of them trying to find a logical way to fit all of the pieces together.

"Wait," Danni said, "Didn't Alex Reed die in that fire with Alina?"

When no one answered her, Danni shrugged, got out, and walked to the house to open the door. She was followed loyally by her husband. Erica turned to Granny.

"It was him, wasn't it?"

"I wouldn't bet my life on it, but yes, I think so." Erica could tell she could hardly believe what she was saying. "What did they want from you?"

"To know how Keith died," Erica lied without knowing exactly why.

Granny nodded. "What did you tell them?"

"That I don't know."

They watched the mourners walk up the driveway and into the house for a moment before Joe Zukowski tapped on the glass on Granny's door. "Need a hand, Vivian?"

Erica looked out her window to see Kyle standing there.

"I suppose we had better go inside," Granny said.

"Can we talk more about this later?"

"Only if there is more to say," Granny let Joe open her door and guide her into the house.

As Erica also exited the car, she was once again flustered by the shortness of her dress. She smoothed out the back before meeting Kyle's determined glance. He reached a hand toward her that she batted away.

"Kyle, it's my uncle's funeral. Whatever you need from me has to wait."

"That's not fair. Everything was fine, and then you ignore me for a week and refuse to talk."

"I've been trying to work through a bit of a family crisis."

"I could have helped."

"We went on one date!"

Judging by the looks Erica was getting from people making her way past them, she said that last part louder than she meant to. She tweaked her mouth into a smile and held the door open. In return, she received understanding nods as people filed past her into the house. She motioned Kyle through as well. She was fed up with being nice. She had too much on her mind to deal with this too.

"I need to change out of this dress." Erica was hoping to throw him off, but he followed her upstairs. She could feel her mother's eyes following them, but there was too much going on for her to care. To give herself some leverage later, she left the door to her room halfway open.

Erica could feel the tension of the last few weeks and months and years—of all the resentment of always putting others before herself, of never being sure of anything—boiling just under her skin. It flashed in her eyes and through her muscles as she turned on Kyle.

"Okay. You have my attention. What do you want to talk about?" Kyle took half a step back and opened then closed his mouth. "You corner me at the funeral, and then here, and now you don't know what you want?"

"I just want to know why you're ignoring me."

"Look, Kyle, I've got things on my mind—big things. Have since I first got here. It's not just Keith. I'm trying to figure out how to be on my own and how to make my own decisions. Do you get that?"

"Sure, but what does that have to do with us?"

"It has everything to do with us because half of us is me! I can't put this weird relationship—not even a relationship—in a box and pretend that nothing that happens around it matters." Erica twirled in frustration, landing hard on her bed. Kyle looked bewildered.

"I'm not asking you to," he said slowly.

"But you are." She balled up her comforter in her hands. "The Erica you like is a little heady, a little complicated, but not a fully realized person. Not the real me."

"I know you," Kyle insisted.

"No, you don't. If you knew me, you'd know that bringing me to that damn logging site was a deal-breaker."

Kyle sighed and raised his eyes to the ceiling. "They've got to print those books you like so much on something."

"Nice try. What kinds of books do I like?"

"Is that a trick question?"

"You say you know me. Who is my favorite author?" She stared at him from the bed, her eyes daring him to guess.

"Does it matter?"

"It matters to me."

Kyle crossed the room and dropped down into the butterfly chair, which was covered in clothes. Under his breath, he muttered, "You said you wanted to go."

Erica couldn't disagree with that, but that didn't mean she wasn't affected by what she saw. If she was honest with herself, though, it wasn't just about the trees. "Look, this is going to come out wrong no matter how I say it."

"You should say it anyway."

"Are you sure?" Kyle nodded. "Okay." She took a deep breath. "The thing is, I don't want to be with somebody because they're a distraction. If I'm going to do this, I want something more. Something real."

Kyle's face hardened. She imagined this was the face he made blocking opponents on the football field in his glory days. Back when he didn't have to work this hard to land a girl like Erica. "So I'm just a distraction?"

"I sound like a bitch."

"A little."

Erica snorted, breaking the tension. "You're great. But we're young, and isn't that when you're supposed to feel this stuff the strongest? If I'm going to take time out from everything I'm supposed to be figuring out, shouldn't it be for more than a little crush?"

"That's harsh. I really like you."

Erica rolled to the end of the bed, laying on her stomach with her chin in her hands. "Answer me honestly. Does thinking about me when I'm not around leave you short of breath? Does your heart skip a beat when you see me?"

Kyle leaned forward in the chair. Their faces were within

inches of each other. She closed her eyes, waiting. When he didn't kiss her, she opened them again. Kyle was shaking his head.

"If we can't even achieve the cliches, what makes you think we'll ever get beyond them into something real?" she asked, holding his gaze. He tried to match her, but his eyes quickly dropped to the floor. Erica sat up again and motioned for him to leave. "I need to get out of this dress."

"You're crazy," Kyle said, but he followed her direction.

"At least you know now."

When he passed her, he paused, their faces inches apart, but he made no move, only asking. "Does this have anything to do with that guy you chased out of the church?"

"Not a thing." She shooed him out and closed the door behind him.

CHAPTER 12

The wake went on for what felt like forever. The people who stayed even after the lunch buffet was empty were mostly drunk, which allowed Erica to escape to a corner of the house with Cora. Erica told her about the confrontation with Kyle, hoping for an ally. Cora stayed annoyingly neutral, responding equally with *sounds like he was kind of a dick* but also *sounds like you were kind of a dick.*

"I think you should give him one more chance, but you're clearly not taking my advice," Cora said, widening her eyes, daring Erica to ask what she meant. When Erica didn't, she sighed. "What was Alex Reed doing at the funeral?"

"He knew Keith," Erica said, looking toward Keith's bedroom, which was tucked under the stairs, its door facing into the living room.

Cora's look of disbelief was so exaggerated that Erica momentarily thought about taking a picture so she could make it into a meme. "Well, shit. Wonders never cease."

Both girls found their gaze drawn back to the door. To visitors who weren't familiar with the house, it probably looked like it led to some kind of storage area or utility closet. Growing up, Erica always loved that about Keith's room. That it was hiding in plain sight.

She was reminiscing about this and only barely registered that Cora asked her if she was doing okay with everything. It was the first time that day someone had asked that question without it annoying her. It was the kind of thing that felt wrong to make small talk out of, but also no one wanted to hear the real answer. Granny's friends hardly wanted to listen to her talk about it, let alone Erica. She wished she could change the whole cultural expectation around death. She doubted Keith would have condoned all of this public mourning. But this was Cora, who always said exactly what was on her mind, which emboldened Erica to be truthful.

"Not really. You know someone moved him, right?"

Cora nodded. It was the talk of the town. "It's weird, right? Not just because it's someone we know. Things like that don't happen here."

"I guess they do now."

Cora pursed her lips and made a little *hmm* sound. "The police haven't said anything yet? No new information?"

"Nothing worth telling me."

"I'll see if my dad knows anything they aren't telling you. Sheriff Denman is a regular on our dinner rotation."

Erica wanted to doubt that a police officer had lips loose enough that he would share case details with civilians, even if they were the mayor. But Juniper Falls was a small town with small-town politics. Bobby might have known something they didn't. She thanked Cora for the offer.

The last of Granny's friends left well after dark. Erica pushed the door closed behind one final little old lady and turned around to survey the room and her family. They all looked exhausted, the circles under their eyes matching their black clothes.

Erica had an idea. "Let me clean up."

"It will be faster if we all do it," Danni said, already heading to the kitchen for a garbage bag.

"No, it's fine. You're tired. You had to plan the funeral and all the food and talk all day. I want to help."

Her parents exchanged a look.

Granny smiled as she got up from one of the recliners. "I'm going to call it a night." She wrapped Erica in her thin arms and held her tight. "Thanks, love."

Erica breathed in the baby powder smell of her grand-mother's hairspray and squeezed back. "Good night, Granny."

As Granny headed for the stairs, Erica turned her attention to her mother. She put on her most determined face and collected plates.

"If you're sure. I feel like I could sleep for fifteen hours." Her mother watched her for a moment as if waiting to be let in on the prank, but Erica continued tidying up the room.

"You'll be up before sunrise," her father joked. He took his wife's hand. "I think I'm going to bed too. I need to meet Joe at the store in the morning."

"Good night," Erica called as they made their way upstairs. Then, without thinking about it, she told her parents she loved them for probably the first time since she left Portland in August.

Her dad replied and even her mother's lips turned upward. "We love you too, kid."

She returned their affectionate gaze until her mother put her hand on her father's back and they disappeared into their room.

Erica didn't move again until she heard the latch on their bedroom door click. She then brought the plates in her hand into the kitchen and methodically moved through the mental checklist of to-dos. She finished collecting plates, took out the trash, and hand-washed the various wine glasses, pint glasses, and even a few champagne flutes that escaped the cupboard over the course of the day. She took a sponge and a dish towel and wiped down surfaces in the living room, working her way through the dining room and back into the kitchen.

When she was satisfied that even her mother couldn't find fault with her effort, she headed to the bottom of the stairs. She stood silently, looking for light under the door frames of the two occupied rooms and listening for the sounds of her parents whispering to each other. Satisfied that they were asleep, Erica tip-toed to the room under the stairs. She turned the round brass handle and was surprised when it gave way easily. She had half been expecting it to be locked or squeak or otherwise make it impossible for her to enter. But the door slid across the carpet, revealing a familiar space.

Keith's room had the same cabin-like feel of the living room—high carpet, a cedar bed frame, off white walls. The only window was small and hung opposite the door with a desk underneath. Her first instinct was to rummage through the desk drawers. She found them to be full of assorted cords and electronics, many of which she recalled him bringing when they went backpacking. Next Erica patted down the large bed with a red comforter and felt under the mattress but came up empty. On either side of the bed were a couple of intricately carved nightstands, but they had no drawers let alone secret compartments.

Erica turned her attention to the wardrobe, which sat between two built-in bookcases. She knew that the wardrobe opened behind the bookcases creating a not-so-secret nook under the stairs. When she was little, Erica begged Keith to swap rooms, but he told her the best he could do was play explorers or Eskimos or any of the other games he and Danni made up when they were kids. Erica spent many hours in Keith's closet only half paying attention as he taught her survivalist techniques for what to do when you get separated from the group climbing Mount Kilimanjaro.

Had the police bothered to look past the hanging clothes into the back of the closet? Had Granny thought to tell them about it? Erica got down on her hands and knees and pushed in. The ceiling sloped rapidly, and Keith's blue work polos and checkered flannel shirts blocked out most of the light. Erica felt into the corner and found what she was looking for—a flashlight, the same one she remembered from growing up. She pushed the squishy button, and a beam of light filled the small room. There wasn't much to see, just a few cardboard boxes and some dusty carpet.

Erica opened the top of the first box. It held memorabilia from Keith's childhood. Some wrestling trophies, yearbooks, a few knick-knacks. She moved it to the side and opened the one underneath, which was full of much the same.

She rummaged through the remaining boxes but couldn't find anything like a journal. She was about ready to give up when she noticed that the far corner of the carpet was slightly raised.

She made herself as small as possible and scooted to the very back of the closet. The carpet came up with relative ease, bringing the multicolored pad with it. Underneath she found two books that fit Alden's exact description.

She ran her fingers over their smooth, light brown covers. It felt wrong to snoop, but she had gone this far. Erica pulled herself out of the closet and crossed the room to quietly shut the door. She went to the desk and turned on a silver reading lamp. She carefully set down both journals and undid the straps holding the top one closed.

There was a name she wasn't familiar with written in large letters. Erica recognized Keith's handwriting from the last few weeks of reviewing accounting logs at the store. A loose newspaper clipping showed that the same person was the Kriners employee who had died under mysterious circumstances a few months before Keith disappeared. On the first several pages were lists of springtime dates followed by long numbers Erica didn't recognize.

The next heading said *Related???* and also had a list of dates and numbers. Under each was a short description.

4/21 - 43°05'38.19"N 123°05'39.97"W - Eviscerated deer left in newly cleared area. Head placed on largest stump.

5/1 - Heard story about engine being torn out of a logging truck parked at the diner overnight. Grill was ripped open and everything torn out.

5/3 - 43°05'38.19"N 123°05'39.97"W - Visited deer site and now covered in trees 2+ feet tall. Replanting??

From what Erica could make out, it appeared that Kriners was getting an early start on their southern Oregon logging operations, and someone had launched a gruesome, aggressive protest. Had Keith been involved somehow? Did one side or the other not appreciate that he was keeping an eye on them? But if he was killed to keep him quiet, why had he been relocated to the cemetery where he was almost sure to be found?

Erica's immediate thought was that she needed to hand this journal over to the police. Surely this was exactly the evidence they needed to forward their investigation that, as best she could tell from overhearing phone calls and whispered conversations between her family, was going nowhere.

Her stomach dropped. What if these journals were the evidence that could implicate Alden and Xander in Keith's murder? She wished Kyle hadn't interrupted her and Granny as they were talking about Alden. The day had been so busy that Erica hadn't had time to process how weird it was that Granny knew Alden and that he was somehow—what? A vampire? No, he had been out in the sunlight today. But what possible explanation could there be for not aging in several decades? Perhaps he was Alden junior and Reed genetics were strong enough to practically spit out a clone. But then wouldn't Xander have introduced him as his cousin?

Erica needed more information about the Reeds, and the best place to dig it up was the internet. Shutting off the lamp and grabbing the journals, she made her way out of Keith's room and upstairs to her bedroom. She leaned back against her pillows and powered on her laptop, tossing the journals on her bed. Into the search bar, she typed *Alexander Reed Juniper Falls*.

The first search result was an article from a local newspaper about the fire she thought killed him. Apparently, she wasn't the only one who had that idea. The image at the top of the article was of a house that she never would have recognized as the blue bungalow from her memories. It was completely black with wisps of gray smoke rising all around it.

A tragic house fire in Juniper Falls last night claimed the lives of Alina Reed, 37, and her son Alexander, 8. Fire trucks were called to the scene around 2 a.m. when a neighbor saw the flames while letting out her dog.

"My husband is a volunteer firefighter," said Mrs. Bertinelli. "I woke him up and he got the boys out here."

Firefighters were able to extinguish the blaze before it spread to neighboring houses. Unfortunately, it was too late to save the family.

"Both residents were found in their beds, indicating death by smoke inhalation," said Sheriff John Denman. "The fire may have been smoking for several hours before it found enough oxygen to blaze up."

Alina Reed, a teacher's aide at Douglas Fir Elementary, was the child of one of Juniper Falls' most beloved families. Her father, Alastair Reed, founded Falls Custom Furniture. Both Alastair and his wife, Nora, passed away when Alina was in her teens. She is survived by her brother, Alden, 58.

A photo of Alex—Xander—and his mom was included with the article. He looked as Erica remembered him, gangly and sandy-haired, smiling while being hugged from behind by Alina. Alina herself had the same yellow hair as Alden, thick and shining. She was a pleasant kind of plump that suggested home-cooked meals and deep laughs. There was no mention of Xander's father and Erica couldn't recall having ever heard of him. She continued reading.

"The Reeds have had a lot of tragedy in their family, starting with Alden getting messed up by that machine when Alina was little," said Jean Taylor, Alex's second-grade teacher and a friend of the family. "Alina was a sweet person and an amazing mother. Alex will be very missed by his classmates."

While the cause of the fire is still unknown, it appears to have started in the kitchen. Most house fires are caused by cooking accidents or faulty electrical wiring. A thorough investigation will be conducted to determine the source.

Then, at the bottom of the article:

Correction, 9/6: While initial reports indicated that Alexander Reed passed away in a house fire on 2/23, he appears to have been in critical condition and has since recovered from his injuries. He continues to reside in Juniper Falls with his maternal uncle, Alden Reed.

Erica stared at the correction. She had moved to Portland in the six months between when Xander supposedly died and when the newspaper noticed he was alive. Her mind raced through the reasons why it would have taken so long to issue a correction. She was sure she remembered more people than just her parents talking like both Alina and Xander had died.

Erica navigated back to her search results. A few other regional news outlets had picked up the original story of the fire. None of them appeared to think it was worth reporting on the mysterious resurrection of a boy who had been dead for half a year.

She changed tactics and looked for Xander's name—in all its potential iterations—on social media sites. She couldn't find him. He was missing too from what should have been his high school graduation announcement. Erica searched for Alden, but he was also a ghost with no online presence.

Erica shut the laptop hard. Who were these people? Alden the unchanging and Xander the undead. She picked up Keith's second journal and undid the leather straps.

The pages were filled with sketches of trees, flowers, and pinecones. Intermixed were some drawings of various wildlife, mostly birds and squirrels. Keith was talented. The sketches looked like they belonged in her biology textbooks. The end of the journal was filled with page after page of the same type of tree with distinctive lobed leaves, their tips reminiscent of butterfly wings. The trees looked familiar to Erica. They were startlingly like the white oaks that stood very near to where Keith's body was found.

CHAPTER 13

The next morning, a tired and confused Erica headed to the store just before opening. When she entered through the office door, she found Joe and her parents settled around the circular laminated table where all important store business was conducted.

"Can we talk to you for a second?" her mother asked.

"Sure." Erica nervously took the seat her mother pointed her to. Were they going to confront her about Kyle again? Did even Joe disapprove?

Danni crossed her arms over her chest and used her business voice. "We are transferring some ownership of the store to Joe. Granny can't go back to working full-time, and you're going back to school, so this way everything is taken care of."

Erica held her face as still as possible so as not to betray her surprise. Joe was nice and worked hard, but he was so passive. He deferred to Keith then Danni, and now even sometimes Erica. She wondered how he would fare without direction. But she knew better than to disagree.

"Oh, okay. Congrats, Joe."

Joe beamed. "You're going to stick around for a bit to make sure I've got everything down, right?"

"Yeah, of course."

"This isn't going to make things awkward between you and Kyle, is it?" her mother asked, in a tone that indicated her clear displeasure at the idea of there being an Erica and Kyle.

"Mom. No. Stop."

Joe chuckled at her discomfort. "It's alright, Danielle. They're just kids."

"Well, I remember being just a kid too," Danni said, looking at Rich. "And look at where that got me."

"It got you the love of your life," said Rich. He knocked his shoulder lightly against his wife's.

"It's not like that!" Erica exclaimed. The men both laughed.

"I hope not, because—," Danni began.

"Give it a rest, babe. She knows." Her father winked at her. "Anyway, we need to get the headstone placed."

This was the second piece of news Erica was unprepared for. "What? Already?"

"Granny bought everyone plots in the cemetery years ago. We're going to make sure the headstone gets up, and then your dad and I are going to go back to Portland," Danni said. "We'll come back down, when, well you know."

"When they put him to rest," her dad said. "Do you want to come?"

Erica sighed. Yesterday had been a bit much for her. She was looking forward to a normal day at the store. They were putting out fall decor, her favorite season. Plus, a headstone made it feel more real in a way the sham funeral didn't. "I think I'll wait to say goodbye until he's here."

In the chaos of getting her parents on the road, Erica convinced her dad to take some of the more offensive merchandise back with them to the Portland store. They slipped ceramic cats and pastel dream catchers into the trunk without Danni noticing. After they left, she unlocked the front door of *Juniper Falls Farm & Feed* and opened the register while Joe piled seasonal merchandise onto a flatbed.

It was a slow morning. Erica wondered if the town was purposely giving them a break. She and Joe talked while they assembled a display of scarecrows, hay bales, pumpkins, and mums. She was surprised to hear that he had some ideas for changes. He was unexpectedly eloquent on the benefits of offering premium dog food brands. As she listened, she got the impression that Joe had been waiting a long time for someone to ask him his opinion, but no one had bothered. Erica knew exactly how this felt and made a mental note to stop underestimating people just because they were quiet.

Joe went home at lunchtime, and Erica was alone until the closer came at five. As she waited out the day, selling a rake here and some bulbs there, there manifested within her a desire not only to visit Keith's headstone after all, but a morbid curiosity to see where his body was found. The white oaks at the top of the Juniper Falls Cemetery were some of the most beautiful trees to be found in a town of nothing but trees, so maybe it wasn't surprising that Keith was drawn to sketch them. But that he had been buried between them was too much of a coincidence to ignore.

After counting her register and signing her paper timesheet for the day—a practice Erica hoped for but did not expect Joe to change—Erica walked back to the house. Granny and Tulip were sitting on the porch together, and Granny was reading Erica's copy of *Great Expectations*.

"Dickens rambles too much for my taste," Granny said.

"A bit. But when he's good, he's so good."

"True, true."

Erica bent down to scratch Tulip behind the ears. "I'm going to head out for a while. Do you want me to grab anything while I'm gone?"

"No. We have all that pity food left in the freezer."

"Not tired of casserole yet?"

Granny rolled her eyes. "Waste not, want not."

Erica went upstairs to change. She tried not to wear her polo and khakis outside of work hours. There was too little differentiation between the store and the rest of her life without walking around with a logo on her chest all day. But a new set of clothes wasn't her only motivation for heading to her bedroom. After changing into skinny jeans and a loose, long-sleeved t-shirt, she grabbed Keith's journals from under her mattress and put them and her usual purse into the dry bag.

Deep down, she hoped that bringing Keith's journals back to the oaks, inhabiting the same space he had not that long ago, would cause some cosmic alignment and help her unlock their secrets. The logical part of her brain said that was crazy and she needed to turn the journals into the police. She wasn't Nancy Drew or Veronica Mars—some teen detective who could solve this case. But something in her gut desperately wanted to trust Xander despite the weirdness surrounding him and his family.

Erica kissed Granny on the cheek on the way out and gave Tulip a rub on her furry, upturned belly. In her car, she turned the Top Forty station down to a pleasant hum as she headed toward the cemetery. It was only a few weeks ago that she had driven into town during this same golden hour. She let everything that happened since wash over her as she admired the sun flashing through the gaps in the trees.

She pulled off at the carved wooden sign that marked the entrance to the cemetery. The parking lot was empty. Erica grabbed her bag and headed up the gravel pathway that led to the top of the hill. Juniper Falls was a small and relatively young town, so the cemetery was sparsely populated with shiny, granite headstones. The town council put restrictions on the height and content of the grave markers, and Erica found the diligent uniformity reassuring. No gaudy angels or gothic crosses here.

She had visited her grandfather's grave before and assumed that was where she should go. She left the main path before it crested the hill and made her way around to the back where the graves overlooked the town rather than the waterfalls. She didn't have to wonder why Granny chose this view. Her family loved Juniper Falls. Though she imagined that when Grampy died, the main source of light at dusk came from the tiny downtown and not the Community Center and strip mall off in the distance.

Erica found Keith's headstone instantly. It was blindingly white with inky black letters. His date of death was included as a month—June—with no day. She knew that even this was a guess. Granny chose the epitaph: *The mountains are calling, and I must go.* The headstone was placed next to her grandfather's, which, she noticed, was half blank, waiting for the day Granny would join him. Between the headstones was a newly planted juniper bush with a handful of cut white lilies placed at its base.

Erica realized that she wasn't sure what she was supposed to do now that she was here. She felt like she already betrayed mourning etiquette by not bringing anything. She also didn't believe in talking to dead people, not that Keith was even buried here. Without any better ideas, she clasped her hands in front of her, closed her eyes, and thought about good times with Keith. She remembered him taking her on hikes in the summer, how he and Granny would wait to cut down a Christmas tree until she and her parents arrived to celebrate, about the time he drove up to Portland to summit Mount Hood with her dad. Tears formed in the corner of her eyes. She opened them and dabbed her face with her sleeve. When she took her wrists away from her eyes, she noticed movement at the top of the hill.

Someone was leaning against the trunk of a white oak, watching her. Tall and slender with dark hair, she recognized immediately that it was Xander. She slowly made her way up the hill, wondering if he followed her here.

"Hey," she said when she reached him.

"Hey."

Erica turned her interest to the disturbed soil between the two trees. She knew from her mother that the area was blocked off for a few days after the discovery of Keith's body, but so many people were interested in peeking at the site that the police tape was taken down when it was clear the area was too contaminated to yield any more secrets.

"So, this is where they found Keith's body." She hoped she would be able to tell from his answer if he harbored any guilt.

"I know." His impassivity annoyed her. She tried a different tactic.

"How did you and Alden know him?"

Xander raised his eyebrows, and Erica momentarily felt bad about interrogating him. There was something about his face, not classically handsome but by no means unpleasant, that drew her eyes. He caught her staring, and she blushed.

"Alden and Keith met hiking. They were both upset about Kriners coming to Juniper Falls. I think they bonded over that."

That sounded true enough. "You guys were close?"

"He came over a lot."

"Alden is your mom's older brother?" Erica asked, emphasizing *older*.

Xander shifted his weight between his feet and feigned interest in the dirt again. Erica had to fight the urge to break the awkward silence by changing the subject. She was so used to being the one who placated, the one who didn't rock the boat. But here in front of her was someone who was oddly invested in keeping information from the police. Someone who was determined to burn through the unearned goodwill she was bestowing on him.

"Did you find Keith's journals?" Xander asked.

Erica's mouth hardened. Answering questions with questions was something her mother always called her out on. She could see now how frustrating it could be. "I did."

"Did you open them?"

"Yes."

"What did you think about what you found?"

"I think it looks suspicious. Kind of like finding you here."

"I figured you would come," Xander said. He gestured with his chin toward Keith's grave, which was visible from their spot on the hill.

"You knew we were putting up Keith's headstone today?"

Xander shrugged. Erica was frustrated by his apparent inability to be forthcoming about anything. But at the same time, she did not get the sense that he was lying to her, merely that he was holding back. She became aware of how close they had moved toward each other before she had the sudden presence of mind to step out of his reach.

"Why do you want the journals so much?"

"Would it help if I told you that I know what's in them?"

"Maybe." Erica crossed her arms, emulating her mother's pose from that morning.

"They're coordinates for locations around Juniper Falls.

Keith was keeping an eye on the Kriners logging operation."

"Coordinates? Is that what the numbers mean?"

"Yeah, GPS coordinates for places where we found things that didn't quite add up."

"We?"

"Keith, Alden, and me. We were all tracking things."

"Together?"

"Yes, Erica, together. I guess we haven't done a very good job of explaining, but Keith was a very good friend to us. To me. I know what you're thinking, but there's no way we would hurt Keith. Exactly the opposite."

"What do you mean?" Erica asked. Xander was quiet again. Another question he wasn't going to answer. "If the journals are tracking shady activity by Kriners, isn't that even more reason to turn them over to the police? If there is nothing in there that can get you in trouble, why do you need them? I mean one of the journals is just drawings. Why are you worried about that?"

Xander sighed. "It's more complicated than that."

"How? What aren't you telling me?"

"Look," he said, "hang on to the journals for now. Ask your logging buddies if they've noticed anything weird happening around their sites. Anything they can't explain. Let's talk again after that and see if you still think I'm the most likely suspect."

Erica considered this. Keith had been dead for months. It couldn't hurt to withhold the journals for a few more days.

"I'll talk to them," she agreed. "But next time we talk, you had better have a lot more answers."

"I'll work on it." A shadow of a smile appeared across his thin lips.

The conversation was over, but neither of them made any motions to leave. Erica was so focused on studying his face—the deep vertical line between his heavy eyebrows and stubble on his cheeks making him look older than she knew he was—that she jumped when she felt his fingers touch her hand that was holding her phone.

"I'll give you my number," he said. Erica's hand opened of its own accord, letting the phone drop. Xander laughed and caught it before it hit the ground. "You don't need to be afraid of me."

"I'm not," Erica protested. To prove it, she took a step toward him, and wrapped her hand over his, slipping her thumb under his to unlock the screen. Xander smiled at the picture of a corgi posed against a backdrop of dahlias that popped up.

"Tulip."

Erica investigated his face, aware of how his lips were now mere inches away. "You know her?"

"I keep telling you. Keith was tight with us."

Erica dropped her hand but didn't move away. She watched him put his number in her phone and breathed in the smell of freshly turned earth that she was starting to associate with him.

"I'll call you after I talk to Kyle and Derek," she said when he handed it back.

"I look forward to it."

She watched him head gracefully back down the hill, and only then did she wonder if those long limbs weren't clouding her judgment.

Back home, Erica decided it was time to talk to Granny. If Keith had been as close to the Reeds as they claimed, she must have known about them. But Granny's surprise at finding Alden at the funeral suggested otherwise. While she waited for Granny to bring them both tea, Erica sent off a text to Kyle:

Erica: Can you and Derek meet me tomorrow? Brunch at the Coffee Stop?

She wasn't surprised to see three little dots show up immediately under her text.

Kyle: I can meet u. Derek tho?

Erica: I have some questions about your job.

Kyle: Don't want to go if ur gonna bitch us out.

Erica: It's not like that. Can you just try to get Derek to meet us? At 11?

Erica watched the dots appear and disappear. She hoped that their last conversation was enough to discourage him from wanting to see her alone.

Kyle: Will see if he's available. See u tomorrow.

She gave it a fifty-fifty chance that he would actually invite Derek. She figured she could cut it short and reach out to Cora if Derek didn't show.

Granny came in with two mugs of chamomile tea. Erica was already tucked in with her feet under her on one corner of the couch. Granny sat down on the other end and threw her legs out between them. Her long white hair was in a braid crown, which, combined with her long cotton nightgown, made her look like an aged-out milkmaid.

"How are you holding up?" Granny asked.

"Better now that the house is quieter."

"Your mom means well."

"Not just that. There have been people in and out of here for a week. It's stressful." Granny nodded her agreement. "I went to the cemetery to see the headstone," Erica continued. "It's nice, Granny. I think he would have liked the saying."

Granny smiled. She was in a good mood despite everything. That was Granny's superpower—the ability to stay calm and comforting in every situation. Erica decided to try her luck. "I ran into Xander Reed while I was there."

"Did you?"

Erica waited for her to elaborate. When she didn't, the floodgates of Erica's overstretched brain burst open with an onslaught of questions. "Did you know Keith knew him? And Alden? Are you sure Alden is supposed to be old? Maybe this guy is a different Alden? They seem to know something about what happened to Keith, but they're not telling me and the whole thing is kind of shady. Did you know that I didn't even realize Xander—Alex— survived the fire that killed his mom?"

If Granny was surprised by this line of questioning, she didn't show it. Erica watched her slowly set her mug down on the coffee table. She appeared to be deciding where to start.

"Well," Granny said at last, "none of us knew about Alex at first. There was a funeral for both of them. Except we didn't know there wasn't a body in Alex's casket. What I heard was that he went missing sometime between when he was put in the ambulance and when that ambulance got to the hospital. You know it's a good twenty minutes away and they weren't in a rush. They thought both he and Alina were dead. Now don't quote me on this because I don't know it for sure, but supposedly the hospital was so embarrassed about losing the body that they just didn't say anything. They figured Alina had no family because Alden hadn't been seen in, what, twenty-five years. I guess they figured no one would ever notice."

"That's impossible. How long was he missing?"

"We all thought he was dead until he showed up for the first day of third grade. We didn't know what to make of it. My friend Lily—you know Lily—Ms. Barton, who manages the office at the elementary school? She said he came in with all the right paperwork. Alden set himself up as his guardian. But, of course, Alden didn't come to the school. Alex showed up all by himself. Everyone in town was talking about it."

"But what did people think happened? I don't remember any of this."

"Your parents were so wrapped up in getting the Portland store off the ground then. I told your mom about it, but I doubt she remembers. The school I guess called Alden and the story he gave was that he had Alex transferred to a different hospital right away and there must have been a mix-up. Supposedly one of the teachers tried to follow Alex home one day but they said he just disappeared into the trees. Besides, he was a different boy when he came back. I don't know if you remember him. He was a loud kid, but he was good at heart. Friendly with everyone."

Erica did have vague memories of being in class with Xander, of recesses playing wall ball and tag, usually boys versus girls. In her memory, he was a blur of constant motion, so unlike the still, quiet person she met in the graveyard today. But she had grown up too. It was unfair to make comparisons against an eight-year-old.

"Losing his mom had to have been rough," Erica said. "I imagine that would change someone."

"I see him around now, mostly at the library. He's polite but reserved. Maybe from a long recovery. Maybe from spending so much time on his own. I never saw him out with friends after he came back." Granny grabbed her tea again and gave it a whirl. She held the mug in her lap. "Did you say he knew Keith? That surprises me, but not as much as that he knew Alden. No one knows Alden anymore. Is that why they were at the funeral?"

Erica had to choose her next words carefully. She wasn't sure yet how much she wanted to give away, but at the same time, what did she know? She was worried that if she told Granny about the journals, she would want to turn them over right away. But it also was important to find out if Granny thought she could trust them.

"Xander and Alden were hiking buddies with Keith. It sounds like they were both interested in what's going on with the new logging stuff."

Granny nodded. "Keith was very against Kriners coming to Juniper Falls. A lot of people were. Some fought it. Wrote letters to the government. Tried to put together a protest. Keith was involved on the periphery of all that. He never was much of a joiner."

"But he didn't protest? No one would have had any reason to want him to keep quiet?" She was surprised when Granny laughed.

"That was the first thing the police asked. But no. He attended a few but he wasn't as vocal as most. I have no reason to think Kriners was out to get Keith. I think that kind of thing only happens in the movies."

This was it. If Erica was going to tell Granny about the journals, it had to be now. For the first time, she wondered if possibly the damaged equipment, the foreboding messages, weren't actions Keith was just observing, but that he was participating in. Was it possible that Keith was some environmentalist vigilante operating in conjunction with the Reeds? Erica tried to impose this version of Keith on top of the one she knew, and it didn't fit. Not to mention Granny didn't think he had it in him to intimidate a giant corporation. Keith was too smart and too pragmatic for that.

Erica was lost in her thoughts and didn't hear the question

Granny asked her. "What was that?"

"I was just wondering why Keith wouldn't have told me he knew Alden. He knew your grandfather and I were friends with the Reeds. Alden and his father made our dining table as a wedding present."

"I never knew that." Then she asked the question she had been pushing to the back of her mind since the car ride back from the funeral. Her gut told her that the answer would push her farther out of her comfort zone than she had ever been before. "Are you sure it was Alden you saw at the funeral? The Alden you knew?"

Granny stared at her. "You know, Erica, I want to tell you without a doubt that it was. And this conversation we're having about Alex—how strange his disappearance and reemergence was—it makes me think that I might not be totally crazy to say that it was him. But you know that I'm not superstitious. I don't believe in spiritual stuff or what have you. So, at the same time, it seems impossible."

Listening to her grandmother, Erica knew that she needed more than rumors pieced together by nosy neighbors. She needed answers about Keith and about Kriners, but most importantly about Xander and Alden themselves.

"Xander wants to meet up again."

Granny frowned in a gesture that was more contemplative than disapproving. "Do you want to?"

"I do." She knew she couldn't stop herself even if she didn't.

"Then do it. I'm sure there is a perfectly good explanation for Alden. And if not, well, you're just the right age for a little intrigue."

Erica and Granny's conversation continued in this way, making guesses about things without getting closer to answers. Erica was glad just to be talking to her grandmother again after she had been so quiet in the wake of discovering Keith's body. She was glad she was there for her in Juniper Falls and not rushing back to Cascades to take some pointless exam. It was important—necessary—for her to play her small part in Granny's recovery. And now to solve the mystery of the Reeds.

CHAPTER 14

Erica woke up early that morning anxious to meet with Kyle and Derek. The night before, she had formulated a plan. She looked up the GPS coordinates of the site where Keith had seen the dead deer. While his journal was full of notes of strange goings-on—slashed truck tires, logs that had been moved overnight to block forest roads—the image of the deer was the one that stayed with her, its disembodied head an unambiguous threat. According to a quick internet search, there was no named road to the site. Erica contemplated how she would figure out getting there when she had a moment of brilliance. She snuck downstairs in the middle of the night and found a handheld GPS stashed among other camouflage-colored electronics in Keith's desk drawer. She stayed up half the night figuring out how to work it, and by morning she was confident she could guide herself where she wanted to go.

Just in case, though, she texted Cora to ride along with her. It was a tough sell. Cora knew about her meet-up with the boys that morning, which Erica took as a good sign that Kyle planned to bring Derek. She invited Cora to come with them and vaguely referenced going for a drive after. Cora was wary after the messy end to their double date, but Erica managed to convince her that they were visiting somewhere special to Keith, which wasn't exactly a lie.

With her plans in place, she started getting ready. Her goal was to look as innocent and non-threatening as possible in the hopes that it would encourage Kyle and Derek to open up. She took the time to round brush her hair and apply the dewy makeup that her mother told her made her look natural but somehow made her feel more done up than the *nighttime* look Danni convinced her to do for prom. Erica sighed over how much of her wardrobe was flannel but settled on a baby pink and blue button-up over a low-cut white tank top and cropped jeans. There was nothing she could do about the severity of her crimson bob, so she pulled it away from her face with a headband.

As she made her way downstairs, it occurred to her that her car might not be the best choice for potential off-roading. She located her grandmother in the kitchen and asked innocently, "Can I borrow Keith's truck today?"

Granny's eyes widened. Erica realized that probably no one had driven it since the police returned it. "For what, love?"

"I'm going hiking with Cora. I'm sorry. I just thought it would be safer. I don't need it."

"You're going hiking like that?" Granny looked skeptical. Erica knew because the face she was making was the one her mother used on her most of the time.

"Um, yes?" Erica said, pulling on one of her sleeves. "But it's fine. I'll take my car."

But Granny's countenance was already softening. She wasn't inclined to be suspicious of Erica. Erica smiled brightly, feeling a little guilty about leaning into Granny's goodwill.

"You know," Granny said at last, "it's fine. It can't sit in the carport forever. The keys are in the bowl by the door. The keychain with the rabbit's foot."

"Thank you!" She wrapped Granny in a hug. Though she would be early, she decided it was best to not let Granny change her mind. She pulled on her hiking boots, fished the keys out of the bowl, and headed outside.

Erica wasn't prepared for the cab of Keith's truck to smell like him—a mix of citrus soap and spearmint gum. She almost couldn't see out of the back window due to the many years of Oregon state and national parks passes that were stuck there.

There were maps all over the dashboard and Tulip's thick hair coated the seats. Erica had to adjust the driver's seat both forward and up to see over the steering wheel. Though she hadn't enjoyed shocking Granny, it felt right to be taking Keith's truck as she researched the contents of his journals, like he was right beside her, guiding her.

The Coffee Stop wasn't much more than a tiny hut in the middle of a gravel parking lot. At some point, they partnered with a cafe in Roseburg that brought them baked goods and simple sandwiches a few times a week. This made it a popular place for locals on mornings when the weather was good and the offerings fresh. To accommodate their newfound popularity, the Coffee Stop erected a large tent on one side of the parking lot with picnic tables to allow guests to enjoy their purchases.

Erica grabbed a triple-shot mocha and ham and egg croissant at the drive-through and managed to park the truck without hitting anything. Navigating the much larger vehicle was a learning experience, but she felt like she was getting the hang of it. Walking over to the picnic tables, she was glad that she was early. The place was predictably busy. She set down her food on the last open table and threw her jacket and purse on the other side, the universal sign for holding a spot.

Cora arrived first, and Erica thought she might have to revise her opinion of Cora as a late person. Cora tried to take the seat opposite her, but Erica grabbed her arm and pulled her next to her in a move she hoped came off as friendly and not desperate. She wanted a clear view of the boys when they arrived.

Derek drove up in a beater station wagon with Alaska plates. He headed straight for them and gave Cora an open-mouthed kiss that made Erica uncomfortable. They went together to the small window designated for walk-ups to keep foot traffic out of the line of cars. Erica saw Kyle's truck get into the drive-through line and waved him over after he parked. He came toward her with a to-go cup in each hand and frowned when he saw one already in front of her.

"Sit down," she said, gesturing across from her. "Cora and Derek are ordering."

"You look nice."

Erica smiled and gestured to the cups. "What did you get me?"

"I took a guess and got a vanilla latte. Skim milk after our conversation about Diet Coke."

"Oh, fat is okay now. It's just sugar that's the enemy." Holding up her cup she said, "Mocha. Whole milk."

"Good to know."

Cora and Derek returned with cups and bags. Derek looked disappointed when he was forced to settle himself across from Cora.

Kyle and Derek bumped fists and the latter asked, "You get mad overtime this week?"

"Yeah, I think I put in almost sixty hours. My crew is putting down an access road. Everything hurts."

"But isn't that new de-limber cool? Taking off all those branches." Derek put his fingertips together and brought them down slowly. "They come off just like that. Crack, crack, crack."

Erica flinched involuntarily.

Derek saw it. "Oh. Sorry."

"No," Erica said, trying to add some levity to her tone. "That's what I wanted to talk about. I've heard that there is some weird stuff going on at your logging sites, and I was wondering if you guys have seen anything unusual."

Kyle and Derek exchanged looks. "Weird how?"

"I don't know. Maybe, like, vandalism." Erica mentally kicked herself for the flick of her hand that accompanied this. It was an unnaturally casual gesture that caused Kyle to squint suspiciously at her as he replied.

"I've heard about some stuff. The guys say it's environmentalist groups. They've seen it before. Shit spray-painted on the trees and the equipment. Stuff like murderers and whatever."

"Have you seen it yourself?"

"Not like that exactly."

"You?" Erica asked, nodding to Derek.

"No spray paint," Derek said. "Our foreman had a dead raccoon left on his truck, though. Its guts were half-eaten by something before we got to it. Pretty gross."

Kyle nodded, then his eyes widened, remembering. "I'm not sure if anyone ever told me if it was an accident or what but we came on site one morning and one of the skidders was knocked over on its side and the arm was all bent up. That would have been hard to do without the keys. Our crew lead was super pissed."

"That's not that weird," Cora interjected. "When they were constructing the community center, my dad said the construction guys would break stuff and try to lie their way out of it."

"Maybe," said Kyle, "but the damage was crazy. Let me show you."

Kyle pulled his phone out of his pocket. The photos must have been taken in the early morning because the light was low. Erica could see that the huge steel arm of the machinery was twisted in a way that even her very limited knowledge of physics told her required an intense amount of force. He scrolled through several photos of the skidder and then talked them through some of the other, more pleasant photos.

"It's so quiet out there first thing in the morning," Kyle said, showing them pictures of dense forest, some with an early morning fog hanging low in the branches. "Here, I took a video."

Kyle pressed play and they all leaned in to watch the camera pan through an eerily silent forest. The fir trees towered over a bed of sword ferns and waxy-leafed plants. Erica wondered how they could be so blasé about destroying something so beautiful. Then she saw something huge and black move in the background at an impossible speed.

"What was that?" she exclaimed, reaching for Kyle's phone, but he kept his hold on it.

"What was what?"

"Behind the trees. Go back!"

Kyle dragged his finger over the screen and pushed the play again. Now that she knew what she was looking for, she poked the screen to pause it when she saw the shadow.

"Do you see that?"

"Weird," said Kyle, squinting at the screen. "We hear something big out in the woods sometimes, but the guys say we make too much noise for anything to try to bother us."

Erica looked up to see Derek who was staring intently at the phone. "What?"

Derek slowly lifted his head to meet her gaze. He looked like he had seen a ghost. "I have this feeling when I'm out there that something is watching us. Sometimes it's so, like, woah, that I have to stop, but I can't ever see it." Derek grabbed the phone from Kyle's hand and brought the screen up to his face.

"You okay, dude?" Kyle asked. "It's probably just an animal or something."

"I don't know. It looks big," Cora said.

"An animal," Derek said, half a statement, half a question. He was so shaken up that Cora got up and wiggled her way onto the boys' side of the bench. She put an arm around Derek and gave Erica a warning look. Erica ignored this and continued asking questions.

"Do you think that thing could have damaged your equipment?"

"Honestly, I'm not even sure that is anything." Kyle slipped his phone back into his pocket. "Just a cloud passing over the sun."

"Yeah," said Cora brightly leaning into Derek. "Just a cloud or something." Erica opened her mouth to remind them of the dense fog in the video but shut it when Cora glared at her and changed the subject. "You know what, Kyle? You'll never guess who I heard was coming back to town to work with you guys!"

Kyle was more than happy to give in to Cora. As they reminisced about former classmates, Erica watched Derek. He gave her a small smile and a shrug before getting up from the table to go smoke a cigarette. She wondered what Cora saw in him. If there was more than met the eye.

After Derek returned to their table, Erica couldn't get much more out of him and Kyle about what was going on at the logging sites. Cora was visibly annoyed whenever she tried to draw the conversation in that direction. It took a kick in the shins for her to finally give up. At least she had confirmation of Keith and Xander's assertions that there was a pattern of weird happenings in the area. She made a mental note to go through Keith's journals to see if he mentioned anything about overgrown wildlife.

With both Erica and Derek's minds elsewhere, the chatter soon petered out. Erica was anxious to get to the next part of her plan for the morning and reminded Cora that they should be going. They said goodbye to the boys in the parking lot. Erica and Kyle hugged stiffly while Cora and Derek shared a sloppy, open-mouthed kiss that Erica wished she didn't have to watch or hear.

Once the doors were shut on Keith's truck, Cora said, "I don't think that was quite the happy reunion Kyle wanted."

Turning on her phone's GPS and making sure the hand-held unit was in the cupholder, Erica backed out of her spot. "I told him—I told you even—that it's not going to work. It's more than the logging job. There's just, I don't know, no spark with us. Unlike you and Derek."

"All spark no fire if you know what I mean," Cora said in a conspiratorial tone. Erica wasn't sure she did know. "Anyway, I think Kyle thinks there's a spark. Plus, you guys looked like you were hitting it off when you first got here."

"I know," Erica sighed. "I feel bad about that. I was thinking it would be nice to have a distraction but then things started happening and it seemed like a worse and worse idea."

"I get that. Derek's just a distraction too. I should probably be thinking about what's next."

"Me too."

They drove in companionable silence for a while. Erica was relieved that Cora didn't push her on why she was asking questions about logging. Cora's interest never lingered too long on topics that she couldn't bring back to herself.

Erica was considering turning the radio up when Cora said, "I heard your mom talking about you going to Cascades at the wake. Is it a done deal?"

"I have to go, but I'm still working on picking a major."

"See, I've got that all figured out. Business Administration to an MBA. I just don't want to waste another four years in Oregon."

"Oregon isn't so bad," Erica countered. She pulled the truck onto the highway, practically flooring it to get up to sixty before she had to merge.

"Portland, maybe," Cora said. "But after a lifetime in Juniper Falls, I can't imagine leaving just to get stuck in Eugene or Corvallis, or worse."

"Worse?"

"One of those tiny colleges that literally no one outside of Oregon knows exists. How am I supposed to make it big with a no-name college on my resume?" This felt like a jab. Cascades wasn't exactly internationally renowned. But Cora was doing her a favor coming out to the woods with her, so she ignored the comment and asked if she was supposed to take the exit, they had just flown by despite knowing the answer.

Cora checked Erica's phone. "No, the next one. Where are we going again?"

"I told you, one of Keith's hiking spots."

"But we don't have to, like, hike, right?" Cora asked. She looked down at her flip-flops.

"I don't think so. We're just checking something out." This time they were at the correct turn, and Erica pulled off the highway onto a worn-down frontage road. "Did you talk to your dad about Officer Denman?"

"Yeah, but he didn't have much. They're floating a theory internally that he was buried by some transients passing through the area. Did you know there's been some weird cult activity in Oregon over the years?"

"The police think Keith was killed by a cult?"

"No, more like he was moved by a cult. Like, as a nice gesture maybe?" Erica rolled her eyes. If the police were floating those kinds of theories after having the body for a week, it was unlikely they were going to solve it.

As expected, the farther they got away from the main road,

the weaker the cell signal got. By the time they made their second to last turn, her phone stopped reading out directions. Erica switched to the handheld, trying to take turns that put her in the direction of the dot that indicated the location from Keith's journal.

"Okay. We just need to keep an eye out for a logging road. It should be on the right."

"Jesus," Cora sighed. "Is this related to you traumatizing Derek earlier?"

"Only kind of," Erica admitted.

"What if that thing from the video is out here?"

She laughed at the look on Cora's face. "I thought you said it was a cloud."

"I was trying to shut you up. This is dumb. What if one of the crews is out there? How are we going to explain just showing up?"

"Don't worry about it," Erica said. "There!" She took a sharp right at a break in the trees. The packed dirt road was overgrown and bumpy, but she was confident she was heading in the right direction. A low branch hung overhead, and Erica made the calculated decision to drive through it.

"Your grandma isn't going to like that," Cora said as the branch scraped across the top of the truck.

"It wasn't that thick."

The road abruptly ended, short of where the GPS said it should have. Erica stopped and shut off the truck. She opened the door and hopped out.

"I thought you said no hiking!" Cora yelled at her.

"I just want to take a look."

Erica walked toward the trees, watching the screen of the GPS as the arrow that indicated where she was drew closer to the destination dot. It looked like every other forested area she had ever been in, ferns and bushes growing right up to the base of tall trees. The landscape flowed out in front of her, rising and falling gently. There was no indication of any further road beyond where she had stopped.

Erica wasn't entirely sure she had the right spot, but she

headed in the direction of the GPS, expecting at any minute to come out into a clearing. Cora was calling to her from the truck, but she pressed on.

She was losing sight of the truck when her foot snagged on a tree root. She fell. The hand she threw out in front of her came down on something hard. Thinking it was a rock, she pulled herself up and touched her hurt hand with her opposite thumb. To her surprise, it was full of splinters.

Erica reached down and pushed the foliage away from what was unmistakably a recently cut stump. Confused, she moved on to the next rise in the ground, pushed back the leaves, and found another stump. It didn't make any sense. The road did not look like it was used recently, and the live trees were far too close to the stumps to not have been damaged during logging. Erica remembered Keith's notes, that the area was supposed to be covered in little saplings, not grown trees towering tens of feet in the air.

She double-checked her GPS. It showed the exact coordinates she had copied from Keith's journal. She had to be in the right place, but how was it this overgrown? Something was going on out here that she suspected Xander and Alden, in their fervor to make sure the journals didn't wind up in the wrong hands, must know about. Xander had even more explaining to do than she thought.

CHAPTER 15

Erica texted Xander after she got back from her exploratory trip to the forest but didn't receive a reply until early the next morning. She wanted to meet right away, but he suggested they wait until her next day off. Part of her wanted to push him, to threaten to go to the police with the journals, but she didn't see the point in holding him to an ultimatum she knew she wouldn't keep. They made plans to meet at Peace Falls early Wednesday morning. She had suggested somewhere more public, like the library, but he was adamant. Erica had to admit that she was a little touched that he wanted to meet where they had first set eyes on each other barely a month ago. The thought made her blush and she had to push it to the back of her mind. It was more likely he just didn't want to be overheard.

She stumbled through the next two days of work, spending most of her off hours studying the drawings and notes in Keith's journals to find the link she was missing. Granny told her they would be releasing Keith's body soon for burial, but that Officer Denman and his team had no new information for them. This information sent Granny back to the same low state she had been in on the day of the funeral. Erica had also thought that finding Keith's body would provide all the answers they needed. But now everything hinged on her next meeting with Xander.

On Wednesday, Erica woke before her alarm. They were meeting early to allow her to sneak out while Granny was with her walking group. Erica was prepared to be honest about where she was when she got back but didn't want to try to lie on her way out.

As she drove toward the falls, Erica tried to keep her heart rate down. She had done her best to look casual like she hadn't put too much thought into her outfit or her hair. She had to remind herself that this was a fact-finding mission and not a date. But her mind wandered more often to Xander touching her hand than she would admit to anyone else. No matter how many times she reminded herself that the whole reason for this meeting was to explain something strange and unnatural, and maybe even dangerous, Erica's heart was racing toward the minute she would see him again. So much so that when it happened, she expected it to be a letdown.

It wasn't. Xander sat straddling a downed log near the edge of the pool. While he must have heard her car arrive, he didn't look in her direction until she had closed her door and was walking toward him. As he had been the first time they met there, he wore a white t-shirt, now accompanied by loose-fitting jeans that were going threadbare in the knees. The deep line between his eyebrows relaxed slightly when their eyes met. Xander scooted down the log to make room for her. Erica thought for a minute about throwing a leg over so that they would be eye-to-eye but chose the ladylike option and sat down facing the falls. She didn't realize she was staring at his mouth until his lips moved.

"What?" she yelled. "I can't hear you over the water."

Xander smiled. "I said I'm glad you came."

"Of course I came." Her heart was pounding, but she tried to play it cool. "Are you ready to talk?"

"What do you want to talk about?" He was being coy on purpose. Erica wasn't sure she appreciated it. She rolled her eyes at him. "I know, I know. What do you want to know?"

"I thought you were dead," Erica said. From his open-mouthed expression, she knew this was not where he expected her to start, but she needed to know more about him, more about Alden, before the rest could make any sense.

"We're going to get right into it then." Xander took a deep

breath and straightened his back. "I have to warn you, things are about to get strange."

"Strange how?"

"Inexplicably strange. I did die in that fire. Or at least, Alex did."

It began with Alden, or so they had long thought, but Xander would get to that later. Alden arrived in Juniper Falls with his parents shortly after the end of World War Two. Alden's father—Alex's grandfather—had been pretty shaken up by the war and wanted to raise his family somewhere quiet. Juniper Falls was more of an idea than a town at the time. Alastair learned how to build houses, then cabinets, then furniture. He taught his trade to his son. From the time Alden could hold a saw, he was a natural at woodworking. He worked alongside his father as the town grew up around them. Eventually the Reeds had Alina, a very late in life surprise for Alden's mother. Alden was happy to stay home with his parents, run the family business, and watch Alina grow up. Erica noted the parallels between him and Keith.

When Alina was about two, Alden took some knotty pine to a friend's house to turn into lumber for a shed he wanted to put up behind the house. He had used the mill a dozen times, but that day he hit a big knot and the log bucked, sending him straight into the blade. It sliced through his shoulder, severing arteries. His friend tried to hold him together, but he bled out on the floor of the shed.

Back then the cemetery was private land held by a couple of families who had come early to Juniper Falls. Alastair thought Alden would hate the idea of being sewn up by a mortician, embalmed, and put into a casket. In his grief, he brought Alden's body to the top of what would become the cemetery hill and spent the entire night digging his grave. He buried Alden and placed in his hands the acorn of an Oregon White Oak, the most beautiful tree he had seen since coming west.

The family was in shock. They knew there was paperwork to file and the business had to keep processing orders, but they shut themselves in, trying to figure out how to move forward. Only a handful of people knew Alden was dead. This turned out to be a blessing when, three days and nights after he was buried, he came home.

"What do you mean he came back?" Erica asked. She was leaning in toward Xander, her eyes wild.

"He came back, Erica. But he wasn't the same," Xander explained. "There wasn't a scratch on him and, in the beginning, he didn't remember much. He couldn't even hold a fork. He was just empty. It took weeks for him to remember who he was."

"He told you that?"

"He didn't have to. It was the same for me."

"What—," Erica began.

"Just wait. You have to let me finish."

Alden eventually recovered. He was never social, but after he came back, he was a recluse. At first it was because being around people made him uncomfortable, but as the years went on, it became apparent he wasn't aging. About ten years after the accident, Alden's father died of cancer, and his mother passed shortly after. He dedicated his life to raising Alina. He hired out-of-towners to do the customer-facing work at the furniture store, and always found a reason to fire them within five years and send them packing. Meanwhile, the oak on the hill grew huge in no time at all.

While Alina was more social than Alden, she learned from him to play her cards close to her chest. She had Alex. He didn't know who his father was, but Alina was good at making it seem like it didn't matter. His childhood was happy. He was too young to notice there might be something off with his family. Then the fire happened.

"I don't remember dying," Xander said. "I just fell asleep one night like usual and woke up three days later—except I wasn't me."

When Alden arrived at Alina's house that bleak morning, two ambulances were already there, along with police cars and fire trucks. All the paramedics were at one of the ambulances. Alina was still showing signs of life and they were working hard to bring her back. The other ambulance sat unattended, its doors open. Alden approached the ambulance, terrified of what he knew he would find. Little eight-year-old Alex was laid out on a gurney. Alden yelled for someone to come help, but the paramedics called out that there was nothing more they could do.

Alden stopped thinking. He took the body in his arms and walked back toward his car. He expected someone to stop him, but they were all trying to save Alina or put out the fire. He put Alex in the backseat and sped toward the cemetery hill. Like his father, Alden dug a hole. It was February and the ground was hard. When he was satisfied it was deep enough, he put Alex's body in it. He plucked one of the acorns that grew on the White Oak no matter the season and put it in the grave.

Xander stopped here. His eyes were glossy like he might cry. Erica moved closer to him. She took one of his big hands in both of hers and rubbed her thumb against his smooth palm. "Tell me what you remember."

"When I woke up, I was sitting against a tree that was maybe ten feet tall. I was naked. I didn't remember anything. My mind was completely blank. It was night. I sat there for what felt like hours. Then I noticed Alden, slumped against the big tree just feet away. I didn't recognize him. He was asleep. I watched him until he woke up."

"Then what?"

"He took me home. He kept calling me Alex. He tried his best to help me remember. We looked through photo albums and he told me stories. But the thing was, I knew that Alex was under that tree. I could feel him in my roots. His body was still soft."

Question after question surged into Erica's brain, but she didn't need to ask them. Now that he had begun, words were spilling out of Xander. He started to shake. Erica pressed her whole body into his, wrapping her arms around him, trying to hold him still.

"I knew I wasn't Alex. I was something else, something new. Even as the memories started coming, they felt like they belonged to someone else. I knew that Alex couldn't feel the things that I could feel, like I was in two places at the same time. Sitting on the top of a hill with the wind blowing through my leaves and worms digging at my roots. But also a boy in a living room, sitting on a scratchy chair, watching a television. I told Alden to call me Xander. He resisted for a long time, but I needed it. I needed a clear marker of the separation between who I was and who I am now."

Xander breathed for what Erica thought may have been the first time in several minutes. When he inhaled, he looked down at her as if surprised to find her so close. She thought he might pull away, but he relaxed and settled his arms around her hips, his hands clasped at the base of her spine.

"So, what does that make you?" Erica asked, her lips brushing the t-shirt that clung to his chest.

"My best guess?" Xander asked. Erica nodded. "A dryad."

Erica pulled back to stare at him. He was watching her closely, their faces inches apart. The worry line between his eyes was deep again. She understood that a lot hinged on this moment—on her reaction—which was why she surprised even herself when she let out a deep genuine laugh. She felt Xander shift away from her, but she grabbed his hands again to keep him on the log. He looked bewildered.

"I'm sorry but some straight-up mythological tree spirit?"

"I mean, if you have any better ideas, I'm all ears."

Erica dropped one of his hands to wipe tears from her eyes. She wasn't sure if they had appeared during Xander's story or during her laughter. "I'm sorry. I know you just told me all this family trauma, but I don't think this is going to work for me."

"How so?" Xander asked, sounding annoyed.

"That's just, well it's just not a thing. You can't be a dryad. That means I have to start believing in, like, fairies and shit, and I just don't think I can do that."

"In my defense, I've never met a fairy. Aside from the fact that my life force is bound to that tree up there," Xander pointed in the direction of the cemetery, the twin oaks just visible, "my supernatural experiences are very limited."

Erica threw her leg over the log so that they were facing each other. "Wait, you're serious, aren't you? About all of it? You really believe you're a—." She couldn't say the word again.

"I don't have the perfect word for it, but yes. Alden and I both died and were reborn as something else."

Erica felt like this was the time to ask those questions she had bottled up, but now that she had heard his explanation, she wasn't sure she was ready for what came next.

As if reading her mind, Xander asked, "You went to the logging site, right? The one from Keith's journals. You saw what happened there. All the new growth."

"I wouldn't call that new growth," Erica said. "It looked like those trees had been there a hundred years. Also, how do you know I was there? Were you following me?"

Xander shrugged. "At a distance."

"What does that mean?" Erica wondered if she should be feeling scared. She had been taken in by his emotion as he told her his story, but the more they talked, the crazier he sounded. Xander didn't seem dangerous, but perhaps he was delusional. She began to regret putting so much faith in him. She went to stand up, but Xander got to his feet instead.

"Here," he said. "Maybe this will help."

Xander knelt and put his hand on the ground. Erica waited for something to happen. Then she saw it. Tiny green tendrils crawled up around his fingers. Xander raised his hand and the tendrils hung on, thickening at the base as they grew before her eyes. Leaves unfurled from the stems like the time-lapse videos she watched in science classes. When he reached waist height, the tendrils sprouted little buds that popped open to show tiny, bright orange flowers.

"How?" Erica whispered as she watched the flowers shrivel. The tendrils withered and fell away from Xander's fingers. By the time they hit the ground, the leaves were already brown and dying.

"I told you. Dryad."

"Wait," she said, her brain attempting to process what felt like its fiftieth emotion in the last ten minutes. "Does that mean you regrew the forest?"

"No. But I think that whatever did may have killed Keith."

"What is it?" Erica asked, not yet sure she could believe him but also starting to see the pieces lock into place.

"Do you trust me enough to show you?"

Erica looked at the plant that had just gone through its full lifecycle in a minute. She nodded.

CHAPTER 16

The atmosphere was tense in the cab of Xander's truck as they took the cemetery road in the opposite direction of town. Erica knew Xander was annoyed at her for laughing at him. But there was no way he expected her to just smile and nod and accept such an impossible situation. She peppered him with questions, trying to get a clearer picture.

"What does it mean to be a dryad?"

"How so?" he asked, keeping his eyes fixed firmly on the road and his mouth in a thin line.

"You can make plants grow, but what else?"

Xander's expression didn't change. Erica wondered if he was going to answer her question. Then he said, "You asked if I was following you when you went to meet your friends. I was. But you didn't notice me because I can, I guess, feel what's going on around me. I tap into the trees and weeds and sort of experience what they experience."

"You could hear my whole conversation?"

"No." He was warming up again, she realized, in response to her being more open. She chastised herself lightly for making light of something that she now realized he may never have told anyone else. "I knew you were there. You were with three people. I could feel you leave and get in your car. I followed you, staying far enough behind that you wouldn't see my truck, but watching you, if that's the right word, from the trees as you passed them."

Xander paused here. He glanced at Erica. She was trying to decide if this sounded like stalker behavior, but she wanted to hear more, so she stayed quiet. When he decided she wasn't going to laugh again, he continued.

"When I figured out where you were going, I pulled off at a shortcut and met you at the end of the logging road. Your face," he said with a slight laugh. "You looked so angry but also confused when you uncovered the stumps. Keith made that face a lot when we were first getting to know him."

"That's a little creepy, but I'll allow it." The comparison to Keith made her feel warm. Plus, she kind of got it. Xander was—continued to be—so mysterious to her that she probably would have stalked him too had she been able. She decided to take it as a compliment.

"I also heal," Xander said, as an afterthought.

"So can I. I don't think that counts."

"No, I mean fast and from anything. Between my tree and me, the tree is the only one that takes any lasting damage."

Erica thought about how freeing it would be to not have to deal with physical consequences. She was such a careful person usually, weighing out risks and rarely finding them worth the reward. "Is that why Alden doesn't age?"

"We don't know. There is a lot we don't know to be honest. When I was first, I guess, reborn, me not aging was kind of a problem. People would notice if I was eight forever. Alden is always trying to commune with his tree, but I find them to be tight-lipped. Still, he made us spend a whole day out there leaning against them, sort of meditating on aging. When we were done, I had grown a few inches and lost some baby fat. So now Alden makes me go spend time every summer trying to age myself up."

"It seems like it's working. Xander had the kind of dark, thick hair that couldn't hold a shave. She thought about Alden's golden mane and wondered if a side effect of being a dryad is looking like you belonged in a shampoo commercial or if the Reeds were just genetically gifted in that department. She blushed at the thought of saying that out loud, and instead asked, "Why doesn't Alden age up?"

"Would you? He would be sixty-eight. Wouldn't you rather be twenty-something forever?"

Erica thought about this. "I don't know. I think maybe I would want to live a normal life. Not have to hide."

Xander tensed again, locking his arms at the ten-and-two position on the steering wheel, which Erica associated with her father when he was stressed out about Portland traffic.

"I mean, being young is probably nice, but my granny said that no one has seen Alden in almost forty years. That must get lonely."

"It is."

A heavy silence sat between them. Erica knew she had hit another nerve and was reluctant to keep poking it. In her cheeriest voice, she said, "But at least he saved your life, so it seems worth it."

"Haven't you been listening?" Xander asked, the anger rising in his voice. "He didn't save my life. Alex died. I'm something different. Something with problems that aren't solved just by looking like everyone else."

"I'm sorry." The need to touch him when he showed emotion was becoming second nature to her. She reached out to put a hand on his arm, but he pulled the steering wheel to the right, dodging her and maneuvering the truck into a gravel pull-out.

"This is our turn. Are you ready to hike?"

Xander's long legs set the pace as they strode into the forest. There was no trail to follow. Erica struggled to keep up as she tried to choose the best place to bring down her feet in the dense underbrush. Xander appeared to be having no such trouble, and she was pretty sure that he was intentionally keeping himself far enough ahead of her to discourage further questions. Now and then she even thought she saw a fern shoot out to slow her down.

They went on this way for half an hour. Erica was about to ask him where they were supposed to be going when they emerged from a dense patch of trees into a wide-open meadow. It was like nothing she had ever seen. Huge cedars, firs, and hemlocks formed an almost perfect circle several hundred feet across. Despite it being late September, grass grew up to her waist and was dotted with blue, white, and yellow wildflowers. But Erica barely saw them because her eyes were drawn to an enormous oak tree in the center of the meadow. Its trunk was as thick as the giant sequoias Erica had visited on a road trip through California. About twenty feet up, it split into a hundred branches, each with a hundred twigs. Some of the branches were as thick as the trees that surrounded the meadow and swooped down so low, they almost touched the ground.

"It's beautiful," Erica said. "But this means—."

"That Alden and I aren't the only dryads in Southern Oregon."

Erica walked toward the magnificent tree. The meadow hummed with the sounds of insects. It was somehow warmer here than in the forest, though that may have just been the sunbeam that shined right onto the center of the tree. She walked around the tree and saw that it had a hollow at its base. The hollow was twice as tall as she was, and she was sure she could walk into it with her arms outstretched. She was about to try when Xander pulled on her shoulder.

"I wouldn't touch it if I were you. I don't know if it knows we're here."

"It? What is it?"

"We're not completely sure. If it's like us, it's really old. Alden's tree hasn't grown in years."

Erica was just beginning to wrap her head around Xander having been reborn and potentially immortal, and now was faced with the idea that there were more unexplained things out in this forest, and maybe other forests, that a couple of hours ago she would have said were myths and legends.

"I told you—we don't have all the answers to whatever all this is." Xander gestured to himself when he said it. "Whatever is attached to this tree may be something different. But it's strange because we never had any idea it existed until after Keith died. I told you that we can feel through the plants? Whatever lives here can hide from that ability."

Xander explained that Alden had long suspected that there

was something in the forest that he couldn't identify. It was as though portions of the forest would drop off the map like a slice was cut out and the open edges were pushed messily back together. In the early days, Alden would go to those edges and traverse the area in between, looking for signs of what or how it had gone momentarily missing. Sometimes he would find things—impossibly large footprints or huge trees pushed over, their snapped roots left dangling in the air—but more often, he found nothing.

Then two years ago Kriners began taking out patches of forest—a few dozen trees here and there. Keith was keeping track of the areas that Kriners was logging because he was pretty sure they didn't have a permit. He wanted to gather enough information to shut them down.

"That's how they met," Xander said. "The dead spots were occurring in the same places Kriners was logging. Alden thought Keith worked for them, but eventually Alden got up the nerve to talk to him. He was surprised to find out that he knew Keith's mother."

"Granny mentioned she knew him. She was shocked to see him at the funeral."

Xander nodded. "I never got the full story from Alden, but he tried avoiding Keith for a while after that. He was anxious about telling our secret. Then something changed between them, and he went from never wanting to see Keith again to him being around all the time."

Erica felt a little glow emanate from inside her as Xander explained how calm Keith could be even when talking about the logging. It would take someone who knew him to see behind his placid expression and realize just how angry he was at the violation of his forest. He was good with animals, not just Tulip. He was always finding injured wildlife and driving them out to the rehabilitation center.

"He talked about you too, you know. He loved it when you came to visit. I felt like I already knew so much about you when you introduced yourself at the library. I'm surprised I didn't recognize you."

They stood together a few feet from the base of the tree and both looked up into its back-lit branches. It was truly unlike anything she had ever seen. This whole moment, standing in this magical place with this magical person, talking about someone she cared so much about, felt like something out of a fairy tale—until she remembered.

"What does the tree have to do with Keith's death?"

Xander's face fell. "I wanted Alden to tell you. But he didn't want—." Xander stopped abruptly. Choosing his words more carefully, he said, "Keith was hiking alone that day. We had been finding more and more weird things in the dead spots. Mostly dead animals on display and ruined equipment. Alden went to check on a dead spot and that's when he found him."

"Wait. You think that this," she waved her arms at the tree, "killed Keith?"

"Yes. We think Keith injured it during whatever happened. It was a long time before we found another dead spot and in between them we found this tree."

In the weeks since Keith's body was found, and especially after the funeral, Erica had been expecting she would be surprised by the truth of what happened to him, whatever it wound up being. But even if she had made a list of a thousand possibilities, this would never have landed among them.

"Alden moved the body."

"Yes."

"You buried him on the hill between your trees."

"Yes."

"You made him a dryad!" Erica yelled, the thought rising up inside her like a hot air balloon. "Why haven't you told me sooner? Where is he?"

Erica looked around as if Keith was hiding somewhere in the meadow. She thought of how funny Keith would find the situation. And how appropriate. Someone who loved the forest so much becoming a fixture of it.

Then she saw Xander looking at the ground and shaking his head. "Erica, I'm so sorry. Alden tried. He wanted to bury Keith right where he found him but I didn't want that for Keith."

"You wanted him to be dead?" She could feel tears tickling the corner of her eyes. It had only been the briefest of moments that she thought he might be alive, but it felt like losing him all over again.

"He was always going to be dead. Keith never expressed any interest in becoming like us. I didn't think we had the right to choose for him. Alden brought him back to his truck and said he was going to take him to the hospital. But he drove him to cemetery hill and tried anyway."

"Then why didn't it work?" Erica asked, her face now glistening with tears.

Xander shook his head. "I don't know. I think he was gone too long."

"And whose fault was that?" Erica felt hot anger rush into her ears. She was about to light into Xander when he shushed her. She stared at him, shocked by his rudeness, but he squeezed her bicep and trained his eyes on the opposite side of the clearing.

Erica turned her head to where he was looking. She strained her ears to pick up anything unusual. She couldn't hear or see anything. She was half-convinced Xander was stalling to avoid the confrontation when she heard the faintest crack of a tree branch.

"We have to go," he said.

He took her hand and ran. This time Erica wasn't imagining it. The brush jumped to the sides and roots sank into the ground making a clear, smooth path for them to run along. Erica could barely keep up. Every time she dropped his hand, he grabbed for hers again and pulled.

It took less than half the time to get back to the truck. Xander threw open the passenger door and helped a winded Erica into the seat. He jumped into the driver's seat, turned the ignition, and pulled a U-turn to head back the way they came.

"Do you really think something was coming for us?" Erica panted.

"Better safe than sorry. It doesn't like coming into developed areas." Despite this assurance, she saw him check the rearview mirror so often that she thought he was paying more attention to what was behind than what was forward.

"I feel like there is a lot you aren't telling me," Erica said once she caught her breath.

"I know. We can talk more later."

"Not now?"

"No. I'm going to drop you off at your car."

They rode in silence back to the Peace Falls parking lot. Erica was both eager to ask more questions and desperately in need of alone time to process. She assumed Xander must have been feeling the latter. When he parked, they both sat in the car as if a spell would be broken if either of them made a noise.

Xander spoke first. "Are you still angry?"

Erica took a moment to consider this question. That Xander could have saved Keith, or at least some version of him, and actively took steps not to weighed on her. But she could also feel the pain in his voice when he talked about how isolating it was for him to be different. She thought of what Keith would want.

"No," she said at last.

Xander exhaled. "I'll text you, then?"

"Sure." Erica got out of the truck and walked over to her blue sedan. The lack of shadows on the ground told her it was only noon. It felt strange to be walking back into a world that made sense again. To get into in her car to head to her own house, back to her Granny who didn't know the secrets of the white oaks. Erica gave Xander a small smile and a wave and drove away.

CHAPTER 17

After the awkwardness of their most recent goodbye, Erica didn't expect to hear from Xander again for a while, if at all. The day had given her emotional whiplash, and she struggled to come to terms with everything she had discovered. She thought through everything Xander had told her—about Alden, about himself, about Keith's death—and tried to poke holes in his stories. His version of events meshed with what Granny had pieced together from town gossip. What was more, she had seen what he was capable of. What she had witnessed by the waterfall was no trick of the light, and she had felt the texture of the ground change beneath her feet as they ran. She had to accept it: Xander was a dryad and Keith had been killed by some immortal tree spirit that lurked around the Kriners logging sites.

Erica realized that she had forgotten to tell Xander about the dark shadow from Kyle's video. If Xander thought that the same thing that killed Keith was responsible for the damaged equipment at the logging sites, that might have also been what Kyle captured on camera. Erica thought about the base of the giant oak with its huge hollow—a hollow that could easily house something the size of what she saw in that video.

She wondered what the protocol was for reaching out to someone who you had just yelled at for not resurrecting your dead relative. She searched her room for her phone, having tossed it somewhere in a distracted haze when she got home. After locating it on the dresser, she texted Xander.

Erica: Is it possible that the giant oak dryad isn't human?

She stared at the phone, willing those three little dots to show up at the bottom of the screen. It took her almost going cross-eyed to give up on waiting for a return text. She pulled her laptop to her and tried to find any information about what was happening at the Kriners job sites. Most of what Erica could find spun Kriners' presence in Southern Oregon as an unmitigated positive. Every article was titled something along the lines of *Resurgence of Logging Operations Adds Hundreds of Jobs in Struggling County.* There were community council notes that listed public protests, but Erica could tell from the meeting minutes that Bobby Hendricks wove a convincing narrative around the benefits of allowing Kriners into the community. There was nothing about them chopping down trees at illegal test sites.

Erica was so intent on her search that she didn't hear the knock on her door. She saw movement in her periphery and turned to see Granny standing in her doorway.

"Hey," Erica said. "Did you get a good walk in this morning?"

"Not really. We did a couple of miles then I decided to stop by the store. It was busy, so I helped run the register for a while."

"You could have called me," Erica said as though she hadn't been deep in the forest discussing impossible things. She closed her laptop and shifted over on her bed, inviting Granny to sit with her. Granny sat down. They both looked up at the marbled texture on the ceiling.

"Did you do anything interesting this morning?" Granny asked.

For a moment, Erica thought about telling her everything. She had more right to know what happened to Keith than anyone. But even though Xander had not asked her to keep his secret, she could tell by the way her stomach twisted into knots at the idea of saying anything that she would feel better if she had explicit permission to do so. Plus, without having experienced what Erica had experienced, how could she expect Granny to believe her?

"No," Erica lied. "Just sat out by the falls."

"What are you reading now?"

"*A Tree Grows in Brooklyn*. But American literature just doesn't hit the spot like British."

"Several hundred fewer years of culture," Granny agreed. Tulip came into the room and tried to jump on the bed, but it was too high, and she was too old. Erica picked her up and put the corgi between her and Granny. She trailed a finger from Tulip's nose up her snout and between her eyes. Tulip breathed a contented little sigh.

"We are going to bury Keith on Saturday. Your parents are coming," Granny said as she also absentmindedly petted the little dog. Erica nodded into her pillow.

They lay together in a comfortable silence until Erica heard the vibration of her phone against wood. She reached across Granny to grab it off the nightstand hoping that she hadn't seen the name.

Xander: I'll call you tomorrow.

"Who is that from?"

"No one," Erica said, fighting the small smile tugging at the corners of her mouth.

Xander did not call her the next day. Nor did he call her by late Friday night when Erica's parents arrived. They made polite small talk about how things were going at the Portland store— busy—before Erica headed to bed disappointed for the second day in a row.

She awoke the next morning and put on yet another somber, dark-colored outfit. As much as she missed Keith, Erica was looking forward to reintroducing color back into her wardrobe. On her way downstairs, she could hear her mother fussing about the late September cloud cover.

"It's going to rain, Mom. Are they going to make us reschedule? I don't know if me and Rich can come back anytime soon. These kids we keep hiring are flakes. We're always training a new one."

"They've already dug the grave, so I can't see them not letting us bury him today," Granny said with a level of patience that Erica thought would earn her sainthood.

"Can you call them to make sure?"

"Danielle, love, I'm sure they would have let us know if they were going to cancel."

Erica took a deep breath and walked into the dining room where her mother and grandmother sat at the round table. She gave everyone a good morning smile before heading into the kitchen for coffee and a couple of the pumpkin nut muffins she could smell had just come out of the oven. Her father came downstairs shortly after, and her mother only gave him time to inhale one muffin before pushing them all out the door.

As a passenger, Erica had the luxury of watching the forest fly past her on the way to the cemetery. While she never took the beauty of Juniper Falls for granted, she couldn't help but see it in a new light now that she had learned just some of the secrets it held. Her heart leaped when the cemetery hill came into view, Xander and Alden's trees reaching up, almost touching the low, dense clouds.

Her family followed the same path from the parking lot that Erica had taken just last week. Only this time when they turned the hill, they saw a huge mound of dirt only semi-hidden by a piece of AstroTurf. The mound sat at the base of the most perfectly rectangular hole Erica had ever seen. Next to it was a casket. It was plain but beautiful—a light pine inlaid with purple heart wood panels and thick, carved handles adorning the sides. Erica thought it was exactly what Keith would have wanted.

"This isn't what we picked out," Granny said to the group of four men in identical black suits, white shirts, and skinny black ties who were milling around the gravesite.

The shortest among them, an older man with a wispy comb-over and full mustache looked taken aback. "I'm sorry, Mrs. Schueller. This casket arrived yesterday with a note that it was for your son. I assumed you sent it."

"I didn't," Granny said. She stepped toward the casket and ran her hand across it.

"Jesus," Danni said. "Please tell me it's at least Keith in there."

"I can assure you we are burying your brother today, Mrs. Wright," the short man said, though he looked nervously around to the other men. They all nodded, and the man looked relieved.

"What do you want to do, Mom?" Erica's mother was doing the impatient shift of her weight between her feet that Erica knew would shortly be accompanied by an outburst unless she was appeased.

Granny appeared to be admiring the craftsmanship of the casket, but Erica saw tears in her eyes. She knelt next to her grandmother and whispered, "I think it's perfect."

Granny turned to face Erica, tears just beginning to fall down her cheeks and nodded. To the man, she said, "If you're sure it's okay."

"Yes, of course!" he said, letting out the breath he must have been holding. "Shall we begin?"

Erica was thrilled that the pastor from the funeral was not present. The short man she assumed must be the funeral director, prompted each of them to say a few words about Keith. Her father went first, but he only made it a few sentences in before he joined Granny in crying. This was enough to set off both Danni and Erica. They huddled together, doing their best to remind each other of their favorite memories of Keith. But whenever one of them would begin, the group would flood with emotion and the tears would fall harder. It was cathartic for Erica. Their collective reactions to that point had been so staid like they were all putting on a brave face for each other. It was right that here at the very end, the last time it would be five of them rather than four, they could finally steep in their loss.

When they had cried themselves out, Granny nodded to the funeral attendants. The men took up the nylon straps that lay under the casket and used them to center and lower it into the grave. Granny was the first to grab a handful of dirt from the pile.

"I will love you forever," she said as she tossed it on top of the casket.

Danni, Rich, and Erica followed her lead. When it was done, the family looked expectantly at the funeral director. He told them they were done here, that someone would monitor the gravesite until the caretaker came to fill it in. There was nothing to do but head back to the car and move on.

They were already starting back when Erica asked, "Can I have a minute?" She expected her mother to be annoyed, but the burial had taken it all out of her.

Danni nodded. "We'll meet you at the car."

Erica broke off from the group and walked to the top of the hill. She wondered which of the white oaks was Xander's. She ran her hand across the thick bark of the tree farthest from town. The texture reminded her of oil paintings, stroke upon stroke of thick, layered paint. This tree was wider than the other and its bark was bleached almost gray by the sunlight. Its branches were heavy with fat green and brown acorns wearing their funny little hats.

She walked over to the other tree, the one that was fullest where it faced the town. This tree was leaner, browner, less gnarled. Putting her hand on the tree, she instantly knew this was his. It was as though the oak pulsed with the same strong heartbeat she felt when she put her hand in Xander's.

Erica put her forehead against the tree and whispered, "We buried Keith." She jumped when seconds later her phone buzzed in her pocket. A text message.

Xander: I'll call you tonight. Promise.

Back at the house, Danni asked if she and Rich should stop by the store to check in on Joe. Both Granny and Erica insisted that everything was running smoothly. Sales were up year-over-year. Thanks to Keith's diligent bookkeeping, they had the right stock for the right season.

"Maybe logging really will be good for this town," Rich said.

"I doubt it," Erica muttered.

Rich shot her a wounded look, not used to being on the receiving end of her sarcasm. Danni looked a little smug for a moment before lifting her eyebrows, remembering something. She went over to the door and pulled an enormous white envelope with the green College of the Cascades logo out of her suspiciously large purse. Erica imagined she brought it just to spring the envelope on her.

"This came for you. You need to make a student portal so you can register on time," Danni said as she handed the envelope to Erica. Of course, it was already open.

"I updated your FAFSA. Turns out all that creative accounting we do for the store is worth some grant money," her dad joked.

Erica pulled out a letter printed on cream-colored paper confirming her attendance for the winter quarter. There was also a shiny welcome booklet.

"There is a new student orientation day that I would like you to attend in November," Danni said. "You can get some academic advising, which you clearly need." Rich placed his hand on Danni's shoulder and gave Erica a sympathetic smile.

"I'll go," Erica said, surprising all of them, not the least of which herself.

"You will?" Her mother had been expecting more of a fight.

"Yes. If you guys are getting out of here, I might go set up that student portal right now."

It seemed prudent to see her parents off on a good note. Erica hugged them goodbye and practically pushed them out the door. Granny wasn't too put off by this. Erica had the suspicion that now that Keith was buried, she was ready to get back to whatever normal was going to look like for her.

Erica took the envelope with her upstairs and shut the door. She flipped through the welcome booklet full of attractive, smiling students and thought that the college might be better off being more honest about its population. Erica wondered if the pages featured pale and sullen-looking students who had not bothered to brush their hair or put on proper pants that she might have an easier time envisioning herself there.

She opened her laptop and navigated to the website indicated in her letter. At first it was easy. Erica double-checked that they had her name and address correct. She was excited to see that her Advanced Placement classes had not been for nothing.

Cascades was going to offer her more than a quarter's worth of credits for them. Erica couldn't wait to bring this up to her mom as proof delaying for three months wasn't the absolute worst thing she could have done.

Then she came to the page she had been dreading. *Please indicate your potential major. Don't worry! We want to pair you with the best advisor. You can change this after enrollment.*

But Erica was worried. She scrolled through the fifty or so programs offered. English continued to be the most tempting option, but she couldn't picture what she would do after college. She loved reading, but she couldn't see herself doing any of the things that popped up when she searched online for *jobs for English majors.* She scrolled back up to the Bs. Biology was so close to Business Administration. She hovered her cursor between the two, feeling like this was the moment that could determine the course of the rest of her life.

Her phone lit up on the bed next to her. Xander's name flashed on the screen. Erica grabbed the phone and swiped up.

"Hello?" She was embarrassed by how loud she had yelled into the phone.

"How did it go? The burial?" Xander asked, his voice unexpectedly warm.

"It was hard. We all got emotional, which isn't really our thing."

"I get that. Alden isn't big on emotions either."

"What about you?" Erica thought about him recounting the story of how he came to be what he is, how he started with his grandparents. If she were telling her story, that is probably where she would start too, with Granny and Grampy getting married and moving west to the land of evergreens.

"Emotions?" Xander asked. "Oh yeah. Just waves and waves of them all the time. Non-stop."

"I can't tell if you're being serious," Erica giggled.

"I am, sadly. I feel way too much. It's another reason I don't read fiction."

"I maintain that you are missing out."

"Maybe. I miss out on a lot."

Erica was already creating a catalog of books she needed to introduce him to and almost missed his last comment. When she realized what he said, her heart sank. She wondered if Xander's openness, his willingness to let her in on his secret, was an attempt to replace Keith with her. To have had a brief reprieve from the company of only Alden day in and day out and then lose it must have been difficult.

She must have been lost in her thoughts too long because Xander switched subjects and asked, "What makes you think the giant oak dryad isn't human?"

Erica told him about Kyle's video and the huge shadow hiding in the tree line. "Unless you and Alden have super strength, I don't think it's a human dryad out there ripping engines out of semi-trucks."

"We're strong, but not that strong. I tried to ask Alden about it, but he keeps telling me to leave it alone. I've been out there hoping to see it. That's why I didn't call you."

"You sat out in the woods by yourself trying to catch a glimpse of something that you know has already killed at least one and probably two people?" The thought of Xander being attacked, alone, with no one to help him, sent a jolt of anxiety through her.

Xander laughed. "I heal, remember? It kind of screws with your sense of danger."

This did not appease Erica. She grabbed a pillow off her bed and held it anxiously against her stomach. She racked her brain for a safer way to track down whatever belonged to that tree. Then she remembered the pile of camo electronics in Keith's desk.

"I think Keith has a trail camera."

"Okay?" Erica could tell from the way Xander's voice went up at the end of the word that he was not following.

"We could go put the camera out facing the giant oak. It takes photos when it detects motion. I remember him telling a whole story about how he got all these hilarious pictures of raccoons getting into our garbage cans."

The line was quiet for a moment. Erica wondered if the

call dropped, but she looked at her phone and they were still connected.

"That could work," Xander said at last.

"I'll see if I can come up with a good excuse to get into his room and meet you tonight?"

"Sure. I can go set it up and hopefully we get something."

Knowing she wouldn't be able to live with herself if something happened to Xander in the forest alone, Erica said, "Oh no. My plan. I'm coming with you."

CHAPTER 18

Erica decided that some version of honesty was the best policy. She told Granny that she was looking for a trail camera to lend to Kyle for deer season. Granny didn't mind Erica disturbing Keith's room, though she had to pretend to look around a bit rather than head straight for the desk drawer where she knew she would find it. She did legitimately have to search for its charging cable, which she found in a cardboard box of assorted electronic accessories in the guest bedroom. When the camera was finally charged and tested using Tulip as a guinea pig, Erica texted Xander. It was getting late, but she was too excited to wait.

Not trusting the clouds that had built up throughout the day, Erica tossed the trail camera into her dry bag and put on her navy-blue rain jacket. After kissing Granny on the cheek and promising she wouldn't be home too late, she took off toward the cemetery for the second time that day. Despite assuring Xander that she could find where they had pulled off together earlier that week, every mile she drove without seeing a gravel turnout convinced her she had missed it a while back. She was usually pretty good with directions, having grown up in the maze that is the Portland suburbs, but she cut herself some slack when she remembered Xander had given her a lot to process on her way out last time. It was not surprising that she hadn't been paying the best attention.

When she was just about to give up and turn around, Erica saw Xander's tan pickup truck parked on the side of the road. He leaned against it wearing a maroon hoodie and, she was pretty sure, the same jeans from the last time she saw him. He waved at her as she pulled in behind him. She shut off her car, and Xander opened her door for her as though trudging through the damp wilderness was his idea of the perfect date. When Erica stepped out, throwing her wet bag over her shoulder, he leaned into her and sniffed, causing a blush to rise against her pale skin.

"Are you wearing perfume?"

"Just a little."

"In the woods? Keith would be ashamed of you."

Erica's blush deepened. Xander crinkled his eyes in amusement. He took her elbow and helped her off the roadway shoulder and down a slight embankment before hitting the forest floor. When he dropped her arm, Erica shot out a hand to grab his bicep. Xander flexed in a move that reminded her less of Kyle's attempts at showing off and more of a response to unfamiliar touch. Xander relaxed his arm slowly and brought it in toward his side, pulling her into him.

They headed into the forest at a much more leisurely pace than days earlier. Having spent so much time recently up close and personal with oak trees, Erica now studied how different they were from the far more common firs that coated the Southern Cascades. Straight branches shot out far, far above her head, and ended in flat needles instead of lush leaves. Both species were majestic in their own way, but the oaks belonged in the novels set in the English countryside that she loved so much. The firs were quintessentially Oregon, like Erica. She wondered if she and Xander pricked their fingers, which one of them was more likely to bleed sap.

Xander stopped suddenly, snapping Erica out of her thoughts. In one quick motion, he wrapped his arm around her waist and pushed her behind him. They stood still, holding their breath.

"What?" Erica asked. Xander shook his head, as he held her firmly against his back.

A small, brown rabbit shot across their path and into the underbrush.

Erica stifled a laugh by shoving her face into Xander's hoodie. "Do you think that was our dryad?"

But Xander was still on high alert. Erica wondered what he was feeling—what it would be like to connect into something as primal as an ancient forest. She came out from behind him and looked straight into his chocolate brown eyes.

"What has you on edge?"

"I wish I knew," he said. "Something feels off, but I can't figure it out. Everything is too quiet, but not dead spot quiet. Somewhere in between."

She could see him rethinking whether it was safe to bring her out here. The worried line between his eyes was as deep as Erica had ever seen it, and she wanted nothing more than to run her finger across it, the same way she relaxed Tulip the dog. The more she tried not to think about his mouth, the harder it was to stop herself from bringing hers up to it.

Before she had the chance, the rain her mother had fretted about that morning let loose upon them. It was as though the sky was cut open with a knife right above their heads.

"We should keep going," Erica said, a little louder than she meant to. "You're going to get soaked."

"I'm a tree, remember?" Xander said without the playfulness she had been hoping would carry throughout the evening.

Erica half expected he would insist on bringing her back to the car, but Xander surprised her by hooking his arm through hers again and continuing forward. Not wanting to make him doubt this decision, she remained silent as they made their way through the forest.

After the initial burst, the rain settled into a proper Pacific Northwest mist. Erica knew they were getting close to the clearing when the trees started growing almost on top of each other. Xander veered them off the generally straight line they had been heading in, skirting around the densest area of trees. Then she saw it, the giant oak tree, its branches reaching toward her from its home in the middle of the meadow.

Erica took the camera out of her dry bag. She hadn't thought about whether the camera strap would fit around the huge trees that encircled the meadow. They found one skinny enough to accommodate it, but Erica shook her head and pointed toward the hollow, adamant that the camera face its direction. From the first time she saw the oak, she had been drawn to that hollow, as if a walk inside would reveal the answers to all their questions. But she heeded Xander's earlier warning not to get too close and now his anxiety kept her at the edge of the clearing.

Through some trial and error, they found a tree that was just barely the right size and got the camera securely attached. Erica opened the front of the camouflage case and turned it on. A red light flashed but was hidden when she closed the case again. She nodded to Xander. They both looked expectantly at the oak as if setting up the camera should have summoned what they were there to photograph.

When nothing appeared, Xander motioned in the direction they had come. It was almost completely dark now, and Erica took her phone from her pocket to turn on the flashlight. Xander touched her hand and whispered, "No." She didn't realize until that moment how much time had passed between them without words. They had worked together easily, supporting each other in their shared task. Being with Xander, even out in a black forest that was home to a nameless threat, Erica felt the calmest and the most herself in as long as she could remember.

His hand still on hers, Erica grabbed the front of Xander's hoodie, stood on the tips of her toes, and kissed him. Erica ran through a catalog of every touch between them beginning with the handshake at the library. But she realized that she had wanted this before even then and hoped he did too. From the first time she saw him at the waterfall, she had imagined her hands on his hard chest, his hollow stomach. Standing in the rain, the water drops traced his jaw and ran down his sinewy neck the same way they had that day.

They relaxed into the kiss at the same time, him opening his mouth in response to her tongue. The kiss was clumsy but satisfying in a way she had never experienced with the handful of other boys she'd done this with. This close to him, she smelled something underneath the earthiness she had become accustomed to—something soft and floral. She drank it in and never wanted to forget it. She was trailing her fingers down his neck when he drew back. Erica opened her eyes, but the view was much the same. The moon was hidden behind a thick layer of clouds, and Erica could just make out Xander's outline only inches in front of her.

"We should go," he whispered huskily. He took her hand and led her on a smooth path out of the forest. It was as though Erica floated over the ground rather than walked. As they went, she listened to the rustle of his jeans and the slight pant in his breathing. She was so aware of him. She imagined his skin under those jeans, the lean muscle under that, and the bones that were at the center of him. She wanted to touch him enough to know what he was made of.

A faint light through the trees told her they were almost to the road. Erica grabbed her keys out of her pocket and unlocked her car. She saw the lights flicker in response. When they reached it, Erica pulled open a rear door and climbed into the car, never letting go of Xander's hand. She was confused when he did not immediately follow her inside. He bent down to put his face even with hers, but just out of reach.

"We should talk about this."

"Please come in. It's raining."

"Only if you promise that we talk before we—," Xander stumbled over his words. "Before we do that again."

Erica smiled. "Does that mean we get to do that again?"

Xander sighed softly, but a smile was forming on his lips. "Talk first?"

Erica feigned a pout but nodded. She scooted across the seat of the car and tucked her legs under her, facing him. Xander folded himself up and sat next to her.

"Hang on," she said. Erica reached across Xander and pulled the lever to move the front seat up. "Any better?"

"Kind of."

Erica settled back into the backseat and tilted her head slightly in what she hoped was a seductive way. All they did was talk. She was ready for a change of pace.

"I'm not totally human," Xander said.

"We've established that."

"Right. Well, that comes with certain limitations."

Erica had no idea where this was going. Her mind went wild with possibilities. Xander didn't want to be forthcoming despite this talk being his idea.

"Limitations?" she repeated, trying to help him along.

"It's like this. In sixth grade, my class planned a trip to the sea lion caves in Florence. I was so excited but when I told Alden, he said I couldn't go. I was a kid, so until that point it wasn't weird that I never really left Juniper Falls. Alden took me out to our trees and explained that they were almost like our hearts, and it's impossible to go anywhere without your heart." Erica nodded like this made sense, but she still wasn't sure what this had to do with her, with this moment she was so desperate to create. Xander breathed out and said quickly, as if it pained him, and said, "That's when I found out I am stuck here."

"Stuck how?"

"We tested it out, and we can only get about twenty miles away from the trees before we start, I don't know, fading." Erica cocked her head to the side again, this time in genuine concern. "I didn't want to believe Alden, so he took me on a drive. We couldn't even make it to I-5 before I felt like I was suffocating. Blood was pounding in my ears. Alden pulled the truck over and told me I would die if I went too far for too long."

Erica was just getting used to the idea that Xander was indestructible and immortal. Far from being the turn-off he seemed to think it was, Erica found that this sudden admittance of fragility made him more accessible, less intimidating, than before.

"I'm sorry," she said. She slid over to bump her leg against his. He shook his head.

"You don't get it. You're smart. You have a good family. I'm sure you're going somewhere in life. College maybe. Not me. I'm stuck in this tiny town forever. At some point, I'm not going to want to age up anymore and that will be it. Just me and Alden. In the woods. Forever."

He dropped his hand, but she kept her eyes trained on his. There was no sign of tears, but she thought she could hear them in his voice. She understood him now. This gorgeous, mysterious, sensitive person thought he had nothing to offer her. The irony of the situation would have made her laugh if it wasn't so sad.

"You can be more than that," she said. "You are more than that." She took his hand in hers and laid them where their thighs met. The need to kiss him again had evaporated, replaced with the need to comfort him. She knocked her shoulder against his. "We'll find you a future."

Xander smiled. And what a smile. It filled her up. "Somehow I believe you."

CHAPTER 19

Erica and Xander sat in the backseat of her car and had their first conversation that wasn't about Keith or the mysterious tree. He explained to her how lonely it was to grow up with only a taciturn old man—in age if not appearance—for a companion and how it was only through books that he understood the parts of the world Alden had given up on long ago. She told him how hard she worked in school and at the store to meet her mother's expectations even though, deep in her heart, she knew it was an impossible goal. As they talked, she forgot about kissing him, but her skin still tingled with every accidental touch.

He listened to her as she poured out her fears about college, about getting lost in a sea of people smarter and more confident than she was. He said the same words as everyone else she had this discussion with, namely that she would be fine, and she was good enough. But whether it was the earnestness in his voice or the fact that they had only just met, she believed them coming from him. They ended up saying goodbye with a squeeze of their hands.

Upon arriving back at Granny's, Erica rushed upstairs to finish setting up her student portal. She decided to select Business Administration. It felt like the choice that required the least commitment now. She had been helping run a business since she could identify numbers on a ten-key. Most conversations her parents had were about the store: what to stock, what to markdown, when to change inventory, tax season. Business classes didn't scare her and that felt like a good place to start.

Back in her room, with the laptop open on her bed, the website assured her again that she would have the opportunity to speak with an academic advisor before she started classes. She rushed through the rest of the set-up process and a confirmation email immediately showed up in her inbox. As she read the email, an idea occurred to her. Erica fished a spiral notebook out of the belongings she brought to Juniper Falls, opened it to a fresh page, and wrote down the list of online degrees offered by Cascades.

Xander was far too doom and gloom about his geographic restrictions. This was the twenty-first century and the internet made everything possible. She kicked herself for not asking what he might be interested in studying. Remembering the biography he was reading in the library, she put a star next to History on her list. She also put a star next to Horticulture, mostly as a joke, but then again maybe the idea had merit. Erica could envision Xander bringing fresh batches of plants every day to *Juniper Falls Farm & Feed*, the greenery growing at such a rapid pace it would turn the lawn and garden area into a jungle.

When she was satisfied that she had enough information to initiate the conversation when she saw him tomorrow, Erica changed into an old t-shirt and sweats and slipped under the thick comforter. She willed herself to sleep so that she could see him again, but the anticipation kept her wide awake. They made plans to meet in the afternoon to see if their camera trick managed to yield the intended results. Xander was going to pick it up in the morning and then text her directions to his house. She was eager to see where he lived and drifted to sleep imagining a thatched roof and ivy growing up whitewashed walls.

Erica woke late the next morning. For a long time, she stayed in bed, letting the images of clandestine forest kisses, entwined legs under Granny's table as they studied together, and picnics on the cemetery hill fill her head.

Before long she heard Granny banging around in the kitchen. Erica did her best to put on a neutral face when she greeted Granny downstairs, but she must have done a poor job.

"Have a good night, love?" Granny asked from her usual spot at the table.

"I did." Erica took one of the heavy ceramic mugs out of the cupboard that the two of them painted at a studio years ago. It was delicately patterned with blue, pink, and white forget-me-nots on a green background. She poured herself a cup of lukewarm coffee and went searching for a pan.

"Kyle was appreciative of the camera?"

For a moment Erica forgot her lie and couldn't draw the connection between Kyle and why last night had been so good. When she remembered, she wanted to laugh at the idea that anything to do with Kyle could make her this happy, but she wasn't sure it was time to give herself away. She nodded noncommittally.

"Eggs?" Erica offered.

"Don't bother. Reheat some of the frittata one of the ladies gave me this morning."

"They're still feeding us?"

"They feel terrible that we still don't have any resolution about what happened to Keith."

Erica scooped some frittata onto a plate and put it in the microwave. She kept her back to Granny, having already been wrong once this morning about her ability to keep a poker face. "Maybe we'll hear something soon."

The microwave dinged, and Erica brought her plate and mug over to the table. She thought Granny was looking better, more lively and engaged. Erica wondered how much she would be able to tell her grandmother if she was able to find out, definitively, what killed her uncle.

Granny took a sip of her coffee before surprising Erica with a request. "I was going to ask if you wanted to attend this fundraiser for me later this week. It's for the high school. Bobby puts it on every year, mostly to show off the community center. It will be boring, but people will notice if none of us are there."

"You don't want to go?"

"I don't think I can take their pity."

Erica's good mood faded slightly. Maybe she was wrong

about Granny making strides. She suddenly felt guilty about having plans to run off today. "I'm happy to go."

"You can see if Kyle wants to go with you," Granny offered, with a sly, sideways look. "It will be a lot of old people getting drunk and bidding too high on silent auction items. I bet I could wrangle you some drink tickets."

"Granny!" Erica cried in mock outrage. She took a bite of the frittata, which was unexpectedly delicious for reheated eggs, before feeling noble and offering to stay home for the day.

But the disappointment must have been obvious in her voice because Granny smiled and shook her head. "No, you go out."

Erica took another big bite and warred with herself over whether to be a good granddaughter or give in to her baser instincts. She rationalized that since she was in pursuit of the truth about Keith she could leave and fulfill both desires.

To be a better granddaughter, Erica spent time with Granny planting spring bulbs in the front flower beds. Yesterday's rain had left the soil damp and pliable. Granny was partial to daffodils. As Erica transferred each delicate, papery bulb into the ground, she tried to feel its potential life within. She thought it was beautiful how something so brown and ordinary could lie dormant for months at a time before suddenly activating to reveal tall green leaves topped with buttery yellow petals.

She did her best to hold up her end of the conversation but was distracted by waiting for her phone to buzz in her pocket. When it did, Erica almost ripped her jeans trying to get to it.

Xander: Ready for you. Head east on Main Street. I'll meet you at the road.

Erica raced upstairs to change, leaving a bemused Granny in her wake. She had been planning her outfit since last night. After scrubbing the dirt off her hands and arms, she put on a dusty rose striped dress with a boatneck top that came in at her waist and flared out just above her knees. It highlighted what she thought were all her best features without being too revealing. At this point, she knew that proper footwear was important when seeing Xander, and this outfit allowed her to wear a pair of well-loved canvas lace-up sneakers in case she found herself hiking again. She finished the look with a light denim jacket.

Before she left her room, she had one final decision to make. Keith's notebooks sat under her mattress, and she wondered if it was time to hand them over to Xander and Alden in a gesture of goodwill. She decided she would put them in her car and see if it felt right.

"You look nice," Granny said as Erica came back out onto the lawn. "Who are you meeting?"

"Just a friend." Erica tried to be casual, but she knew she was grinning.

"I know everyone in this town. Who is this friend?"

Erica shrugged and scurried over to her car to avoid further questioning. If she told Granny she was meeting Xander it would lead to a whole conversation she wasn't ready for.

She waved at Granny as she backed out of the driveway and headed toward Main Street where, across from *Farm & Feed*, she took a right. She rarely had a reason to go this way. All the development since the founding of downtown took place north and west, nearer the highway. It struck Erica as strange that Xander didn't live closer to the cemetery where he could keep an eye on his tree, but she remembered that area was almost all state forest land.

Erica followed the winding road for a few miles before she saw Xander standing in front of a narrow driveway. The well-worn tire tracks were more dirt than gravel, and greenery grew between and around them. Erica pulled over and lowered the passenger window.

"Need a lift?" she asked.

Xander smiled and got into the car. She pushed down her nerves at seeing him again and her disappointment that he didn't so much as brush against her hand sitting on the gearshift. His demeanor was warm and loose, and she hoped for a sign that, after their kiss and getting to know each other better, there would be something more between them. She felt ridiculously overdressed next to his t-shirt and jeans, which she was starting to believe made up his entire wardrobe.

"Did you download the photos?" she asked in an attempt to ease the tension that was boiling up inside her. She started the car slowly down the driveway, worried that her sedan didn't have the necessary ground clearance.

"It didn't feel right to do it without you."

Erica noticed out of the corner of her eye that his left hand was fidgeting. She willed him to place it on her bare knee.

"How far am I going?"

"You'll see." There was mischief in his voice. He threw his arm behind her seat, his twitchy hand just barely grazing her shoulder, but sending a bolt of lightning down her spine.

She went a few hundred more feet down the driveway before she found herself blocked by a dense thicket of what looked like salmonberry. Woody stalks she knew to be covered with fine thorns grew out of the ground in any direction. It appeared impenetrable. She looked at Xander who smiled.

"No worries."

Erica watched as the berry bushes slowly drifted to either side, leaving just enough room for her car.

"Impressive," she said.

"Just wait."

Erica drove through the thicket. The newly vacated ground was soft, and the car sank into it. She was so focused on not getting stuck that it took her a moment to realize they had entered a huge clearing. On the other side of the salmonberries, it had been autumn and the leaves were just starting to change color. On this side, it was spring. The driveway was u-shaped, and in the middle lay a dense lawn filled with wildflowers of every color. After the bend sat a workshop made of rough-hewn logs with a glass roller door in the frarnt. Deep blue clematis with flowers the size of her hand grew on one side. She pulled her car next to Xander's truck, which was parked in front of a matching log cabin with a green metal roof and a farm porch that took up the entire front of the house. Erica got out of the car and walked directly into the field of wildflowers with Xander close behind her.

She threw her arms out and twirled like she was Maria in

The Sound of Music, a favorite film of her mother's that she must have watched a hundred times growing up. "Does it always look like this?"

"I may have embellished a few things."

"For me?" she asked, her voice teasing but the question serious.

Xander slipped his arm around her waist and smiled. A wave of relief washed over her. It wasn't just her. This thing between them was real. She threw her arms around his neck and hugged him, his signature scent indistinguishable from that of the flowers that grew around him.

"What changed your mind?" There had been no real resolution after he tried to warn her off him in her car. As happy as she was at this moment, she didn't want to push him.

"You were right. It might be nice to try living a little. And you seem like someone very full of life."

Erica wasn't sure if it was the sun or her emotions that blinded her, but when she came back to her senses, Xander was gesturing toward the workshop, eager to take her on a tour. She grabbed his hand as he explained that Alden bought this land before his accident, before he changed, and that he raised the buildings by hand over many years. As far back as Xander could remember, the property was surrounded by a wall of brambles to keep out unwanted visitors. Alden had all sorts of expensive tools in his workshop but more importantly, this was where he tested the limits of his abilities as a dryad.

They walked behind the workshop where there stood the most unusual sculpture garden Erica had ever seen. Trees grew in the shape of chairs, of people, of insects and forest creatures. Some pieces were just bare branches, weaving in and out of each other in artful tangles. Others had plants growing over them, like skin over bone, filling them in and providing depth. Flowers bloomed in the perfect locations to provide eyes and noses. Erica's favorite was a red Japanese maple that perfectly imitated a fox on the prowl.

"Alden does these?"

"He's more creative than I am."

Xander brought her into the workshop and showed her the pieces Alden had in progress. She knew from his storefront that Alden specialized in living wood furniture—allowing the imperfections and rough edges to inform the shape and function of the pieces. But in addition to the minimalist tables and benches that lined the walls of the shop, there were a few select carved pieces that stood out to Erica. There was a leaf pattern on several works in progress that Erica recognized from the nightstands in Keith's room.

As she explored deeper into the space, she found wood chips brushed into a corner. They looked like they had been dipped in red wine up to the last inch, which was so light it was almost white. Erica picked up a piece of the purple wood and held it out to Xander.

"Did Alden make that casket for Keith?" When Xander nodded, she continued, "Seems like they were closer than you are letting on."

Xander shrugged and redirected her attention toward the cabin. "Let's go see if the camera caught anything."

Erica wrapped her fingers around the wood chip. What did the casket mean? Was it an apology? She felt like she was missing something, but she didn't want to ruin the moment. She let Xander tug on her dress and lead her back through the wildflowers and onto the porch.

There were two rocking chairs with a table between them in what Erica now recognized as Alden's style. Xander opened the door, and Erica followed him inside. The cabin had one large room that served as a kitchen, living room, and office. On the far side was a wall with three doors. Xander explained that these were two bedrooms with a bathroom between them. Everywhere she looked was the same golden tone used to stain the furniture, walls, and floor.

The furnishings were sparse—a sofa, some chairs, a smattering of various sizes of tables, and an ornate desk on top of which sat a large monitor and the trail camera. There was a bookshelf filled with books, mostly biographies of historical figures that she assumed belonged to Xander, but also translations of Greek poetry and dramas. Some of the names she recognized—Homer and Ovid—but others she had never heard of—Aristophanes and Nonnus.

Xander sat in the computer chair, the only piece of furniture in the cabin that wasn't made of wood, and Erica pulled over one of the chairs to sit beside him.

"After the disastrous sixth-grade field trip, I begged Alden to let me be homeschooled. He was pissed about having to figure out how to run internet out here." Xander bent down and pushed the power button on the PC tower sitting next to the desk. "But he's embraced it now. His Etsy store is doing pretty well."

Erica sat in the wood chair. It had a rough wool cushion and was so deep that she couldn't sit back and have her feet on the floor at the same time. "I didn't realize you stopped going to school."

"I just felt too different. I probably ostracized myself." He was quiet for a moment before he brought his eyes up to hers. "Honestly, you're the first person who has made me feel like I belong since—."

They let the unsaid hang in the air. Erica remembered how Cora had had been almost frightened to talk about Xander. She wondered what the town thought of him. He wasn't hiding away like Alden—not yet anyway—but it was clear he didn't push himself to interact either. She wondered if she should try to get him a job at the store. The image of her mother came into her mind at that thought, and she reminded herself how much she hated Danni's constant pushing, how she always knew better. Erica promised herself she would figure out what Xander wanted and make sure he was open to having her help to achieve it. She decided to leave her college research for another day.

Xander fumbled with the camera before handing it to Erica to figure out how to take out the SD card. She opened the case and found the tiny slot. Xander put it into the computer. They were rewarded with dozens of image files sitting in the folder with today's date.

"Hopefully it's not just squirrels," Xander said.

He clicked on the first image and waited for it to load. The color was so desaturated and the pixelation high that they could only just make out the giant oak in the background. There was no sign of any wildlife. Xander clicked the arrow to the next picture.

"I think I see something," Erica said. She pointed to a dark spot coming into view on the left side of the picture.

"What is it?"

"I can't tell yet. Keep going."

Xander clicked again, and the blob got bigger. With each new photo, it took up more and more of the side of the frame. Then, with the next click, a face came into view.

"Oh my god," Erica said. "It's a bear." Even with the poor picture quality, the distinct muzzle and rounded ears of a black bear were unmistakable. But this bear was at least four times bigger than any black bear Erica had ever seen—bigger even than the grizzly bears she saw on her trip to the wildlife safari in Roseburg.

Xander clicked through more of the photos. The bear kept emerging. Erica's eyes were locked on the deadly claws at the ends of its unnaturally large paws when the front door opened, and Alden strode into the room. He was wearing waders over a dirty white shirt and had mud up to his knees. His long golden hair was held back in a thick ponytail, and it looked like he had run a mud-streaked hand through it at some point.

"This explains the performance happening outside," he said, staring pointedly at where Xander and Erica's legs were nestled together after they squeezed in to examine the photos. Then, switching his gaze to the computer, he growled, "What are you looking at?"

Xander backed away from the monitor and showed Alden the picture of the bear. Alden's face immediately hardened, his cheeks going ruddy under his deep tan.

"What are you thinking? Destroy those!"

"You know what this is?" Xander asked.

"Of course I do. You're not the only one who sneaks out at night." Xander and Erica's eyebrows shot up as they exchanged a look.

"But why wouldn't you tell me?" Xander demanded.

Alden pointed at Erica. "Since they found Keith's body, she is all you talk about. I told you not to tell her. Remember what happened last time we involved someone else in our business?" That took the wind out of him. Alden dropped into the other chair and put his head in his hands. "So now you know. What are you going to do?"

Erica looked at Alden and thought of the purple wood chips in his workshop. "You found him."

"I did."

"Do you know what happened? Why it killed him?" Alden didn't move or look at her. Erica knew he didn't want her here asking questions about things she shouldn't know. She looked at Xander for help.

"She's his niece, Alden," Xander said softly.

Alden sighed and sat back in the chair. "I know that."

"Please. My family, my grandma, she's desperate to know. If you tell me the truth, we can figure out what to say to them that will help them move on."

Alden's eyes searched her face. He must have found what he was looking for.

"It was the most damage Kriners had done by far up to that point. They cleared at least five acres. We didn't know it at the time, but the spot was within a few hundred yards of its tree. Keith overheard some guys at The Diner talking about where they had been that day, and he wanted to check it out. The bear must have been there already. It must have been enraged. I don't know what happened, but I do know that Keith carried an old Smith and Wesson, and there were a couple of bullets missing when I found him."

So that was it, Erica thought. The last piece to the puzzle. The reason Keith's body was shredded to pieces. And here, before her, was the man who tried to undo all that. He looked broken, the way he slouched in the chair. He ran a hand across his hairline, brushing some of the mud off his face.

"Thank you for telling me. I want to do what's best for both of you. But the logging isn't going to stop. I've seen a video of this," she pointed to the computer screen, "stalking work sites. It's getting bolder as the loggers move into the forest."

"What do you want us to do about it?" Alden asked, more than a hint of incredulity in his tone. "Do you think if we walked into Kriners headquarters and explained that there is an ancient bear that's angry they're clear cutting its land, they'll just go away?"

Erica wasn't sure what she expected. She thought back to Officer Denman explaining the damage that had been done to Keith. She hadn't let herself think until this moment just how horrible it must have been to die that way, torn into and bleeding out in the middle of nowhere.

"This thing already killed Keith and probably the Kriners biologist," Erica said. "I don't care about it breaking into trucks or whatever, but now that we know about it, aren't we responsible if we just let it go after someone else?"

"Absolutely not," Alden said. "If those guys want to destroy the forest, there should be a price to pay."

This shocked Erica. She looked to Xander for support, but he seemed lost, either unable to collect his thoughts or unwilling to take sides. "You think Keith was just paying the price?"

"Of course not. Keith was trying to find enough evidence of their illegal practice to shut them down, or at least slow them down."

"But he didn't and now people are going out there every day, friends of mine, who might be at risk."

Erica wasn't sure when she had stood up, but she found herself now looking down at both of them. She was reminded how much they had at stake, how difficult things would be for them if who they were, what they were, got out. Erica's resolve softened. She sat down again and reached for Xander. He slid his chair closer to her and took her hand, their fingers tightly entangled.

"I don't want anyone else to get hurt, but what are we going to do?" Xander asked, squeezing her hand. "Cut down the giant oak?"

"No," Alden growled. "That's not happening."

Erica wondered what Keith would do in this situation. He had explained to her when she was little that animals would be animals and that people were almost always to blame for accidents involving them in the wild. He would shake his head at the arrogance of humans who thought their place in the food chain bought them a level of protection no matter where they were or what they did. Were the rules of engagement with an everyday bear different than when dealing with an ancient tree spirit? Either way, Erica couldn't imagine Keith advocating for anything that would cause harm to an animal defending its territory.

"What if you guys moved the tree like Xander did with the bushes out front?"

Xander snorted, a stand-in for an inappropriate laugh. Erica swore she saw Alden roll his eyes.

"First of all," Alden said, "moving roots that big would take days even if it was a normal tree. The damage it would do to the surrounding ecosystem would be devastating. You've seen those firs around it. Where are they going to go? Anyway, it's not a normal tree. It's a dryad tree. It wouldn't listen to us."

It was off topic, but Erica couldn't help but ask, "Can you move your own trees?"

Alden and Xander shook their heads in sync. "That's the thing about being a dryad. The tree is the one in control," Xander said.

Erica couldn't come up with another solution. She needed time to think, to come back to them with a better plan, even if leaving it here made her uneasy.

"Okay," Erica said. "We do nothing for now." She didn't think Alden was seeing the threat clearly, but she also felt powerless to protect everyone she desired to. She wished she had someone to talk through everything she had learned in the last few weeks, someone whose even temperament and advice had never led her astray.

Then she had an idea.

"Just a second," Erica said. The two men looked confused as she walked out the door. She took Keith's journals out of the back seat of her car and brought them inside.

"I think you wanted these," she said, as she placed them in Alden's hands. He brushed his fingers over the covers. Alden opened the journal with the drawings and flipped through the first few pages, his face softening.

"Thank you," he said shakily. "You don't know what this means."

"See?" Xander said. "She won't tell anyone."

"I won't," Erica said, then to Alden added, "but I'm hoping you will."

CHAPTER 20

Erica told Alden that the price for her silence was that he had to tell Granny everything. As Keith's mother, she was owed the truth about his death, but more than that, Erica needed the peace of mind that came from not being the only one burdened with so many secrets. She expected him to put up much more of a fight, but, having brought Keith and Erica into their confidence, Alden resigned himself quickly to the idea.

"I trust Vivian more than you anyway," Alden said as she left the cabin that night.

The Reed who was giving her quite a bit of resistance was Xander. She suggested he accompany her to the fundraiser Thursday night. She presented numerous compelling reasons why he should go. First, that she knew Granny would be home, so it was a good time for Alden to talk to her. She wasn't sure how to prepare Granny for the conversation without starting down the path of a million questions, so she figured her best course of action was to spring him on her and hope for the best. Second, that she thought it would be good for Xander to be around people. Unlike Alden, he was still actually young, not just in appearance, and there was no point in locking himself away from the world already. Third, she heard from Cora that Kyle would be there, and she thought she could avoid some unpleasant banter if she had a date.

"You went out with Kyle Zukowski?" Xander asked during one of their good night phone calls. "That cocky kid from elementary school."

"He's not that cocky. And we only went on a date when I first came down. We were not dating."

This was the deciding factor for Xander. Thursday just before six-thirty, he texted Erica that they were on their way. She tried to hide her nerves for Alden's arrival under the guise of getting ready for the fundraiser. Granny lent her a champagne cocktail dress with a gathered bodice and tulle sleeves and skirt. The last time Granny recalled wearing this dress was to a wedding in the late 1980s, but Erica figured that was old enough for it to be in style again. Erica wished she owned a pair of heels since she could wear them without being taller than Xander, but she settled for a nice pair of Granny's sandals even though her toes stuck out over the ends.

Erica sat nervously at the edge of the couch trying to swallow her guilt over the shock Granny was about to receive. She heard a truck pull up in front of the house and, seconds later, a knock on the door. Tulip jumped up from her bed by the fireplace and barked like she did whenever anyone came over. Granny made a move toward the door, but Erica beat her to it. Granny had assumed that Kyle was accompanying her to the fundraiser, and she had been careful not to confirm or deny this. When she swung the door open to reveal Xander, Erica only registered the surprise on Granny's face for a moment before all her attention was taken up by two buttons left undone at the top of Xander's black dress shirt. She had first seen him at the waterfall in just a pair of swim trunks, but here in front of her, clean-shaven in dark jeans, muscles and tendons spilling out of his too-small shirt, she had to stop her knees from buckling. She wanted to rush forward and put her hands on every inch of exposed skin, but she held herself back.

"Oh, Alex," Granny said. "I wasn't expecting you."

"Xander," Erica and Xander said at the same time.

Granny's eyes widened and she turned her head toward Erica as if asking if at least one of them knew why this boy was at their house. But before Erica could explain, Alden arrived in the doorframe.

"Hi Vivian," he said. "I thought we could talk."

Erica stepped back and let them into the living room. Granny's eyes were wide as Alden looked sheepishly around the room. The corners of his mouth sagged when his gaze landed on the door under the stairs, but they picked up again as Tulip sauntered over and dropped herself at his feet. Alden bent down to pet the little dog who flopped right over on her back to accept a belly rub, something she would never do for a stranger. Granny looked from the dog to Alden, and Erica wished she knew what she was thinking.

"Can I get you some tea?" Granny asked at last.

"That would be nice," Alden replied.

Erica waited for someone to head toward the kitchen, but Alden and Granny kept their places, him crouching and her staring. When she let her eyes land back on Xander, he was holding himself straight and tense, not at all helping the awkwardness of the situation.

"I'll get it," Erica said. She grabbed Xander's hand and pulled him into the kitchen with her. Xander tried to hover in the entrance to keep an eye on their family members in the living room, but Erica put him to work picking out a tea bag for Alden as she warmed the kettle.

"Your grandma looks sterner than I expected."

"It's just the gray hair. She's the sweetest," Erica promised.

Despite this assurance, they both stood with their hands against the countertops listening for signs of trouble from the other room. They relaxed in tandem when they heard polite whispers. Erica decided to fight against her nature and be optimistic. She had to put faith in Granny's even temperament and open mind. She was sure that if Xander could convince her as easily as he did that Alden would have no trouble. As Xander said, Alden was the creative one.

Erica picked her favorite mugs and poured boiling water over the tea bags they had chosen—soothing peppermint green tea for Granny and oolong for Alden. When she brought them out, the whispering stopped. The mood in the room was tense but not unfriendly. Erica handed them their mugs.

"We're going to go," Erica said tentatively, taking Xander's arm. "Granny, are you going to be okay?"

Granny nodded and flicked her hand toward the door, shooing them out. "Sure, love. Alden and I have some catching up to do," she said.

Not wanting to wait for her to change her mind, Erica shoved Xander back out the door and closed it behind them. Outside, they grinned at each other, as though they had gotten away with something.

"Your poor grandmother."

"I'm glad she's in good health."

They watched the door for a few moments, but it didn't look like Granny was going to kick Alden out. Erica took Xander's hand and led him toward her car.

"This isn't how I imagined my first date," Xander said. Then he lifted their hands above her head and twirled her around. "Except for this part. You look amazing."

Erica giggled as she regained her center. "This is your first date?" Xander shot her a look and she remembered who she was talking to. "Oh god, right. Well now I feel awful. I wish I was taking you somewhere other than the community center."

"Not much nightlife in Juniper Falls." Xander opened her door—the driver's side—and settled her into the car. Once he was beside her, they took one last look at the house and backed out of the driveway. Keeping her eyes determinedly on the road, Erica took the hand that wasn't on the steering wheel and ran a finger down Xander's bare forearm. She felt him shiver at her touch and her heart surged.

"I like you," she murmured.

She was embarrassed the second the words crossed her lips. She could barely believe she said them out loud. She was thankful for the road in front of her so that she didn't have to look at Xander. But then again, he had to know, right? As if it wasn't obvious from the way she couldn't keep her hands off him. As if when he dropped in at the store earlier that week on the pretense of buying pruning shears, she hadn't immediately taken her lunch and strolled downtown with him for an hour. As if she wasn't, at this very moment, subconsciously tracing hearts on the tendons of his wrist.

Erica came to a stop sign and turned to confront Xander for his non-response. She found him smiling, not his usual close-lipped smirk, but a genuine, white-toothed smile. He slowly placed his big hands on either side of her face and kissed her hard. Erica reciprocated, leaning into him as far as her seatbelt would let her go.

"Erica," Xander said.

"Yes?"

"You're rolling through the intersection."

Erica snapped her eyes forward and slammed her foot on the brake so hard that they both jerked forward. Xander laughed, a low deep rumble of a sound that made her chest feel full. She pretended to be angry with him the rest of the way to the community center, but it was impossible when he looked that good and when, for the first time, he had been the one to kiss her.

There was an attendant directing traffic even though just a few cars were trickling in and the parking lot was only half full. That was Bobby Hendricks' style, a little bigger, a little flashier than was necessary in a place like Juniper Falls. Erica could see him and his wife Lucia welcoming guests as she and Xander made their way toward the door. Lucia, in a gold column gown, looked expensive and elegant next to Bobby who was both very tall and very fat, his ginger hair going gray at the temples.

"Erica!" Bobby cried when he saw her. "I really didn't think your grandmother was going to skip this, but I guess she has a lot going on."

"She's sorry she had to miss it."

"How is she?" Lucia asked, pulling Erica in for a hug.

"Mostly fine," Erica said, hoping it was true. She wondered how far Alden had made it into his story by now.

"And you brought a friend," Lucia said. Erica caught the quick look of surprise she shot her husband. She saw that Xander did too. His back straightened to bring him up almost to equal height with Bobby.

"Thank you for having me," Xander said, holding out a hand. Bobby shook it.

"Of course, uh—." Bobby was searching for the name.

"Xander Reed."

"Oh!" Bobby yelped. He was much less subtle than his wife. "You Reeds don't get out much. Well, enjoy. Go say hi to Cora. You went to school together, right?"

Erica pasted on a smile and steered Xander away from the Hendrickses and into the party. She supposed she should have expected this, but they were off to an awkward start.

"I'm sorry," she said to Xander as they followed signs leading them to where the event was held on the basketball courts.

"It's okay," he said, but she wasn't convinced.

One side of the room was set up with a buffet and a couple dozen cocktail tables draped in black with a single gold balloon rising out of each as a centerpiece. The other side had rectangular tables holding various auction items—books, baskets, and trinkets. A hundred or so people were milling about, some carrying drinks and others food. Xander set his face into a look of flat resignation.

"Where should we start? Silent auction or buffet?" Erica asked.

"I don't eat," Xander said in a deadpan voice like this was the most obvious thing in the world. Erica stared at him.

"What do you mean you don't eat?"

"Alden taught me. We can't die, right? So we don't have to eat. The first few weeks are horrible, but then you get used to it. Sometimes I can't help myself and I'll get a hamburger or something. It's so not worth it. It feels great while you're eating it, but going back to the not eating? Excruciating."

Somehow of all the crazy things Erica had been forced to come to terms with in the last few weeks, this was by far the hardest to swallow. As if on cue, a server walked by with a plate of shrimp cocktails.

"But I love eating," Erica said.

"Go for it."

"That feels, I don't know, rude." This did not stop her from grabbing a shot glass with a single shrimp and a napkin. "Are you sure?"

"Yes."

He watched as she bit into the shrimp. She was self-conscious when a bit of juice exploded from the side of her mouth. She wiped her lips and tipped back the cocktail sauce like a shot. When she was done, she looked sheepishly at him.

"Was it that good?" he asked. Erica nodded modestly. "Good, because that was so mean. If there are brownies, I may have to say to hell with it and suffer the consequences."

"I feel so bad!" Erica said with a laugh. "This was a terrible idea. I'm sorry if you hate it. We can go bid on some stuff we'll never win and get out of here." Though Granny had made her promise to spend at least a hundred dollars to keep Bobby from asking for more later, Erica was seriously considering bailing on the event. She had a feeling she and Xander would have a better night if they drove out somewhere quiet than if they stayed here.

Just as she made a move toward the silent auction tables, Erica saw a rush of fuchsia headed toward them. Cora's dress was off-the-shoulder with a full skirt that ended above the knee. Erica thought she looked adorable and was planning to tell her so when Cora grabbed Erica's arm and dragged her toward the back of the room. Erica shot an apologetic look at Xander who stood anchored to the spot.

"What are you doing bringing him here?" Cora spat.

"He's my date," Erica said, pulling her arm out of Cora's grip. "I don't know what you have against him."

"He's weird, Erica. You weren't here when he came back after his mom died. He stopped talking and would just sit there and watch everyone. And it never got better. Then he just disappeared with his supposed uncle who half of us are convinced is dead."

"Xander's uncle is visiting my granny right now."

Cora's eyes widened, and she took a half step backward in surprise. "Okay, but have you heard the stories about—."

"I don't care," Erica said, cutting her off. "You should give him a chance. He had a hard childhood, but he's great. He's smart and funny and really sweet." Erica knew she would want to punch herself in the face if she could see the mushy grin, she was making talking about him.

Cora stared at her so hard that Erica had to look away. She caught eyes with Xander who had moved closer to her but not quite within earshot. The concern on his face made her feel warm and cared for.

"Jesus Christ. You're together, aren't you?" Cora said, looking between them.

"Yeah, I guess so." Erica could feel herself being pulled back to him like a magnet. "Let's go out again. Us and Derek."

"Oh, no. Me and Derek? That's not happening anymore."

"What happened?" Erica asked, but she was only half-listening. She waved Xander over, unable to stop herself from touching him when he was within her reach again.

Cora didn't acknowledge Xander's arrival other than to angle her body away from him. "What usually happens? Things just fizzle out. We were just having fun."

Erica wouldn't let her ignore him. She leaned into Xander and asked, "You know Cora?"

Xander nodded. "Hey."

"Hi," Cora responded flatly.

They stood together awkwardly as Erica searched her brain for a topic of conversation that would interest them both. She was saved, however, by the screech of a microphone coming from the direction of the buffet. Erica hadn't noticed earlier that there was a small stage set up where Cora's father was now standing.

"Thank you all for coming to this fundraising event to purchase an electric sign reader for Paul Bunyan High School." Bobby's voice reverberated through the large room. "Go Lumberjacks!" There was a small smattering of applause, but Bobby carried on as strong as before. "I don't want to distract you for too long from our smorgasbord, but I did want to introduce you to tonight's largest donor. Kriners Lumber has generously donated five thousand dollars to our goal, and their Regional Vice President, Mitchell Watters, is here to talk about other investments Kriners is looking to make in the community."

A nondescript businessman of medium build wearing a well-fitted navy suit thanked Bobby and took the microphone from him. His thinning hair was slicked back on the sides. Erica expected Mitchell's speech to be as boring as he looked, and she was taken aback when he spoke with the authority and decisiveness of a late-night televangelist.

"Now I know not all of you are happy about having the logging industry back in your town, but Kriners wants you to know that we are deeply committed to sustainable practices. That includes giving back to the communities where our employees live, work, and play. We will be working with the Town of Juniper Falls," here he nodded conspiratorially at Bobby, "to fund a downtown revitalization project that will have a lasting impact on this and future generations. We will be hosting a booth with the town at the upcoming Harvest Festival and look forward to hearing directly from you about how we can improve life in Juniper Falls."

The words that he spoke should have been warm, but their delivery made Erica uncomfortable. She appeared to be one of the few who felt this way, as after a few more minutes of Mitchell carrying on in the same vein, he received healthy applause from the crowd. Mitchell stepped back from the microphone and shook Bobby's hand.

"Don't forget that they also need money to cover up the fact that people are going missing," said a voice behind Erica.

Erica and Xander spun around to face the voice. It was Kyle. He too was wearing a suit and an enamel pin of the Kriners logo—crossed axes over a log round.

"Who is going missing?" Xander asked. Kyle sized him up, his displeasure at finding Erica cozied up to someone else written on his face. Kyle maneuvered himself in a flimsy attempt to block Xander from the conversation.

"Remember when we talked a couple of weeks ago with the broken equipment and other weird stuff?" Kyle asked. "It's gotten worse since then. Three guys have just disappeared off job sites."

Xander squeezed Erica's hand and she knew what he was thinking. Kriners was shady, but they had no reason to harm their workforce. They both knew there was another explanation.

"You guys haven't seen anything?" Erica asked.

Kyle shook his head. "Ever since you pointed out that thing in the video, I can't shake the feeling that we're being watched. But no. We're on a buddy system now, but they're trying hard to convince us that those dudes are fine."

"What are they saying happened to them?"

"That they got called to headquarters. But I was on one of the crews where a guy didn't come back after wandering off to take a piss. Something is going on in the woods."

Cora asked a follow-up question, but Xander was already pulling Erica toward the door. Erica heard Kyle ask, "is she okay?" as she followed Xander out of the room, running to match his long stride.

"We have to tell Alden," Xander said as they wound their way through the halls and back out into the parking lot. As they drove home, Erica wondered how Granny was going to take a second round of troubling news in the span of a single evening.

CHAPTER 21

Alden's truck was still parked on the road when Erica and Xander pulled back into the driveway of Granny's house. Erica was nervous about what they would walk in on. She steeled herself as Xander rushed out of the car toward the door. When he realized she wasn't at his side, he turned back to look for her, a confused expression on his handsome face. Xander was so worried that being with him would be boring for her, but in Erica's experience so far, it might be more exciting than she could handle.

Erica had come to terms with Keith's death before she discovered its exact circumstances, so it had been easier to swallow than the fact that others were disappearing, and she could prevent it. It was a level of responsibility she hadn't asked for and didn't want. The urge to put the key in the ignition and drive to Portland was overwhelming. At that moment, she couldn't even remember what she had run from in the first place. The problems she left up north were so commonplace, so solvable, compared to what she had unearthed in Juniper Falls.

But it took just one look at Xander, the line between his eyebrows growing deeper by the second, for Erica to quickly reprimanded herself for trying to take the easy way out. She wasn't going to be able to run from the difficult parts of life forever. Even though she had so far been unable to find the fortitude to fight for herself, the boy standing on the doorstep deserved someone stronger, more capable. He had been through so much. She had to be better than she was. She had to be better for him.

Erica slowly got out of the car and joined Xander at the door. He raised his eyebrows at her, but she just shook her head and put her hand on the doorknob. She drew a deep breath and opened the door.

Granny was sitting on the sofa with a couple of white tissues in her hand. Across from her, Alden sat at the edge of a recliner, leaning toward her. They had walked in on an intense conversation, and Erica hoped that Alden had gotten through enough that she didn't have to hear all the gory details again.

She walked over to the sofa and sat down next to Granny. "Did he tell you?"

"Yes." Granny's eyes were red, but her voice was clear.

"All of it?" Erica asked, this time looking at Alden. He nodded. Erica put a hand on one of Granny's and squeezed. They sat like that, staring at their interlocked hands for several moments until Xander cleared his throat.

"What are you doing back so soon?" Granny asked, taking note of Xander's presence for the first time.

Xander shifted in place. "I need to talk to Alden."

"About what? What happened?" Alden was alarmed. Erica could see the possibilities playing across his face.

"I think we should go," Xander said. Erica was surprised by this. She had just convinced herself that they were a team. She tried to read Xander's expression to understand why he wanted to cut her out now, after everything he had told her. He avoided her gaze and focused on trying to get Alden out the door. Part of her wanted to let them go, to throw her hands up and say she tried. But the bigger part of her wanted to show Xander that he wasn't alone anymore.

"It's the giant oak," Erica said. "The bear. It's killing people. Logging workers."

Alden jumped up from the chair. "They know?"

"They don't know about the bear specifically but it's obvious, isn't it? Why else would people be disappearing in the forest?"

"Lots of reasons. Accidents happen in that industry. I'm proof of that" Alden grabbed his shoulder reflexively.

This was not how Erica expected any of this to go. She had been counting on a call to action, some decision-making overseen by an informed adult. Erica looked to Xander to back her up. She knew that they had made the same assumption about the cause of the disappearances and wanted him to say so. He didn't meet her eye.

"We have to do something about it," Erica insisted.

"Like what?" Alden asked. "I'm not hearing any proof that the dryad is responsible for what may have happened to those people. And even if it was, how are we supposed to reason with a bear? Unless you're implying something else."

"Can't we, I don't know, trap it? Limit its range somehow?"

Alden laughed coldly. "If you want to try to trap a thousand-pound ancient forest spirit that can rip apart a semi with ease, be my guest."

"Alden," Granny interjected, having caught up with the conversation. "We are talking about the thing that killed Keith. I didn't see his body, but I did hear about its condition from Officer Denman. If it's doing that to other people, it must be stopped."

"This was all a huge mistake," Alden said, taking two long strides so that he could look Xander straight in the eye. "This is your fault."

Alden opened the door and stalked toward the truck. Xander stood in the open door frame, his shoulders slumped. He looked between Alden and Erica several times before whispering, "I'm sorry," and following Alden, carefully shutting the door behind him.

"He always was a hothead," Granny said, watching through the windows as Xander and Alden argued their way toward the truck.

Erica slumped back into the sofa, trying to process what just transpired. Maybe Xander's desire to leave as fast as possible was his attempt at protecting her from Alden's wrath. But without knowing there was a plan for how to contain the bear, she was putting all those people at risk. Erica told them that she would keep their secret, but could she do that at the cost of people's lives? Potentially Kyle and Derek's lives?

"What should we do?" Erica muttered, expecting it to be a rhetorical question.

But Granny answered. "Alden said you've seen it. Do you think it's dangerous?"

"Just pictures," Erica said. "Yesterday I would have said Keith was in the wrong place at the wrong time. But this? It sounds like it's targeting loggers."

"Then I guess you have to ask yourself if you trust him."

"Who? Alden?"

"No, love, Xander. Alden may be too caught up in being what he is, but it sounds like Xander can still see things from a, for lack of a better word, human perspective."

Erica considered this. Xander had inspired trust in her since before she knew anything about him. From the very beginning, he had wanted to do right by her. He could have gotten Keith's journals through any means, but he chose honesty. He must have a reason for being so unwilling to stand up against Alden tonight, for wanting to have this conversation away from her. She had no choice but to trust him.

"I'll call him tomorrow," Erica said. "Maybe he can get through to Alden."

"I wouldn't mind having the boy over again. I have some follow-up questions."

In the fervor of the evening, Erica almost forgot that Granny just received a lot of strange and disturbing news. "I'm sorry we dumped all this on you out of the blue. I didn't think you would believe me if I tried to prepare you."

"I probably wouldn't have," Granny said with a smile in her voice.

"How did he convince you?"

Granny pointed to an orchid in a square glass container that was given to her after Keith's funeral. Someone had put it on a table on the far side of the room away from the windows, and Erica was positive neither she nor Granny so much as watered it since then. She vaguely remembered meaning to throw it away a few days ago when she noticed the blooms had fallen and the leaves were more yellow than green. Now it was double the size, its leaves thick and glossy, with a dozen plump white flowers on its stem.

"Oh, sure," Erica said. "They like that trick."

Granny laughed.

Erica opened the store by herself the next morning. There was some busy work left to do to prepare for the Harvest Festival, so she set herself up behind the counter stapling coupons to plantable paper imbued with native wildflower seeds. Every year during the second weekend of October, downtown Juniper Falls put on a street fair to celebrate the last few days before temperatures dropped and rain fell. Part art walk, part farmers market, residents put up tents on the sidewalks and local businesses offered freebies and refreshments.

Erica loved the Harvest Festival when she was growing up. Every year she got her face painted and left with a balloon and a funnel cake. She had fond memories of Keith manning the grill in the store parking lot and handing out bratwurst piled high with onions for adults and smothered in ketchup for the kids. She was using these thoughts to distract herself from what she learned last night, and from how little she slept in its aftermath when the door chime announced her first customer of the day.

She looked up to see Xander slouch into the store. She could instantly tell he had a worse night than she did. He was back in his maroon hoodie and the stubble on his chin was thick. Erica had been planning to freeze him out for a little while to express her displeasure at being excluded from whatever conversation he and Alden had after they left. One look at his face wiped that idea right out of her head. She put down her stapler and made her way around the counter. When she got to him, she wrapped her arms around him and held him tight. He melted into her as he hugged her back.

"Rough night?" she breathed into his chest.

"Alden is on the warpath."

Erica leaned back so she could see his face, letting her arms fall around his hips. "He's going to do something about the bear?"

"No," Xander sighed. "He's pissed that you know and that you talked him into telling Vivian."

"He seemed to want to."

"I think he did. But he's convinced that this dryad is tied to us maybe or to the forest. He probably takes Greek mythology more seriously than the Greeks did."

"It's killing people, Xander."

"I know, but what can I do? We don't know how any of this works. What if Alden is right? What if taking it down does more harm than good?"

Erica let go of Xander and walked back to the counter. She bounced her fist against the linoleum a few times, trying to think of other solutions. "Can't we figure out how to contain it?"

"With what? It's been able to rip through metal no problem."

"Some kind of fence?" Erica said, thinking of the black bears that roamed around a spacious enclosure at the Oregon Zoo.

"I don't think it would give us enough time to build a fence around it before, well, you know." Xander formed his hand into a claw and scratched through the air. He had a point.

"We could tranquilize it."

"And then what? Lock it up in Alden's workshop? It's not like we can relocate it. Its range seems a lot larger than ours, but it's still a dryad. It has to be near its tree."

It was Erica's turn to sigh. "So we're not going to do anything?"

Xander came up next to her and leaned into the counter. They looked out at the empty store with its neat rows of merchandise, a little bit of order in a chaotic world. "I can try to track it," he said. "It's been getting sloppier. I can catch glimpses of something now and then that must be the bear. I might be able to at least warn people."

"Maybe Kyle could help sound the alarm or something."

Xander made a face, but he nodded. "Yeah, I could text him when it's nearby."

This was not the perfect solution Erica had been hoping for, but she had a feeling it was as much as she was going to get out of him today. With any luck, it would be enough. She tilted her head onto his chest. "Be careful, though, okay?"

"You keep forgetting who you're talking to." Xander put his arm around her and kissed the top of her head. "The only thing I'm scared of is losing you."

"I'm right here."

"For now."

CHAPTER 22

Over the next week, Xander intercepted Erica at least once a day at random intervals. He would show up at her house and the store, but also when she was shopping for groceries with Granny or returning a book at the library. On her day off, she was craving a fast-food hamburger and a new pair of jeans and decided to drive into Roseburg for the afternoon. The leaves on the trees were changing color and Erica admired the yellow, orange, and red dotted among the firs and cedars as she drove. She hadn't made it half an hour out of town when she got a text from Xander. *I can't find you.*

Erica didn't mind that Xander was using her to hone his tracking skills. She thought it was good for him to lean into the useful aspects of his abilities rather than see them only as a burden. The more time they spent together, the more obvious it became that Xander battled constantly against a dark melancholy rooted in his loneliness and exacerbated by being an outsider in his hometown. Erica's heart broke for him, and she resolved to be as normal with him as possible.

This was difficult when so much of their conversation was centered around updates on how Xander's tracking was progressing. At first, he had only been able to feel his way through tree roots and large, woody shrubs. He would lose Erica when she was in developed areas. They spent one whole day sitting on a bench downtown until Xander could tap into the network of dandelion roots and decorative annuals to tell her the location of each shopper on the sidewalk.

Despite his best efforts, Xander was still having trouble keeping tabs on the bear's movements. He could glimpse it now and then like an apparition floating on the periphery of the town. Luckily it was staying away from the logging sites. Only once did Xander text her a potential location. He drove to where he thought he felt it, roaming the perimeter of where a Kriners crew was working. Erica had kept her finger over the call button, trying to figure out what she was going to tell Kyle if it came to that. She was relieved when Xander told her it was nothing. In her mind, she played the conversation she was going to be forced to have with Kyle eventually. No matter how she phrased it, she sounded crazy.

Kyle was helping Erica, Granny, and Joe run the Harvest Festival booth that weekend. She would have to find a way to fill him into the point that he would trust her warnings, but not ask too many questions. She should have done it before, but she had already caused so many problems between Alden and Xander. The potential of screwing up her conversation with Kyle, of giving away too much, held her back. She knew that at least part of the reason Xander kept showing up wherever she was, was to avoid being home and being ignored by Alden.

Xander was sitting at her dining room table reading a thick book and watching her and Granny eat when Erica decided the time was right to bring up her college research. He had been having a particularly hard time keeping up his smiling veneer that evening, and she decided that making progress toward the future she promised him the night they first kissed was a good way to cheer him up. Xander told her that Alden was waiting for him to show some interest, let alone proficiency, in his wood-working business. For his part, Xander was convinced that one day he would wake up and that would be what he wanted to do. Erica got the feeling that neither of them had ever considered other options.

"I have something for you. Hang on a second," Erica said. She ran upstairs and grabbed the spiral notebook in which she had scribbled various pieces of relevant information—tuition, scholarships, application deadlines. Back downstairs, she opened it to the list of degrees and slid it toward Xander. She saw him exchange a look of confusion with Granny.

"What is this?" he asked.

"I was thinking you could go to school with me, but online."

Xander furrowed his brows. Erica thought she saw Granny roll her eyes from the periphery. Xander scanned the list she provided and flipped the page, reading through her notes.

"Very thorough," he said in a flat tone.

Erica tried her best not to be disappointed. "I figured since you finished high school online, you might be interested."

"What am I supposed to do with a college degree?"

"It depends on what you want to study. You're always reading, so I thought maybe you could be a teacher or a tutor."

"There are three schools in Juniper Falls. I think they would notice if I didn't age. That's if they would even hire me given what this town thinks of me and Alden."

Granny let out a little tsk that Erica couldn't decipher. She chose to believe that Granny was trying to contradict the town's opinion about Xander.

"You could teach online too!" Erica said. "I was reading all about it. More and more high school and college kids are attending online classes for all sorts of reasons." Erica was ready to launch into a speech about online education, but Xander cut her off. He pushed the notebook back at her.

"This is a waste of time, Erica."

"All you have is time!" she said, perhaps more forcefully than she intended.

Xander stared at her, his normally warm face gone cold. She knew she had hit a nerve. Erica tried to put her hand on top of his, but he grabbed his book and stood up. "I think I'm going to go."

Erica followed him to the door and hovered while he tied his shoelaces. "I'm sorry," she said. "I thought you'd be excited."

Xander bent down and gave her a quick kiss on the forehead but did not respond.

"I'll see you tomorrow?" she asked. He gave a non-committal nod before slipping out the door. Erica watched him walk across the lawn and get into his truck. She had gone about this all wrong. She had meant to challenge and inspire him. What had come out sounded like a mandate.

Erica took her seat at the table again. She picked up her fork and stabbed it into the salad on her plate.

Granny watched her over a forkful of lettuce. "You know who you sound like."

"Don't say it," Erica sighed.

Though they hadn't discussed it, Erica expected Xander to come to help set up for the Harvest Festival. It had been two days since he walked out of her house after their disagreement. He was picking up his phone and responding to texts but blamed bear tracking for not seeing her. Erica tried to apologize but he insisted there was nothing to be sorry about. She hinted that there would be a lot of heavy lifting involved in getting everything ready Saturday morning, but the truth was that she missed him—his touch, his face, his rare but rewarding laugh. She was careful, however, not to push him to see her. Pushing was what had got them here.

Erica and Granny walked to the store just as the sun came up and pulled tables and chairs out of the storeroom. *Juniper Falls Farm & Feed* sat at the far end of downtown and had a large parking lot that over the years had become the designated place for putting your feet up and enjoying the food collected on the way down. It was Erica's grandfather who began handing out sausages to hungry festivalgoers. Now it was tradition.

They were wrapping the folding tables in plastic gingham tablecloths when Joe and Kyle arrived with a big, round, pellet grill in the back of his new truck. Erica noticed that Granny was having an easier time talking about Keith since her chat with Alden. Nowhere was this more apparent than when she announced her intention of giving Joe his truck. As an official co-owner of the store, Granny decided it was only appropriate that Joe drive a company car. Not to mention that she did

not need two big trucks. Erica and Granny had spent an afternoon cleaning it out, peeling parks stickers off the windows, and
doing their best to get Tulip's hair out of the upholstery. Joe had
been close to tears when Granny presented him with the keys.

Joe pulled the truck up to the side of the store and dropped
the tailgate.

"Couldn't even have the tents up for us yet?" Kyle joked.

"Excuse me," Erica said. "Do you think these tables went
up themselves?"

"Leaving the hard work to the men, I see. Not very femi-
nist of you."

Erica elbowed him in the ribs. "I guess I won't be giving
you a hand getting that grill out."

True to her word, Erica watched Joe and Kyle struggle to
get the grill onto the asphalt without damaging either it or the
truck. In their defense, it was more awkward than heavy. She
wished Xander would show up. She took her phone out to text
him but thought better of it and put it away.

Once the grill was in place, Erica and Kyle dragged out the
half dozen coolers full of sausages, toppings, and condiments
while Joe fired up the grill. Erica set up the table for their give-
aways. She kept looking for an opening to pull Kyle aside and
talk to him about her and Xander's plan to keep the loggers safe,
but every time she got him alone, one or the other of them was
handed another task. He slipped out before the event officially
started, promising to come back to help his dad with the lunch
rush. Erica told herself she had to grab him when she saw him
again.

The festival was in full swing by ten o'clock. Erica expected to
be stuck in the store behind the cash register most of the day,
so when Granny offered to cover her at the store for a while
so that she could visit the rest of the festival, Erica was more
than happy to seize the opportunity. The street was closed to
car traffic, and blue and white pop-up tents dotted the roadway.
Erica smiled at the vendors that had been coming for as long
she could remember. Perennial favorites included stalls featuring

chunky silver jewelry, laser-engraved wooden signs, and hand-made cards. New additions included food carts that came from Eugene to peddle beignets and artisan tacos. At another of the new stalls, Erica bought Xander a leather bracelet branded with the outlines of acorns. It was thick, soft, and had an unfinished look that reminded her of him in more ways than one.

All the stores had merchandise spilling onto the side-walks. The grocery store went all out creating a cornucopia out of canned goods that they intended to donate to a local food bank. Neither Alden nor Xander could be found at *Falls Custom Furniture*, but Erica noted that their window display included ornaments made of the same purple heartwood as Keith's casket. Erica peered through the window and caught a glimpse of a middle-aged woman she didn't recognize showing some live edge pieces to a chic young couple.

Erica's last stop before returning to the store was to visit Cora at her parents' gas station. As usual, they had set up a small beer garden next to the liquor store that didn't open until noon. In the front part of the gas station, there was a new booth. It gave off a different feel than the others, which had the unpol-ished, homegrown feel that Erica associated with Juniper Falls. Ironically, this booth was manned by Bobby Hendricks on behalf of the town. A bright white tablecloth and banner bore a logo she had never seen before—a waterfall flowing down a tree-lined hill with *Town of Juniper Falls* written in a bold, modern font. Half of the table was taken up by leaflets advertising municipal ser-vices. The other half was filled with informational flyers about public meetings related to the proposed development project Erica had heard about at the fundraiser. *Kriners supports local com-munities*, Erica read on one flier that prominently displayed the new Juniper Falls logo alongside Kriners' crossed axes.

"Wow, what's all this?" she asked Bobby.

"Isn't it great?" the big man said brightly. "Kriners has been a huge help in teaching us about marketing. They are invested in putting Juniper Falls on the map."

"I designed the logo!" said a voice from behind Erica. She turned around to find Cora standing with Mitchell Watters.

"With a little help from corporate," Mitchell said.

"Well, the concept was mine."

Mitchell was wearing a bright red polo, carefully pressed slacks, and recently oiled patent loafers. He had on a large, shiny, silver watch that reflected the sun whenever he moved. They sized each other up, and Mitchell took note of her dark blue polo with its silver stitching.

"You work next door," Mitchell said in his smooth preacher's voice. "I've been trying to get your grandmother to join the coalition of businesses in support of our improvement plan. Imagine how much more inviting this festival could be with better lighting, some benches, and landscaping."

"I think it's perfect how it is," Erica told him, partly because it was true but mostly because she knew it would annoy him.

Mitchell gave a flat smile that made his lips disappear completely.

"Erica is from Portland," Cora said. "She romanticizes life out in the boonies."

"Juniper Falls is a wonderful town. We're committed to helping it be the best version of itself," Mitchell said. He grabbed one of the pamphlets off the table and handed it to her. "We would love to see you at a meeting."

Erica wanted to ask him what he thought about the workers who went missing from his job sites, but she knew that wasn't fair. Keeping the disappearances quiet was just the latest in a series of shady dealings involving Kriners, but as far as she knew they weren't killing anyone. Having grown up in a small business, Erica had a healthy distrust for the practices of large corporations. While she had a feeling that this wasn't the last time, she was going to be disappointed in Kriners, she had no reason to pick a fight today.

"Thank you," Erica said, taking the pamphlet. "I'll think about it."

Mitchell gave her an indulgent nod and went to take a seat next to Bobby. Cora followed Erica as she made her way back to the *Farm & Feed* parking lot, which was filling up with hungry shoppers.

"What was that about?" Erica asked.

"I know they're laying it on a bit thick, but this town could use some help," Cora said. "Dad built that damn community center, and he needed a new project. He's probably going to zone himself out of being able to have a liquor store here in the name of beautification."

"What Kyle told us the other night doesn't bother you?"

"He seems pretty convinced that there is something in the woods that has nothing to do with Kriners."

"But don't you think they should be doing more to make sure they're safe? You know they were out doing test sites before their permits were finalized."

Cora laughed. "Yeah, that sounds like Mitch. But they got them, right? No one is going to pretend that Kriners isn't here to make money, but it wouldn't be the worst if some of it trickles down."

Erica and Cora rounded the *Farm & Feed* barn and spotted Derek and Kyle sitting at one of the tables nearest the grill. They had four bratwursts on a plate between them, not counting the one in Kyle's hand that was already half-eaten.

"Ugh," Cora said, motioning to Derek. "I don't want to deal with that right now."

"I get it."

"Where is your boyfriend by the way?" Cora's tone when she said the word *boyfriend* told Erica that she hadn't quite come around to the idea of her and Xander.

"I'm not sure." Erica took her phone out of her pocket and unlocked the screen. Xander had called her three times within the last five minutes. His name flashed up again as she held the phone.

"That's him," Erica said. She answered the phone with an upward swipe. Xander was talking before she could get a word out.

"Erica, it's headed for you. It's coming right for downtown." The words spilled out fast, his voice panicked. Erica froze on the spot, both her body and her brain trying to process what he was saying.

"What?" she whispered into the phone. Cora raised an eyebrow in concern.

"I've felt it strong all day. It was sort of near the festival, but far enough away that I wasn't worried about it. Then something spooked it. I'm trying to make it to you first, but—."

Erica didn't catch the rest of what he said. She was focused on a scream from up the road. Still holding the phone to her ear, she ran back toward the street with Cora right behind her. The crowd was so thick that she couldn't see anything. Then a white tent went flying, sending custom craft projects flying in every direction.

"Xander, get here now," she said and hung up.

More screams filled the air. The mood among those nearest Erica was more of curiosity than fear as they craned their necks to see what was causing the commotion. She fought her way through them when a guttural roar echoed between the buildings. It was as loud as thunder. And if that wasn't enough to convince them there was something very wrong, they finally saw it.

The bear reared itself up on its hind legs and let out several long, low grunts. It was bigger than Erica had imagined from the pictures, at least fifteen feet tall. Its fur was so dark it reflected no light, the claws at the end of its paws like obsidian swords. It fell back down again onto all fours, and that was the queue for the crowd to run. They came at Erica so fast that she had to plaster herself against the side of a building to stop from being trampled.

The first gunshot rang through the air. This was rural Oregon after all, where the number of concealed carry permits almost equaled driver's licenses. The bear didn't react as the bullet entered its body. It continued its path of destruction, ripping apart canvas and throwing metal through glass windows.

The street was emptying, and Erica wondered what she thought she was going to do if it came down to her versus the bear. It had felt so important to be in the thick of the action, to prove she was someone who knew something. She lost Cora at some point, but what help would she have been anyway? Erica flattened her hands against the brick at her back and tried to come up with a plan. She heard another gunshot, but she knew it was no use. They had to go for the tree.

Erica felt herself be pulled back into an alleyway. The force almost ripped her arm from its socket. She spun around to see Xander, his face ashen and eyes wild.

"Are you okay?" he asked. He patted her down like she was in the security line of an airport. When he was satisfied she wasn't bleeding, he took her up into his arms so that her feet left the ground. He held her so tight she had to gasp to make him let go. Xander put her down, motioned for her to stay, and peered around the corner of the building out into the street. "This is very bad."

"We have to kill it."

"Erica," he sighed.

She took Xander's hand and pulled him back into the alley. She ran her finger up the bridge of his nose and tapped it between his eyes. "We have to."

"Alden will literally never forgive me."

"After this, I don't think there is a choice."

Xander slumped against the wall. The sounds of people had died down, but they could still hear the bear growling and grunting as it unleashed its anger upon the Harvest Festival. Erica looked pleadingly into his eyes. Xander's own darted between her face and the chaos in the streets. She watched his resolve melt.

"How are we going to do this?"

CHAPTER 23

Erica and Xander followed the alley in the opposite direction of where the bear was rampaging. They kicked up gravel as they ran behind building after building to get to the blue barn.

"Please let them be here," she said as she opened the door to the *Farm & Feed* storeroom. They ran past pallets of potting soil and mulch, sawdust and cat litter. Erica threw herself through the double doors onto the sales floor. Dozens of people had barricaded themselves in the store. Several men were pushing heavy shelving units in front of the glass doors. Erica scanned the crowd looking for the one person who might be able to help.

"Kyle," she yelled. "Kyle!"

"Erica?" said a voice behind her. Kyle was standing in the double doors with a thick wooden fence post under each arm. She must have run right past him on her way in.

"Do you have a chainsaw?" she asked.

Kyle scrunched his face in confusion as if trying to figure out how this could be relevant to their current situation. "I just picked up Derek. His is in the back of my truck."

"Where is Derek?"

"Right here," Derek called from the front of the store.

"We need to go," Erica said.

She was headed for the office door behind the counter when she caught Granny's eye. Erica paused. Her plan had to be clear to Granny. If it was a bad one, this was her last chance to change course. Granny gave her a quick nod but turned a sympathetic glance at Xander. That was enough for Erica. She pushed through the door with Xander and Kyle already on her heels.

Derek caught up as she ran to the small, smudged window that looked onto the parking lot. "What are we doing with my chainsaw?"

"It's hard to explain," Xander said.

Kyle only just registered Xander's presence. "Why is he here?"

"Let's just get to the truck," Erica said. "Where is it?"

"Your house."

Erica turned to face the boys who were lined up obediently. "My house?"

"There was no parking downtown," Kyle protested.

Getting to Erica's house meant crossing the street and putting themselves in the exact path of the bear. She could see that Xander was thinking the same thing.

"My truck is just a couple of blocks away," Xander said.

"Does your truck have a chainsaw in it?" Erica snapped. Xander pursed his lips. "We're just going to have to run for it then."

Looking out onto the parking lot, no one would have known that anything strange was happening on the other side of the barn. The scene was set like the tail end of a good party. Red drink cups were strewn lazily on tables, and a few had made their way to the ground. The grill was still smoking slightly. Erica was sure she would smell the hickory as soon as she stepped outside. There was no discernable danger from their vantage point, but this did not comfort Erica. As she looked between her companions' faces, she could tell it did nothing for them either. Each of them appeared to be hoping someone else was brave enough to take the first step outside.

"People said it's a bear," Derek said.

"You didn't see it?" Erica asked.

Kyle shook his head. "We were getting people inside when the screaming started."

"If it's a bear, I might have an idea," Derek said. He started to pull his black long-sleeve shirt over his head, revealing a sunken stomach with a trail of black hair below his navel.

"What are you doing?" Erica whispered. "Keep your clothes on!"

"But—," Derek started.

"Let's just go," Xander said. He pushed open the door and listened.

Erica put a hand on his back and ignored Kyle's raised eyebrows. "Can you feel it?"

"I can feel it everywhere. I can't pinpoint it."

Kyle and Derek exchanged a look but didn't ask. Xander walked further out, keeping just the tips of his fingers on the edge of the frame. Erica took one big step and was outside. She ran her hand against the building as she made her way forward. After holding the door open for Kyle and Derek, Xander positioned himself in front of her so that he was the first one to look out onto the street. He peeked around the edge of the barn before stepping fully onto the sidewalk.

"Can you see it?" Erica asked. Xander waved them forward.

Erica, Kyle, and Derek slowly made their way into the open. Where there had previously been stalls, stands, and carts, there was now a jungle. The decorative sunflowers and hanging baskets of pansies that lined the walkways had grown several times their original size. Their engorged roots and stems punched through windows. Firs tens of feet tall stood in the middle of the road. The pavement was replaced by a tangle of tree roots. The bear was nowhere to be seen.

They almost made it across the road when a roar came from the middle of the copse. This sent them running for Erica's house. Erica refused to look behind her. If this was the end, if it was coming for her, she didn't want to know. It wasn't until her hand was safely on the blue truck, Keith's truck, that she took stock. All three boys were huddled around her, panting. They had not been followed.

Erica looked in the back of the truck and saw an orange chainsaw with a blade that was almost as long as she was tall. She knew there was a smaller version in the tool shed attached to the carport. She rushed over and waded through the buckets, hedge trimmers, and other gardening supplies until she found it. The chainsaw was old and rusted but better than nothing. She grabbed it and the gas canister for the lawnmower and threw them both in the back of the truck.

"Seriously, Erica, what are we doing?" Kyle asked through jagged breaths.

"I will tell you when we get there."

"Get where?"

"Give me your keys."

"Tell me where we're going first."

"Give her the keys," Xander said, stepping between them. He drew himself up to his full height, even popping his chin up for the best effect. Erica was not amused.

"Is this a joke?" Kyle said, puffing out his chest.

"You both need to just stop. Keys. Now."

Kyle slipped his hand into his pocket and held out the keys to Erica without taking his eyes off of Xander. Erica was exhausted by the useless posturing going on in front of her. She opened the driver's side door and slid the seat forward.

"Someone get in," she said. Derek was more than happy to squish himself into the cramped backseat, away from the tension. It struck Erica that Derek's total willingness to go along with the unspoken plan of a person he barely knew was odd, but then he was an odd guy. She didn't have time to question his motives.

Xander and Kyle opted to sit up front with her. In a different situation, Erica would have laughed at Xander trying to fold himself into the middle of the bench seat. His legs were spread so wide that he probably could have pushed the gas pedal. Kyle was frowning as he tried to sit almost side-saddle in his seat to avoid touching Xander.

"Comfortable?" Erica asked as she put the truck into reverse. No one responded.

Erica sped through the residential roads as fast as she safely could. Every stop sign she rolled through and turn signal she didn't bother to use pained her inner rule follower, but adrenaline won out. Her passengers must have felt her tension because they stayed quiet until she hit the main road. The instant she relaxed slightly, going ten miles per hour over the speed limit but no longer worried about taking out stray toddlers, Kyle started in on her again.

"Where are we going?" He was trying to stare past Xander to see Erica but was not having much luck. Xander slipped his hand onto her thigh and tapped his fingers against her clenched muscle as if she needed reminding that he wasn't keen on Kyle knowing his secret.

"To cut down a tree," she said.

"And that has something to do with what is happening downtown?" Kyle asked. She could hear the mockery in his voice but ignored it.

"Yes."

"Wild," Derek said from the backseat.

"This has something to do with you, doesn't it?" Kyle asked Xander. Xander stared straight ahead and responded with an almost imperceptible shrug of his shoulders. Erica expected more questions, but Kyle was getting the hint that answers were going to be hard to come by.

They watched the forest on either side of them fly by in a green and brown blur. The sun was still high and the sky was perfectly clear. Erica thought back to the last time she was out this way, to her and Xander kissing in the car after getting caught in the rain. She pulled the truck into the gravel turnout she was becoming very familiar with.

Erica hopped down from the truck, grabbed the rusty chainsaw out of the bed, and headed for the forest.

"How far in are we going?" Kyle asked as he carefully extracted the much larger chainsaw.

"A little over a mile," Xander replied. Kyle snorted. "I can carry that for you if you want," Xander said, keeping the smile off his face if not out of his voice. Kyle rolled his eyes and followed Erica.

Erica kept trying to pick up the pace as they headed toward the giant oak, but without Xander smoothing out the path for them, it was tough going. There was no trail, and the chainsaw was awkward to hold on to. Erica was annoyed at Xander for playing his cards this close to his chest when there was so much at stake. Though Kyle had calmed down for now, she thought it was impossible for them to get through this ordeal without an explanation.

After Erica stumbled for the fifth time and almost impaled herself on the blade of the chainsaw, Xander wordlessly traded her for the gas canister, which was only a quarter full. He took her over as the leader of the group and pushed them to the right. She must have been guiding them off course in her rush to get to the tree.

Erica knew they were getting close but before she was quite ready for it, they were in the meadow. This time nothing was blooming but neither was it dead. Every leaf and blade of grass sat perfectly still. The hum of insects was gone, and Erica couldn't feel even the slightest breeze. It was as though when they left the line of trees, they had set foot in a glass globe, the oak a mere ceramic figure glued to its base. The leaves on the giant tree were still green, untouched by the change of season.

"That's the tree we're cutting down?" Kyle asked. His eyes were wide as he took in the enormity of the task Erica set him.

"Dude," Derek said appreciatively.

Kyle and Derek moved toward the tree. Erica expected Xander to warn them, to give them directions, to react in some way. He hung back holding the old chainsaw and staring at the oak as if seeing it for the first time.

"Don't touch it," she called out.

"Isn't that what we're here for?" Kyle asked.

"Just give me a second."

Kyle rolled his eyes, but he and Derek circled the tree, figuring out where they would even start, but they listened to Erica's warning and left just enough distance between themselves and the tree's lowest branches. Erica came up to Xander, putting her hand on his forearm and giving it a light squeeze.

"Anything we should know?" she asked.

"I don't think I can do this."

"It made a forest on Main Street. It may have hurt more people." Xander nodded, his eyes still fixed straight ahead. Erica continued, "It's out in the open now. They're going to find out they can't hurt it. What if they trace it back here? To you?"

"I don't know."

"Xander." She reached up and cupped her hand around his chin, bringing his face to hers. "They could come for you. For your trees."

Xander's eyes widened. She thought of how lonely he must feel, even at this moment, how being what he was made him the outsider in every situation. As much as he wanted to do no harm, taking down the bear was the lesser evil. He had to see that.

So quick that she felt it before she saw it, Xander closed the gap between their faces and kissed her on the lips. He took a deep breath and made his way forward to intercept Kyle and Derek on their second trip around the oak.

"Here's the thing," he told them. "As soon as you touch the tree, the bear is going to know. It is going to come for us. We're eight-ish miles from downtown. I'd say we have twenty minutes to bring it down."

Derek and Kyle responded at the same time but with very different sentiments. From Derek, "So it is a bear." From Kyle, "What the hell are you talking about?"

"The tree dies, the bear dies," Xander said. "That's all you need to know."

Kyle opened his mouth to protest, but no one heard him after Xander yanked the pull start of his chainsaw and it came noisily to life. He approached the oak tree and made a deep cut level with the ground. He held the chainsaw there as it bucked in his hands, trying to push it through the hardwood.

Derek ran to Xander's side and waved his arms wildly. Xander pulled the chainsaw out of the tree and stumbled backward. Derek reached in and slammed the switch to shut it off.

"You have no idea what you're doing, man. You're going to hurt yourself."

"The clock is ticking," Xander said. He handed Derek the

chainsaw and looked pointedly at Kyle as if daring him to run out their time on stupid questions.

"Goddamn it," Kyle said under his breath. To Derek, he asked, "You notch, I'll fell?"

"I guess," Derek said, looking down at the sad, old piece of equipment he was saddled with.

They started their chainsaws and got to work. Sawdust sprayed in all directions. Derek was working on deepening two parallel cuts while Kyle slowly worked his way in a half-circle around the trunk.

"This thing brings a whole new context to the definition of hardwood," Kyle yelled over the drone of the saws. Erica could tell from the tightness of their grips as they tried to move the blades through the tree that this was going to be much more challenging than she had hoped. She wished she could help, but all she could do was watch. Derek held the saw even and pulled out a wedge-shaped section of wood, as though serving a piece of cake. Its rings were too numerous to count. Even if the only life they were taking was that of the tree, it still would have been sad to see something so old, so magnificent fall.

From the corner of her eye, Erica saw Xander suddenly turn to face the direction they had come. He focused on a spot in the distance. A chill ran up Erica's spine. They had miscalculated. It was here.

Xander ran toward the bear as it burst through the trees, sending branches and pine needles in every direction. Erica watched in horror as Xander tried to distract the bear from Kyle and Derek. He had his hands on the forest floor and tendrils shot in all directions. For a few seconds, it appeared to work. The bear slowed its pace and focused on Xander. He stood up, pulling the tendrils from the earth with him. He flicked his hands as if willing the vines to go forward, but they fell lamely to the ground. The bear advanced, and Xander turned his attention, for the merest moment, to make sure Erica was safe. Xander's eyes were locked with hers when the bear swiped with one of its paws the size of a garbage lid and tore its claws straight through Xander.

Erica screamed as bright red blood flew through the air. Xander did an almost graceful pirouette as his body absorbed the impact of the blow. He fell to the ground. Erica couldn't look away but was too terrified to do anything else. She couldn't make sense of the purple mass that lay beside him until she realized Xander's entire abdomen was cut open. The familiar muscles of his stomach, that she had run her hands over so recently, were in shreds.

If it were possible, she would have jumped out of her skin when she felt an elbow in her side. The bear was coming for them again, but the elbow belonged to Derek. He thrust the live chainsaw in her hands and walked toward the bear, stripping off his shirt and kicking off his shoes. Confused, Erica backed away in the direction of the tree. When Derek's hand went for his belt buckle, she spun around, barely avoiding taking her chainsaw to Kyle who was still cutting into the thinner wood of the hollow.

"Go in from the opposite side!" Kyle yelled over the noise. "This had better fucking work!"

Erica crossed to the other side of the hollow. An unpleasant odor filled her lungs as she tried to peer into the darkness. But she couldn't let herself be distracted. She shoved the chainsaw into the tree. The sensation was unlike anything she had ever felt. Vibrations pulsed through her, making her aware of the absorbent powers of the rubber soles of her shoes. It was almost impossible for her to make any progress, and she wasn't sure whether to blame the dullness of the blade, the thickness of the tree, or her arms, weak from shock. She could hear the bear roaring close by, too close, though she thought she could pick out two distinct grunting sounds, one a little less deep but more urgent.

A sharp cracking noise came from deep within the tree.

"Push!" Kyle yelled. He tossed his chainsaw to the side and threw all his weight against the tree. Erica leaned her back against it and pushed with every muscle she could muster. The cracking continued. Kyle picked his chainsaw back up and made one final, deep cut.

The tree was falling in the direction of Xander and the bear. Except now there were two bears—the huge black bear and a smaller, skinny brown one. The latter had matted, chestnut-colored fur and a distinctive hump at its shoulders. It was bleeding but holding its ground, shuffling from side to side to keep its body between the tree and the black bear.

At first, the long branches of the oak slowed its fall, but they soon collapsed under the weight. Erica heard snapping and grunting all around her as she ran toward Xander's body. She threw herself on top of him as the tree came down around them, burying them in a pile of silky, lobed leaves. She stayed there, wrapped around Xander's head and chest, until it was quiet again.

CHAPTER 24

Erica did not realize she was squeezing her eyes shut until she opened them to see a familiar hand laying in a pool of blood. Xander's palm was white, too white, against the dark green leaves. She pulled herself into as much of a crouch as the branches overhead would allow. Her blue polo and khakis were soaked in dark red. She put her fingers on Xander's wrist, but even if he had a pulse, she wouldn't be able to tell over how fast her own blood was pumping. So far, she had avoided looking too long at his face. The quick flashes she glimpsed were already burned into her mind—glassy eyes, a half-open mouth. She wasn't sure she could ever unsee it.

Erica put one hand on his chest and the other in front of his mouth and nose. She closed her eyes again and concentrated, hoping to detect even the shallowest breath. There was nothing. He had led her to believe that he couldn't die. Whether she was conscious of it or not, that assurance had made her brave, had extended to her a feeling of invincibility that led to this moment. This stupid moment when she would have given the lives of everyone in Juniper Falls to have him back. She should have listened. Xander did not want to do this. And now he was gone.

"I love you," she said. She had been thinking it for weeks, too afraid to say it out loud. It was stupid, loving someone she barely knew who couldn't follow her in the life she was just starting to build. But as she curled her fingers around his limp wrist, she knew it was true. She loved him as she had never loved anyone else.

Somehow, despite the emotion rushing through her, his skin went paler with every passing second. Blood pooled around her, and Erica's sadness turned to panic. She couldn't be there anymore. It was like being trapped in a grave. She tried to stand up, fighting through the branches and twigs, searching for daylight. She put her foot on what felt like a branch thick enough to hold her weight only for it to snap and her to fall back down again. Her hands were sticky with blood and fast becoming caked with dirt as she pushed her way toward what she hoped was the top of the tree.

At last, her head popped out through the foliage and she found herself close to the pines that circled the meadow. To her left, she saw three men standing around the body of the black bear. Kyle was farthest away, the chainsaw quiet but back in his hands as though he thought the bear would get up at any moment. Derek was closer. He was using his shirt to mop at the blood weeping from a large cut that began at his shoulder and ran across his chest to his opposite armpit. Kneeling to inspect the body was a man with hair like woven sunlight who could only be Alden. Erica's throat felt like it was swelling shut as she pushed her way out of the rest of the tree and made her way toward them.

Kyle spotted her first. He looked her up and down and lifted his eyebrows, unable to ask the question. Erica shook her head. She sidled up to Derek.

"Hey," he said, as though this were just another normal day. As though she hadn't just seen him become a grizzly.

Erica was too stunned to ask the question, but Kyle did it for her. "You're a—?"

"Werebear. What was that?" he asked, pointing to the animal in front of them.

"Dryad," Erica said.

At hearing her say the word, Alden snapped his head around, gearing up for a fight. He deflated the moment he saw Erica covered in blood. "What happened?"

"He tried to protect us," Erica said.

"Where is he?"

"Under the tree." The tears were hot behind her eyes now. In a thick voice and pointing to the bear, she asked, "Is it dead?"

Alden stood and faced her. She never thought he looked much like Xander, but when she studied him up this close, she saw the similarities. If he let himself get old enough, Xander would have the same creases at the corners of his mouth, the same overgrown eyebrows. But he was never going to be older.

"It's dead," Alden said.

The tension in Erica's muscles released and the sobs started immediately. They took hold and racked her body, buckling her knees and bringing her to the ground. She watched Alden make his way toward the fallen tree, walking quickly at first and then running when he spotted blood on the ground. He tore through wood and leaves until he found him. Even as far away as Alden was, she felt the sharp intake of his breath in the depths of her soul.

Erica couldn't remember much of what happened the rest of that afternoon. She had a general outline of it—the walk back through the woods, Kyle driving her home, explaining to Granny in short, halting sentences what had happened. She stripped her clothes off in the doorway, took a hot shower, and laid in bed for what may have been an entire day. The few hours of sleep she managed were plagued by dreams that left her feeling anxious and exhausted.

Slowly the world came back into focus. It was bright. Light bounced around her room with its white furniture and off-white walls. It was far too comfortable a place in which to mourn. Erica pulled herself out of bed, put on some sweats that were lying on the floor, and went downstairs to curl up in a recliner and stare at the brick fireplace for a change of scenery.

Tulip wandered over and leaned against the chair, demanding to be petted. Erica reached down with one hand and scratched the dog's thick mane. She used her other hand to unlock her phone. There were missed calls from her mother,

Kyle, and Cora. The latter two also texted her several times. Kyle's last text read, *Call me. I got some info.* Hoping against hope that Kyle heard something about Xander, Erica pushed the call button immediately.

"You're alive," he said after the first ring. It was a bad joke and immediately put Erica on the defensive.

"What did you find out?"

"Kriners was logging just outside the town limits yesterday. The bear thrashed their site before being driven into town."

"Are they permitted to work there?" Erica asked, though she already knew the answer.

"Who knows."

Rage built within Erica. Her ethical opposition to Kriners' activities had become a moral issue. Something had to change. "We have to stop this. Do you see that now? I told you from the very beginning that the logging was wrong. Now Keith and Xander and an ancient supernatural creature are dead. For what? Toilet paper?"

"Xander is really dead, then?" Kyle asked, his voice higher and quieter than normal.

"You saw what happened."

"Sure, but I thought maybe, with the bear, and I guess Derek is also a bear—that's crazy by the way—and then I looked up dryads, and I thought maybe he was okay?"

Erica didn't answer this. She saw what she saw. She felt Xander's lifeless body under her hands. But Kyle had a point— he could be okay. An idea came to her so fast that she was already fishing her keys from the bowl by the door when she said, "I have to go," and hung up the phone. Not even bothering to locate her purse, Erica got into her car and drove straight to the cemetery. She could see Xander's tree from the road. The leaves had changed color, but Erica couldn't tell if they were orange and crimson as they should have been this time of year or dead and brown.

Gravel sprayed from Erica's tires as she threw her car into park and ran up the hill. Clouds were gathering from the west, dark gray and ominous. Erica was suddenly afraid of lightning in a way she had never been before. She cursed Alden's father for burying his son in such a vulnerable place.

Erica crested the hill and stood panting before Xander's white oak. She reached up and touched the leaves. They were soft and supple, not dry. She ran her hand across the bark, searching for the heartbeat she had found there before and wondering if she imagined it last time. She thought she felt it, faint but present. A spark of possibility lit within her, battling back the tiniest bit of her despair.

Erica held her lips right up to the trunk and pleaded, "If you can hear me, I love you, I love you, I love you. Send me a sign that you're okay."

She stepped back and watched but the only movement was leaves swaying in the slight breeze. She kicked her shoes off and concentrated hard on trying to feel the roots beneath her. Nothing. Frustrated, Erica sat in the grass at the base of the tree and leaned against it, the crackled bark digging into her skin.

"I miss you. I need to know if you're alright. I can't keep having people ripped out of my life, Xander. It's not fair."

Erica knocked the back of her head against the tree a few times, admonishing him for leaving her. She sighed, fighting back the tears that she knew were coming. The clouds were moving quickly and were almost overhead. It was going to rain.

She kissed the bark lightly and ran her fingers across it as she stood up. "I'll be back tomorrow. And the next day and the next day as long as this tree is still standing."

On her way out the door the next morning, her hair hidden in a bandana and wearing her grubbiest jeans, Granny asked Erica if she wanted to participate in the downtown clean-up efforts. Having several large fir trees in the middle of Main Street was proving to be bad for business. Erica knew she should be there for the store, but Granny was understanding. She had been good, maybe too good, about giving Erica her space.

Just as Granny shut the door behind her, Erica had an idea. "Do you mind if I walk down with you?"

Granny smiled and gave her a one-armed hug.

It was another overcast day, but Erica was thankful for the bite in the air. Warm days felt like they belonged to a different Erica, one who had seen and felt less. She thought she was prepared for what downtown would look like, having glimpsed it briefly on her way to bring down the bear. Now much of the overgrown foliage had been cleared away, revealing the extent of the damage. She counted six trees of varying sizes growing out of what once was Main Street. The road was torn up where roots had sprung out of nowhere. Black, palm-sized crumbles of asphalt were mixed with concrete rubble and shards of glass. Erica counted six storefronts that were missing windows, at least one of which had a tree branch punched through it. *Farm & Feed* was thankfully untouched.

"What do people think happened?"

"Lots of guesses," Granny said. "None of them anywhere near the mark."

"I'm surprised there aren't news crews crawling all over the place."

"I'm sure someone has tried, but who is going to believe them?"

Erica was relieved. She worried that Alden would break if people started poking around Juniper Falls asking too many questions. Though she would not be surprised if what happened to Xander already pushed him so far into seclusion as to stop caring.

Erica dropped Granny off with a group of older women and continued another block to the library. Cardboard covered a lower windowpane and the flowers in the planter box underneath it had been cut level with the soil, but otherwise it appeared to have been spared from the worst of the wreckage. She opened the doors and headed to the desk intending to ask Mrs. Shields for a history book recommendation when she realized the bronze plaque on the wall bore a startling resemblance to someone she knew. She studied it closer and read, *In Memory of Alastair Reed, Juniper Falls Library's First Patron.* Peering around at the bookshelves, Erica could see them serving as inspiration for Alden's later creations. Each shelf varied slightly in depth and thickness. The edges were left uncut and allowed to sport knots and imperfections that others might have removed. They were lacquered to a glossy sheen that held up over decades. It seemed the Reeds would haunt this town forever.

Mrs. Shields came over from the stacks and asked if she could help. Erica opened her mouth to ask her question but changed her mind.

"I think I know what I'm looking for." She wandered into the fiction section for a novel she had read a dozen times before, her book equivalent of comfort food, the antidote for many a broken heart.

As Erica exited the building, she ran into the last person she expected to see walking into a library. Derek looked exactly like he always did in a band t-shirt and dirty jeans, his black hair plastered to his head like he just woke up. She was sure that the events of the weekend were written all over her face, that everyone who saw her knew she was changed. But here was Derek looking as relaxed and unaffected as ever, even though she knew he was as full of secrets as Xander.

"Jane Austen. Nice," Derek said, gesturing to her book.

"You read Austen?"

"Winters are long in Alaska."

They both looked at their feet. Erica knew she owed him so much, but it was hard to find the words.

"Are you okay?" she asked. Erica drew a line across her chest to indicate where he was swiped by the bear dryad.

"Oh, yeah, healing," he said, pulling down the collar of his shirt to show her a raised ruby scab about an inch thick.

"That doesn't look great."

"Better than some."

Erica knew he meant Xander, and her eyes burned as she tried to hold back tears.

"No. No, sorry," Derek said. He moved toward her like he was going to hug her, but hesitated. Erica stepped into him, clasping her hands around the back of his thin shoulders. He squeezed her for just a moment, and she knew from that small gesture that he was feeling some of the same things she was.

"Thank you," she said as she let go.

"Sure thing." They made to go in opposite directions, but Derek hesitated. "Look, Erica, you probably want to know about what you saw back there."

"Only what you want to tell."

Derek nodded. She could tell that this was a long story that, if she was in a better state of mind, she very much wanted to know. She wasn't sure how to tell him that she needed a clearer mind to do him the justice of really hearing him. Then they heard the voices of the clean-up crew laughing from down the street. They both jumped and exchanged a look of understanding that this wasn't the place for this conversation.

"I'll text you. We'll meet up," Derek said. "Maybe you can bring that blonde dude. I have some questions for him."

Before Erica could tell him that she didn't think Alden was going to want anything to do with her anytime soon, Derek slipped into the library. The mention of Alden, though, spurred an idea she couldn't believe she hadn't thought of before. There was one more place to look for Xander.

Erica walked briskly back to her car and threw the book in the passenger seat. Heading back toward downtown, she took a right onto Main Street and followed the road, keeping an eye out for Xander's driveway. She kept driving even after she was sure she had passed it before turning around and looking again. When she just about reached Main Street, she tried again, this time driving out farther than she thought Xander would even be able to go. While she passed the occasional house sat next to the road, there was no evidence of the overgrown driveway.

Confused, Erica doubled back again before parking her car and walking along the road where she thought the entrance to Alden's cabin should be. She walked several hundred feet on the narrow shoulder before finding some faint tire tracks in the gravel. She pushed her way just barely into the forest before she was met with briars in every direction. Erica was sure she had the wrong spot until the branches reached for her, wrapping painfully around her arm. When she ripped herself away, a thorn tore a hole in the sleeve of her shirt.

"Alden!" she yelled. "Let me see him!"

In response, small green berries grew on the still-advancing branches. They swelled, turned dark orange, and exploded with little pops all around her.

"It wasn't my fault!" she screamed. But even as the words left her lips, she wasn't sure she believed them. She was the one who led them into the forest. She was the one who stood by and let Xander face up against something he was no match for.

Erica ran back out to the road and watched as the brambles chased her just to the edge of the trees. There was going to be no commiserating with Alden, no warm words exchanged over a shared tragedy. A sob burst forth from Erica as she cried for what felt like the millionth time in two short days. Any moment now she thought she might cry her last tear and her body would shrivel into a dry husk.

Tears still falling down her face, Erica got back in her car and drove to the cemetery. As she made her way up the hill, she was dismayed by the number of leaves that had fallen since yesterday. The red circle forming around the base of Xander's tree was entirely too familiar. She tried to reassure herself that Alden's tree looked similar. It was all she could do not to count the leaves to check if Xander was fading faster, but she stopped herself.

"I'm sorry," Erica whispered, resting her forehead against the bark. "For all of it. For pushing you. For making Alden hate me. I promise if you come back, I'll be better."

Erica tossed on the ground the cushion she stole from some unsold patio furniture at the store and the umbrella she brought in case the clouds above her burst. She sat down and leaned against the tree.

"I was going to read you something you like, but I decided that it's not your fault that no one taught you to love fiction. I guess that's me being selfish again, but it's the last time. I swear." Erica took a deep breath and settled herself into a more comfortable position. "Okay. Are you ready for this? *It is a truth universally acknowledged, that a single man in possession of a good fortune, must be in want of a wife.*"

True to her word, Erica visited Xander's tree every day. The number of leaves at the base of the white oak appeared to double between visits. Erica found herself searching on the internet for signs a tree was dying only to learn that they are exceptionally good at hiding problems. She thought of all the books she would have to read, sitting in the cemetery, often in the rain, hoping that its leaves would bud in spring.

As Erica made her way through *Pride and Prejudice*, she stopped occasionally to offer commentary ranging from whether the concept of class structure had improved since Georgian times to which actors she liked best from the various film and television adaptations. She learned that a tree was surprisingly good company in the absence of the person she wanted most. Visitors to the cemetery were rare, and none of them seemed to find Erica's presence there unusual. And Keith was nearby, which was comforting.

Erica couldn't put off work any longer after the pines were taken down on Main Street and steel plates placed temporarily over the cracks. It was after sunset that she rushed up the hill with a flashlight, the cushion, and her book. The night was clear, and the brightest stars were just starting to shine through the indigo sky.

"I don't mean to ruin anything for you," Erica said as she settled in, "but this next chapter is amazing. It sets off this whole change between Elizbeth and Darcy. He's already in love with her, but she starts falling for him."

"No spoilers," said a voice close to her, a voice she knew. Erica shined her flashlight in the direction of Alden's tree. There he was, as tall, as handsome, as whole as she remembered him.

Erica screamed unintelligible words and dropped the flashlight. She ran to him and leaped into his arms. He fell back against the tree but caught her and held her.

"I knew it. I knew it," she said over and over again between kisses. Xander's laugh tickled her lips. He put her down, but she stayed pressed into him running her hands down his stomach and under his shirt, feeling for any vestige of what they had been through. His skin was smooth, soft, and warm.

"I'm fine," he said, their mouths so close she could taste his sweet breath on her tongue. "It took a while but I'm fine."

Erica kissed him harder, her hands trying to find purchase in his short hair. He kissed her back for a moment before pushing on her shoulders and holding her at arms' length. She looked into his eyes, and they had the same life, the same sparkle she remembered. She did her best not to think about what they looked like on the forest floor under the branches of the giant oak.

"I have something to tell you," Xander said, his tone serious. Erica's knees almost failed. She couldn't take more bad news. She grabbed his elbows so they buckled, and she could wrap her arms around his broad chest.

"Say it."

"I love you too."

AUTHOR BIO

Kelsey Parpart grew up in Washington state before moving to Oregon then Alaska and finally settling in the Blue Ridge Mountains of North Carolina. She holds a bachelor's in English from Washington State University and is a graduate of Portland State University's Book Publishing program. When not writing, she works in marketing in the engineering and construction industry and makes slow but steady progress on building her dream hobby farm. The White Oak Trilogy is her first series.

If you enjoyed this book, please leave a review on Amazon or Goodreads.